TALES OF LOST SOUTHTOWN

Erik Bosse

FLOWERSONG
PRESS

CONTENTS

MUSHROOMS AND CANDY CORN (OCT. 31)

"Here, let me help you with that," Kat said. She blew into the latex glove and nodded to me. I held up my left hand, allowing her to slide on the glove with a professional expertise. Next, she did my other hand. "You could do with a haircut," she said, as she adjusted my surgical mask. She appraised me from head to toe, then shrugged. "Good enough."

After she unbuttoned the starched white blouse of her nurse's uniform down to her navel, she repositioned her black push-up bra until it held her bosom in a firm grip. "Showtime," she said in a low voice.

We stepped out onto my front porch.

Kat likes to perform, and it makes little difference whether she performs on a stage, or, as was the case tonight, to the children who were walking from house to house in search of Halloween candy.

We first met some years back during a casting call for a short film I had been hired to shoot. She didn't get the part, but we exchanged cards and ended up working on a few projects together. At some point over the years, it had become a tradition for Kat to phone me up as autumn approached to make certain I had kept my calendar reserved for her on that important date. October 31.

This is all because of where I live—that region just south of downtown San Antonio often referred to as Southtown. It encompasses several neighborhoods. Kat's attracted to the area for the same reasons as the kids who come every year to trick-or-treat. The homes are old and spooky-looking. And because many of the people who live here are rich, they can afford the good candies. So children from all over the city make their way to my street to load up.

I could understand the aesthetic appeal. That was why I moved here, and why I continue the struggle to pay the rising rent with my unpredictable and somewhat unorthodox income streams. Where else in Texas could one find a neighborhood with so many buildings from the nineteenth century? Shady, tree-lined streets of cottages and mansions, galleries and coffee shops, and the whole place half-dozing under the scent of jasmine, whose vines spill over the fences and climb the telephone poles. There is a soft bruising of Southern Gothic neglect that you can't ignore once you spot it huddled behind the flimsy facade of upward mobility. I do fear, however, that the whole idyllic milieu will not survive the hipster onslaught, with the infestation of real estate speculators, Airbnb rentals, and artisanal gelato parlors.

I have been here for ten years, longer than I've lived anywhere. I've seen those changes up close.

The neighbors on my block of East Guenther Street do their best to squint just right, so as to only see those things which originally had brought them to the neighborhood, and not the newer amenities which lure in the current batch of young, energetic trendsetters.

Kat has little or no concern about the vicissitudes of gentrification. Mostly, she likes to dress up.

Last year, Kat sat out on the front porch of my little duplex with me, and we handed out treats to hundreds of kids. She was a mermaid, in a tight black vinyl outfit, complete with tail. I was, well, just me.

This year I decided to play dress-up as well. We were back on my porch. I sported medical scrubs and a surgeon's mask. The mask didn't completely cover the week's worth of stubble on my face. I wondered aloud if I should have shaved. Kat said it made me look "distinguished," by which I suspect she meant old. Though I will admit to being well into my forties, I don't feel old; however when I'm in Kat's frenetic company, I often think of myself as creaky. Maybe craggy. Kat, though barely younger than me, still has that firm bloom of youth, and she was taking advantage of it with her revealing nurse's outfit, complete with white stockings and garter belt, mini skirt and stethoscope. We stood at a medical examining table, looking down at a mannequin. As the timid kids crept up the steps, I used a pair of forceps to pull back the sheet, displaying an opened abdominal cavity filled with "entrails" and bags of candy corn.

Earlier in the year, I picked up the examining table from Kat. She was moving to a bigger place in Olmos Park. She wanted my assistance because I had a truck, and also because she knew me to be discreet.

You see, Kat works as a dominatrix. Acting can't pay the bills, so she does what she can to make ends meet. Anyway, she needed someone to help empty her dungeon so that she could then allow her father to supervise the movers.

Daddy doesn't know what she does to make the rent.

I took her cages, racks, and restraint tables to a storage facility on the southside. But she didn't want to keep the examining table.

"I'm done with that naughty nurse bullshit!"

I told her I'd take it. And so I did.

Of course, for tonight, Kat *had* reprised her naughty nurse role (though Halloween has a way of dialing down sexuality to a soft PG rating, even when push-up bras are involved).

"Come on, sweetie," Kat said to a cautious toddler in a ballerina outfit who looked up at us on the porch. Candles in red glass holders burned all around.

"We have candy," Kat added.

That still failed to encourage the child.

The father laughed. He scooped up his little ballet dancer and held the baffled girl over the body with the gaping belly wound. She grabbed her candy, and they headed to the next house.

"Wasn't she the cutest?" Kat gushed.

I nodded, even though cute is not my thing.

***

There was another Halloween. It must have been over twenty years ago. I was living in San Francisco, working in the warehouse of Rough Trade Records. After work, I was hanging out with three of the women who worked the phones, placing and receiving orders. We were tossing back a few drinks at the Metro Bar before heading to the I-Beam for some punk show. Jill had the whole dark goth look to the hilt, which wasn't her normal style. But it *was* Halloween. Frankie worked a butch angle, like Brando in *The Wild One*. Actually, she dressed that way most days. And Erin? Erin had on this pink tutu with matching ballet shoes. She started out the night with a tiara, but a tipsy drag queen bought it off her with a bag of mushrooms.

The four of us took turns heading off to the restrooms at the Metro to choke down the mushrooms. They were dusty, leathery, and tasted like dirt.

Erin held back some for her boyfriend, Derrick. But when he finally arrived, he was so wound up on meth that he didn't care about much of anything. Except that we should finish up our drinks and grab a cab because he was sure the I-Beam would fill up fast. He glanced at the mushrooms with impatient disdain.

Their effects had begun, ever so gently. To my eyes, Derrick looked like some evil robot, fixated on a single, pointless task.

Erin seemed of the same mind as me. She leaned away from her boyfriend, who stood tugging at his watch band. Erin swiveled on her barstool and helped herself to my drink. She began, indiscreetly, to eat up all of Derrick's share of the mushrooms, washing them down with my cheap draft beer.

The bartender, Donny, clutched at his throat melodramatically.

"Girl, put that in a Denver omelet and it'll go down a lot easier."

Erin threw a ten on the bar.

"Okay," she said, turning to Derrick. "Let's go find your fucking cab."

Jill and Frankie laughed and followed Derrick outside. I grabbed Erin, and she stiffened like she could stab me if she had a knife.

"Be like that Denver omelet," I whispered into her ear. "Warm and savory."

She relaxed and tilted back her head. She looked up at me with a playful smile. "You want me to be all hammy and sweet peas?"

"You get locked into some nonsense with Derrick, it'll be a long night for us all."

"I'll be like a soufflé," she squealed.

I turned to Donny. "She's a soufflé!" And I fluffed up Erin's tutu.

Outside, Derrick hustled Jill and Frankie into the back of a cab. I jumped in to join them. Derrick pushed Erin in after me. She slid across, lying atop our laps. We all started laughing. Derrick took the passenger seat up front. We were off. The girls were singing a Woodentops song. I gauged the strength of the mushrooms by looking at the fabric of the headrest in front of me, and seeing how busy the patterns were shifting. And then I heard Erin shout. "Stop the car!"

At first I thought it was a Woodentops reference. But Erin sat up in my lap and reached over to open the door. The cab driver pulled to the curb. We were on Haight Street at Buena Vista Park. Erin took off at a run up the hill. The street lights made her pink outfit all orange. I noticed that sequins had been sewn into her tutu, they splashed light like a puppy shaking off water. Halfway up the hill, she stopped running. She gave us a little hop and began dancing in a slow, serpentine manner. Soon she was lost in herself. Not dancing for anyone.

"Christ," Derrick muttered. "Who's going to go get her?"

He actually looked at me.

"Hey!" I said. "She's a soufflé, fully risen and off the leash." That made me laugh, and I turned to Jill. "I mixed my metaphors." Jill ignored me. She was staring at the lighted radio dial on the dashboard.

"It's like Jesus," she gasped. She turned to me. "A light. You know? In the darkness." And she grabbed my arm, grinning. "I'm so fucked up."

Frankie trudged up the hill. When she got to Erin, she sat down and watched her dance.

I squeezed Jill's knee. She focused on my face with a questioning smile. I pointed up the hill.

"There's a show up there."

Jill looked up and saw Erin and Frankie. She got out of the cab. I followed. Soon we were seated on the grass watching Erin dance—slow and lost and happy. The cab driver sat next to me with a grin. He lit up a cigarette. Derrick stood over us, glowering.

"Is this how it's going to be?"

The cab driver looked up, puzzled. "Well, she sure is a pretty thing, isn't she?"

Derrick zipped up his jacket. "I'll go ahead, right?"

We nodded. And we waved to him.

"Okay," he grumbled. Finally, he left.

We never did make it to the I-Beam. In fact, I never saw Derrick again. But what I do remember is that a couple of white guys in dreadlocks were out walking their Dachshund. For some reason, they both carried drums. One had bongos, the other a djembe. They joined us. They provided a beat, and soon it wasn't only Erin dancing.

***

Halloween is now over. At least on my block of East Guenther Street. Kat has headed home, the candy-seeking children are all tucked into their beds, and even my neighbors have closed down their parties and shut off their lights. I have nothing else to do but sit at my desk in the glow of my laptop. I probably would have made a cup of hot chocolate with some marshmallows on top if I had any of that stuff in my pantry. That would go nicely with this pile of leftover candy corn. Instead, I just nibble on candy and add to my online journal of thoughts and impressions from the day. Mooning over my pathetic desire to return to the sweet irresponsibility of a youth long left behind.

I still want edgy. I want Dionysian. Or so I tell myself. Tonight, however, the strongest thing coursing through my blood is the sugar rush from the candy corn. Even Kat couldn't have been bothered with anything more exciting than occasionally sipping from her bottle of Boone's Farm. It all seems so innocent. What have I come to? Spending my Halloween on a porch in a proper, polite neighborhood, dispensing candy to kids? And it isn't even as if I belong here. Not on this street surrounded by neighbors who warmly embrace their domesticity. I have no plan, no partner, nothing much in the way of a sense of community. I decide to stop overthinking. Instead, I replay the image in my head of the last child to visit the porch tonight.

It happened just as I was thinking of gathering up everything and heading inside. Kat elbowed me, drawing my attention to a young couple leading a child up to the porch. "It's Winnie-the-Pooh!" Kat whispered, pulling on my sleeve. "Isn't he adorable?" As I leaned over the mannequin with my forceps and revealed the colorful candy for the little yellow bear, I could only agree.

GUERRILLA NIGHT RIDE (NOV. 8)

I leaned out the tenth floor window of the Maverick building and looked below at the streets of downtown San Antonio. Ethan pressed close beside me. He directed my gaze upward. A few stars peeked through the wisps of clouds. "See," said Ethan. "It's not so easy to get to the top." Outside the window was the grated platform and railing of the fire escape. The metal ladder to go up was attached to the outer portion of the railing. About ten feet above, at the edge of the roof, the rungs curved into an arch shape. I now understood Ethan's warning from the other day. To make it to the roof, you needed to pivot around and climb up the outside of the ladder. If you slipped, there was nothing underneath you for ten stories.

I pulled myself back in to look along the hallway at the dancers. This was the last location for the evening's video shoot. I hoped none of the women wanted to go up because I sure as hell didn't. I turned to the dancer closest to me, Laura. She shook her head.

"I don't want to die tonight."

"Well, he's done it before," I said, pointing to Ethan, who lived in one of the apartments down the hall.

"Sure," Ethan said. "But I'm comfortable with heights."

"Yeah," Laura said. "I've seen him do all that shit up on his trapeze. Me, I'm no circus performer."

"That's fine," I said, sensing a way out. "We can find another location." But Mona was already out the window, heading up the ladder. Although she's about my age, mid-forties, she's also ex-military and enjoys posting pictures of herself on social media jumping out of airplanes. I was now committed. Brenda, Paula, and, finally, Tamara (the leader of the tribal fusion belly dance ensemble) followed Mona up. The other six members stayed behind in the hallway. Ethan tried to keep them quiet. It was past midnight and at least one of the apartment doors had already cracked open. An unhappy tenant gave us a scowl before withdrawing.

I was wearing all my camera equipment in a backpack, even my monopod was tied to the shoulder straps. After I took one last glimpse into the tenth floor hallway at the half dozen bored, exhausted women in heavy makeup and festive costumes, I stepped out onto the rusty grating. Ethan gave me a weak smile, which I translated into "make it quick and get these women out of my building before someone calls the management company." My disdain for heights doesn't quite make it into full-blown phobia territory, but it comes close. Keeping my eyes focused on my hands, I gripped the ladder, swung around to the outside, and began my slow, methodical ascent. It was a clear night. Warm for early November. I could hear the buses one block over on Houston Street. Suddenly I wished I was down there with the buses. Maybe this hadn't been the best idea.

I had begun moving away from doing film work. But it wasn't to avoid these sorts of extreme and impulsive shoots on rooftops. It had mainly been due to an accumulated weariness of working with people I just didn't like. I found myself drifting into theater work. The pay wasn't any better, but I was surrounded by kinder and more thoughtful collaborators. However, that had not stopped me from taking a meeting when Tamara contacted me a few weeks back. She wanted help producing a promotional film for her dance troupe. She envisioned it in the style of a music video, cut to the tune "La Bruja," one of the songs her group performed to. It sounded fun, and I immediately agreed. Tamara and her dancers were awesome to work with—even if their fearless impulsivity was threatening to shorten my life with an unnerving climb up the side of a building.

We had already spent a long, exhausting night riding bicycles around downtown—a nimble and mobile band. Me shooting, them performing. All went smoothly. We began in one of the eastside cemeteries, just after sunset. The group of ethnically diverse dancers were lit by flashlights, votive candles, and tiki torches as they performed among the gravestones. We continued on to other locations such as the Alamodome, the sidewalk in front of the Southwest Workers Union, a parking lot where food trucks set up, and across the street from the Alamo. Guerrilla filmmaking at its finest.

It was exactly the type of work I loved to do. Even the craziness of ascending a spindly fire escape ladder. But it was when I was making that awkward maneuver at the top, where you had to navigate the curve of the ladder, that it became obvious to me that going down would be a lot more difficult. Oh, well. Too late now. Mona and Tamara reached out to help me onto the roof.

It was lovely up there. The view went on forever. I placed a couple of small battery-powered lights on tiny three-legged stands as the women rehearsed to the music playing on Tamara's phone. A light breeze came in from the south, ruffling their hair and costumes. I snapped my camera onto the monopod to check out the image. I had on a wide-angle lens and was shooting with an open aperture. The lights from the buildings all around were in soft focus—everything seemed lush and alive.

On nights like this, I asked myself where else could I spend an evening bicycling around town with a group of beautiful women, shooting a film in cemeteries and on rooftops? However, I had come to know the city too well. My father would have called even the harrowing clamber up that ladder an "adventure mild," like when you ordered something with jalapeños, but "on the side." Playing it safe was shrinking my world. Bringing the horizons in too close. I wanted my adventures to be in surroundings new to me.

I looked up and out. The Hilton Hotel and the Tower Life Building were both lit up in reds and greens for Christmas. Beyond those buildings, I knew what was out there. To the southwest, I could make out the Pioneer Flour Mills complex, the elevated portion of Highway 90, the lights from the football field of Burbank High School, and far out in the darkness I saw, in my mind's eye, the smooth roll of the South Texas fields, occasionally broken by little towns like Pearsall and Cotulla. If there were exotic horizons beyond, I had forgotten about them.

Tamara noticed I was ready. "Give us a minute to check ourselves," she told me. Tamara paired up with Brenda, and Paula with Mona. They fussed with one another's makeup, adjusting shoulder straps, headpieces, and such. It was much like when I showed up earlier that evening at the cemetery. "Okay, girls, put on your layers," Tamara had instructed her ensemble. They began doing just that, layering their costumes, each one with a slightly different style. I would sum up the overall aesthetic as trashy gothic gypsy with a sprinkle of chola punk thrown in for attitude. I had roamed around with my camera, picking up close shots of the women getting dressed in the light of the tiki torches, pulling up fishnet stockings, lacing combat boots, or buckling patent leather Mary Janes. There were scarlet bustiers, feather boas, a silk hibiscus to put in the hair, animal print belts, rebozos and babushkas, fingerless gloves, beads and bangles, and leather and studs. Fortunately, it was warm, because there was still plenty of exposed skin—the better to see the tattoos and piercings.

And there, atop the gravel and tar roof of the Maverick Building, the preening was complete. "We're good," Tamara said, turning to face me. All four lined up in position, the nighttime skyline glowing from all around. The music had just ended. It would loop again in a second.

"Then I'm rolling," I said, shifting the camera laterally as the music started back up, cuing the women to lean fluidly into the opening choreography. I moved around them, keeping close, racking focus when needed, all the while trying to capture bits of iconic buildings in the background. My plan was to edit a series of hard cuts with no real attempt for smooth continuity, so I felt confident I had recorded more than enough intriguing shots after two run-throughs.

The women helped me break down and pack up my gear. We moved quickly and efficiently. And when we made our way back down the fire escape, we all kept watch over another to make the descent as safe as possible. Somehow I managed it all without any incident. Navigating my way backward over that hump at the top of the ladder unnerved me, though I suppressed my whimpers. I returned to the tenth floor hallway alive, my masculinity unsullied. A relieved Ethan hustled us all to the elevator.

Eleven bicycles were still waiting for us downstairs. Many were wrapped with strings of flashing multicolored LED lights which had been left on, so the whole tiled lobby pulsated with a festive holiday vibe. A young professional couple returning to their apartment building after a late dinner appeared more perplexed than delighted. They pushed their way past us to the elevator as the dancers, still in high spirits, joked and teased one another. We rolled our bikes out onto Losoya Street, causing less curiosity among the thin stream of pedestrians than I thought we warranted.

Everyone said their goodnights and sped off in different directions. I cinched up my backpack and monopod, hopped on my bike, and headed west on Houston Street. The night was still young. I wondered what might be happening over at Main Plaza.

THE GHOST TURKEY OF CONTRABANDO CANYON (NOV. 16)

Last night I was dragged out to a party. The event was put together by a local film organization so that they could show off their new studio space downtown, where aspiring auteurs could rent production offices or hold auditions. I knew most of the folks who were involved with the group, though I had little interest in their organization. However, my actress friend Kat wanted to attend. She needed a date. "But not like that," she made a point of clarifying. "You know these people, and I don't."

So, she wanted an introduction. I said yes because not only do I like Kat, but also because she was a member of a particular theater company that had recently invited me to join. I felt an obligation to help a fellow ensemble member.

The party was just as I expected. Lukewarm snacks. Light jazz. And a lot of self-important aspirational producers yammering on about strategies to fund their upcoming "passion" projects.

The moment we entered the studio, I was overwhelmed with the desire to grind it into reverse and get the hell out of there. I certainly didn't want to talk with those folks. Luckily, I soon realized that Kat *did* know many of the people there. Good. I left her to schmooze, and, after loading up with a plastic cup of white wine and a paper plate piled with finger foods, I went in search of a corner table where I could wait it out on my own, nibbling on pigs in a blanket in private.

When I saw Vincent Lopez sitting by himself, I changed my plans and decided to join him. I'd describe him as rather aloof. Which I suppose is how most people think of me. Vincent is one of the better camera operators around, and as he has no problems landing gigs of a serious stature, he's rarely spotted among the bloviating amateurs who were mingling about us tonight. "I heard you were shooting some art film for Annette Nelson in Mexico," he said as I sat down beside him.

"Shooting? Naw. I was running audio on that one," I said.

"Didn't know you did that."

"We all wear multiple hats, right?" I said. I added that I was supposed to write a play by spring, so I guessed I did that, too.

That's correct. Me, a playwright.

Good lord. What was I thinking?

Well, in truth, I hadn't been thinking. Like many things in life, it'd come about through a series of disjointed events. A series of events which were plausible enough when seen individually. It was only when they were linked together that an odd reality coalesced—a reality wherein I was expected to write a play that would be produced by the Prometheus Performance Company. By March!

This is the same theater company I mentioned earlier. The one that Kat belongs to.

It all began innocently enough. Years ago, when I arrived in San Antonio as a novice filmmaker with the usual elevated aspirations, I set about looking for actors. That meant—at least as I understood things—making frequent visits to local theaters. There were quite a few, but the Prometheus quickly became my favorite. They produced original work, most of which was weird and unusual. I guess you could call it avant-garde.

I found myself helping out as a volunteer. Ushering. Designing promotional materials. Set construction. I even took to the stage to act on several occasions. And when the executive director discovered I did video work, I was hired to create video designs to be projected during many of their productions.

When I learned back in the spring that they had an unexpected hole in their season of performances because an international guest artist had her visa revoked, I submitted a proposal for a replacement play.

I had not expected that my hastily scribbled synopsis would be accepted. Nor had I been prepared to be voted in as a company member.

It was all very daunting. But for the first time in years, I felt excited by the thought of doing creative work. I'd arrived at the conclusion that the local film production scene was seething with uninspired narcissists and tedious jackasses. Sure, it usually paid more than theater work, but my life has already begun to improve as I move away from the petty drama of the worst of those people.

My friend Rachel—who is also a member of Prometheus—has warned me that I'm still in the honeymoon phase with theater. "Bad work ethic can be found everywhere," she'd told me. "And don't for a second think theater is immune from assholes."

I don't doubt she's right. Nonetheless, I'll bask in that honeymoon warmth for as long as it lasts.

Me, a theater person!

Who would have thought? But the unexpected and intriguing are always welcomed in my life.

Vincent was also finding this new chapter in my life unexpected and intriguing. I knew because he was grinning.

"A play?" he asked. "You're writing a play? Like for the theater?" He wanted to know all about it. But because I didn't want to get into all that, I turned it around and asked about *his* work. Besides, I wasn't absolutely sure what the play I was now expected to write would even be about.

So I was happy that he launched into telling me how he'd just returned from a week in Marfa, where he had been hired to shoot some b-roll of the town and surrounding countryside as well as conduct a few on-camera interviews with a few locals for a show called *The Uncanny and the Inexplicable* on the History Channel.

"The episode is about the Marfa Lights." He shrugged. "Fair enough. No trouble getting anyone out there to talk about their experiences. Mystery Lights. Ghost Lights. Call them what you will. Everyone in town has seen them. My problem was trying to capture those things on camera. I was camped out there at the observation overlook on the highway, freezing my butt off every night. But did I see anything? Nope. Zilch. Probably they'll digitally insert them. At least I got paid."

I was no stranger to Marfa, Texas. Over the years, I had stopped at that roadside viewing area on at least half a dozen occasions when the sun was down. I guess I'd been lucky, because I had seen the lights every time. They're intriguing, if unremarkable. They dance and flit about far in the distance, low to the horizon. I hear that the accepted theory is piezoelectricity, a sort of static discharge that comes up from the ground because of subterranean minerals under pressure. Something like that.

I didn't share any of that with Vincent.

"The lights appear throughout the Big Bend region," I told him instead. "Further down south, along the Rio Grande, they're a part of the local folklore. But they don't attribute them to ghosts or aliens."

"Do tell," he said.

So I did.

***

Years ago, I lived in a tiny town in the Chihuahua Desert a hundred miles south of Marfa, just across the river from Mexico. The place is called Vado Rojo. There wasn't much to do, so I found myself drifting into the daily patterns of the locals. Mostly that meant celebrating the arrival of the afternoon mail.

One day I stepped out of my tiny sun-bleached mobile home, walked down the dusty drive, across the two-lane highway, and into the whitewashed cinderblock building that served not only as the town's post office, but also as a gas station and convenience store. When the bell over the door jingled to announce me, Rogelio looked up from where he sat at the post office counter. He mentioned something about the mail truck not having shown up yet, and he returned to listlessly flipping through a fishing magazine. He rubbed at the gray stubble on his jaw. His wife, Carolina, busied herself toward the back of the store stacking cans of sweetened condensed milk on a shelf.

I pulled a bottle of strawberry soda from the low metal cooler, popped the cap with the bottle opener bolted to the wall, and left a pile of coins on the table beside the little electronic cash register. Carolina looked across at me with a nod of thanks. I took a seat on a worn wooden bench. I would wait. The evaporative cooler rattled from overhead. A cool, moist breeze blew across me.

"I saw some lights last night," I said. Rogelio only grunted. Carolina paused and turned to me. "I was sitting on my steps," I added. "Two of them. Floating over the hills. Just like the Marfa Lights. What do they call them? Ghost lights, right?"

"They're not ghosts," Rogelio said, leaning in closer to study an ad for an outboard motor. "They're witches." He laughed and looked at me. "That's what we called them when I was a kid. Guess that's what kids still say."

The bell over the door chimed again. Rogelio shifted his gaze. He sighed, returning to his magazine, muttering to the newcomer that the truck was late today. I twisted around. It was Frank Alvarado, a spindly old man who owned a little ranch a couple of miles downriver. For some reason, he and Rogelio didn't care for one another. Carolina, however, adored Frank. She rushed over to take his hand.

"Frank," she said with a grin, "this young man was just talking about ghosts!" I guess back then I might have legitimately qualified as a young man. Before I could clarify things, Carolina demanded that Frank tell us his ghost story. Rogelio sighed and said something, but this time too low for me to decipher his words.

"Qué cosa!" Frank gasped melodramatically as he turned his attention to me. "That infernal specter haunts me to this day. If only someone had warned me all those years ago when I built my house there in the mouth of Contrabando Canyon. I was not prepared for the screams and the cries throughout the night. The impact this manifestation would have on my cattle! My goats! The toll it would take on my *own* constitution."

"Wait one moment," Rogelio interrupted. We all turned to look in his direction. He ran his tongue across his thin lips and then laughed without humor. "Tell this man what kind of ghost you're talking about."

"A troubled, diabolical spirit," Frank Alvarado said, shaking his head in pained dismay. "One which is bent on the enraged retribution for—"

"It's a turkey," Rogelio said, his eyes on mine. "The ghost of a turkey."

"If that wretched bird was one half as loathsome alive as it is now in death, may the good Lord protect anyone who might encounter its descendants."

Rogelio grunted and flipped the page of the magazine.

"Tell him about the professional exorcist you brought in from Carlsbad," Carolina said.

Frank stepped closer to me.

"Ah, Sister Sophia. She came highly recommended. I mean, I was desperate. That damn ghost turkey scratching on the roof, chattering at my windows. I couldn't get any sleep. When Sister Sophia arrived, she began the seance straight away. And what she saw—some sort of psychic vision—well, it was a sad tale, indeed."

"Second sight," Carolina said.

Frank nodded.

"That's right. It seems that over a hundred years ago, a young couple lived on my land. They kept losing their goats to coyotes and mountain lions. The man finally had a plan. He caught a wild turkey to use as bait. He tied it out there in the desert, and at night, he hid behind a tree and shot every coyote and lion that came sneaking up to eat the turkey. That poor bird. The constant gun shots directed its way. The terror of those predators sneaking up on it. The biting, the clawing, the mauling. But it lived for weeks, enduring all this. Until one day, it just couldn't go on. It expired, traumatized and enraged at those days and nights of indignities. Could you blame it?"

Frank Alvarado stared at me, as if expecting me to disagree.

"Did it work?" I asked. "The exorcism?"

"Sister Sophia gave me the history," he said, before taking in and then letting out a deep breath. "But I'm afraid her rituals—her candles and incense and prayers—were not strong enough to send that beast off to its final resting place. It remains in the canyon to this day. I fear I had to seek out a prescription for sleeping pills."

Frank shook his head, overwhelmed by the enormity of his tale. He pulled a pack of cigarettes from his shirt pocket and shook one loose, catching it expertly as it fell out. Rogelio slapped his hand on the counter and pointed up at the *No Smoking* sign above him. Frank headed to the door.

"Don't let me catch you doing it near the gas pumps," Rogelio warned with a growl. Frank nodded and walked outside. Rogelio watched the man cross the dusty parking lot and light up his cigarette in the shade of a cottonwood tree. Rogelio grumbled under his breath, "Frank Alvarado's the biggest liar in the county."

***

Vincent laughed at my tale. "We should shoot that story! Just us. To hell with that *Uncanny and Inexplicable* garbage. What happened to the History Channel?" That *did* sound attractive. I knew he was kidding, but what a lovely thought, to head out to the Big Bend and make a documentary about a ghost turkey. God, I missed the desert. This town was closing in on me.

Vincent headed off to freshen his drink. Kat drifted by, and with a sort of phony embarrassment, explained that she was heading out to an "after party" with Leroy (Leroy being a director of straight-to-DVD features, which makes him a legitimate big fish for San Antonio) and she'd see me later. Fine by me. I unceremoniously slipped out the back exit just as I noticed someone setting up a karaoke machine.

ATOMIC ORISHAS (NOV. 22)

I had gotten up before the sun this morning to help Johnny move his sister's washing machine. She was leaving her husband, who didn't know it yet. The reason we were rushing around at such an early hour was because hubby had booked the early flight in from Tulsa, where he'd been attending a structural engineering convention. My part in this? Well, the lesson here is, don't tell people you own a truck. Though I could hardly hide that fact from Johnny. He and his wife rent the other side of my duplex. And the night before, when Johnny asked for help, I didn't have time to come up with a plausible excuse. So, in the morning, after a short drive through the empty predawn streets to the Palm Heights neighborhood, Johnny and I fell to work unhooking and loading up the washing machine.

"Cheap son of a bitch," Elvira grumbled, leaning into her car to fasten the seatbelt for her little girl. "He's saving twenty dollars to make it home by 6:45 in the morning. If he wasn't such a pinche—" she covered her daughter's ears with her hands "—shithead, we'd be doing this at a reasonable hour." She looked over at me and Johnny. We were in the bed of my truck, strapping down the white front-loading monstrosity. "Johnny," she said loud enough to set off a neighbor's dog. "We ready?" Johnny ignored his sister as he used duct tape to secure the door of the washer. "Juan Esparza," she hissed. "Answer me!"

"Yeah, Vira. We're good." Johnny turned to me with a shrug. "Let's roll on out of here."

The rest was quick and fairly painless. It could have been worse because

Elvira had never warmed to me. Once, when I mentioned that I was agnostic, she suggested I prepare myself for an "inevitable and eternal misery in perdition." Luckily today she was too preoccupied by other matters to waste any words on me.

After we arrived at her new place, a garage apartment near Harlandale High School, all Johnny and I had to do was trundle the washer to the covered breezeway beside a utility shed. No need to attach the machine, as there was neither a suitable plumbing connection nor a 220 outlet. All she really wanted was "to make sure that unfaithful dog has to buy a new machine to wash the dingy bras of his whore!"

Elvira wandered off into the kitchen to prepare pinole for her daughter. She did not invite us to stay for breakfast. Johnny caught my eye. He mouthed the words, "let's get outta here." We climbed into my truck and drove away.

The sun had cleared the horizon, but I couldn't see it. There was this weird autumn morning fog everywhere. It was a dim ghostly light—the world made all soft and diffused. We drove along South Flores Street, heading toward downtown. "Man, I'm starving," Johnny said. "Let's stop here. My treat." He pointed to a small bakery with a faded yellow facade. I'd never noticed it before. I pulled into the dirt parking lot. "The woman who owns this place is my aunt," Johnny said. Then he turned to me. "You're not going to put this into your blog, are you? That whole thing with Elvira?"

"What do you mean?"

"Don't play coy. I read it. Every so often."

"Oh?" I was surprised. "I didn't think anyone knew about it."

"You should change people's names," he warned me. "You're gonna get sued one day. Or sucker punched." Johnny got out of the truck and headed to the entrance of the bakery. I followed. Even though I'd never before stepped foot in the place, when we entered, it seemed strangely familiar. The girl standing behind the counter smiled at us. She had tiny hearts painted on her fingernails, all iridescent and sparkling. Johnny ordered two conchas, topped with pink icing, and a large yellow shortbread cookie. I scanned the pastries and cookies in the glass case.

"Two empanadas de queso," I said. "Oh, and one of those marranitos," I added, pointing.

As the girl bagged up our selection, Johnny asked her something in Spanish so quickly I didn't really get it. It sounded like he wanted two cups of coffee so we could eat and drink on the patio. I saw no patio. She paused, with her fingers still poised above the buttons of the cash register.

"Doña Estella es mi tía," Johnny said.

The girl nodded, letting us know she'd bring the coffee out to us. Johnny handed her a few dollars. I followed him down a corridor behind the display counter. We walked out into a simple garden. Across from us, on the far side of the yard, was a Quonset hut. Johnny told me that was where they did the baking. To the left was a cottage painted blue and covered with flowering vines. The little house couldn't have been more than three rooms. That was where Johnny's aunt lived. On the right side was a wrought-iron fence covered in ivy, which hid the auto transmission repair shop next door. Almost swallowed up by a stand of bamboo at the back of the yard was a shack made from scrap wood and gypsum board. It looked like it'd fall into a dusty heap if you slammed the door too hard—but it had no door, just a heavy yellow oilcloth hanging over the entrance.

"I haven't been here since I was a kid," Johnny said, his voice softened with nostalgia. We sat down at one of three picnic tables in the garden. Just then, the girl with the heart-tipped fingers came out and placed two huge steaming mugs of coffee in front of us. There was sugar and creamer already on the table. I watched Johnny tear open the bag of pastries so we could help ourselves to what we had ordered. The empanadas were good, and the marranito, that little ginger pig, was still hot from the oven.

I savored it all, taking little sips of strong sugared coffee to accentuate the flavors. That was when Doña Estella walked out of her small house and came up to us.

"My little Juanito!" she cried out. The woman was seventy or eighty, but she moved with a firm, fluid grace. Her long braided white hair was piled up on her head. She wore a white kaftan which went down to her sandaled feet. A light blue woolen rebozo was gathered at her shoulders. Before Johnny had time to stand, she pulled him to his feet and gave him a warm embrace. Doña Estella was slim, about a head taller than Johnny.

He introduced me to her. Estella took my hands in both of hers. She spoke to Johnny in Spanish, pointing back to the shack. Then she leaned low over the table to inhale a deep lungful of steam off Johnny's coffee. "That's what has been missing from my morning," she said. "I'll get a cup and come out to join you."

As she walked away, I asked Johnny what she had been talking about. "She said something about *preparing the temple.* Did I hear that right?"

"Yeah. She's a spiritual leader. Sort of."

"Okay." I looked at the shack. "And that's her church back there?"

Johnny took a moment to finish chewing a pastry. "It's a small congregation." He laughed and took a sip of coffee. "That back there is a temple to the Orishas."

"You mean Santería? Your aunt's a cult leader?"

"You make it sound so much more interesting," Johnny said with a shrug. "It's just a lot of candles, prayers, and, honestly, more Catholicism than you'd expect."

"Hey, I know this place," I said. It all fell together. This place looked familiar because I had seen some video of the bakery on the news last month. "This is that Voodoo bakery where the owner was sacrificing all those cats in the back."

"Whoa," Johnny said, his voice stern. "Let's make this clear before Estella comes back. That was the work of a group of primitive Pentecostals from over on Pleasanton Road. They threw some dead cats over the fence one night and then called the news stations. The car repair guys next door were hanging out drinking beer after hours. They saw it happen. But the reporters don't care about the truth."

"Sorry."

"It really upset my aunt. She loves cats." Johnny shook his head. "There's so much bigotry about the old religions. Yahweh, Jesus, la Virgen, those Orishas. It's all the same. Harmless stories to give people comfort."

"That's rough. Did the story hurt her bakery business?"

"I don't know about that. But it's no secret what she does back here. If folks around the neighborhood are okay with her sacrificing chickens to the ancient gods, what's a cat or two?"

"Wait. What?"

Johnny put his finger to his lips. I turned around and saw Estella walking up with a mug of coffee in one hand and a paper plate in the other. The plate held a strawberry kolache. She sat down beside me, placing the plate and cup in front of her with ceremonious deliberation before lowering her head in a short, silent prayer. Then she sat up straight and looked from Johnny to me. "I'll bet you're too young," she said. "Both of you. But today marks an important anniversary in this country's history."

"You mean the death of Kennedy?" I asked.

Estella's eyes widened. "You were quick with that."

"It's a big thing where I'm from," I explained. "Dallas being famous as the *city that killed Kennedy*."

"That's because San Antonio botched the job." Estella took a bite of her kolache.

"What?" If it was a joke, I didn't get it. "Not a fan?"

"Oh, but I was! He was the best thing to happen to this country." She licked a bit of strawberry jam off her finger. "All that talk about Jack and Jackie being American royalty?" she continued. "Absolutely! Everyone in San Antonio at the time had two pictures in their homes. The Pope. And Kennedy. So when he made his visit here, the day before his fateful stop in Dallas, the streets were lined with cheering people. Democrats, Republicans, it didn't matter. Along the entire motorcade route from the San Antonio International Airport down into the southside."

Estella reached out, placing a hand on Johnny's arm. "I was in the crowd with your aunt Miranda," she continued, "drinking root beer and waving an American flag as he rolled by with Jackie and Connelly and the lot." She turned to me. "Pretty much a preview of what you folks in Dallas got. Well, without the blood. We were in Roosevelt Park. We wanted to be up on the railroad bridge, but the Secret Service were chasing people off. So exciting! The motorcade continued past us, down to Brooks Air Force Base, to show off the troops and all that. Then all the way out to Kelly Field to fly out. People were nuts along the entire route. It was like Fiesta. Drive a president through San Antonio, and everyone forgets about the nuclear explosion in town just a week earlier."

"The what?" asked Johnny, leaning forward. I had no idea where this woman was going with her story. But it was clear she was enjoying herself. She took another bite from her pastry and sipped some coffee, all for dramatic effect.

"Look it up," she finally said, leveling her eyes at us. A challenge. "It was in all the papers. You see, the Atomic Energy Commission had a top secret operation that of course everyone knew about. Medina Base. It was adjacent to Kelly Field. So when on November 13, 1963, a huge explosion rocked the city, breaking windows as far away as Alamo Heights and sending up a gigantic mushroom cloud, oh it made the news. It was a big deal. The official report was 13 tons of TNT ignited by accident. But my parents' military friends were telling a different story. When the blast went off that morning, it was like the end of the world. A mushroom cloud, just like in the movies, so they said. I still believe it was a nuclear bomb that went off eight days premature in an underground facility."

Johnny poked me in the ribs with his elbow. "Are you hearing this?" he whispered. Johnny is obsessed with his personal theory concerning a network of mysterious, secret tunnels under the streets of San Antonio. It's a topic, along with flying saucers and abominable snowmen, on which he'll hold forth for hours after a few drinks.

"Imagine had it gone off on the surface as the motorcade passed along Military Drive on its way to Kelly Field," Estella added. "*We* would be the city that killed Kennedy."

"You see?" Johnny said, his voice rising. "More sinister activity down there in the tunnels!"

"Johnny!" Estella shook her head. "You and your tunnels." She lifted her hands and smoothed down the front of her kaftan, shifting roles from beloved aunt to priestess. "These tunnels you obsess over?" she said, tilting back her head. "They are nothing more than our shared histories and our interconnectedness. However, if there are, beneath our feet, prehistoric tunnels built by super intelligent dinosaurs living in the center of the earth, I'll be the first to nominate you for a Nobel Prize. Until you have proof, though, please don't be telling these stories to your nieces and nephews." Estella turned to me. "Their parents have to spend hours setting those children straight."

"Hey," Johnny murmured. "That's not fair."

Estella smiled as she leaned in closer to me. "If this one here knew the number of matches I've gone through over the years lighting candles for his wayward soul, well, he'd swoon!"

Johnny sighed. "Never said anything about dinosaurs."

Estella pivoted around and ran her fingers through Johnny's hair. "Swoon!" Then she took a deep breath, pushing away her plate and mug. "Just ask those families living downwind from the Medina Base how many of their relatives have died of the cancer. It's all been downhill since Cabeza de Vaca came through. Now we're surrounded by the church, the military, Walmart. It's amazing that we can get any honest work done around here."

Estella stood up. She placed a hand on my shoulder and dipped down to kiss Johnny on the head. "Well, I'll leave you be," she told us. "I've a busy day ahead of me." Johnny forced a smile. We watched Estella walk to the tiny building. She pushed her way inside; the oilcloth slapped shut behind her.

Johnny's smile faded, and he turned to me. "I don't know where she gets this stuff about talking dinosaurs from the middle of the Earth." I considered telling Johnny that I was quite familiar with *his* online writings. I wasn't the only one with a blog. Johnny had created a website he called *The Cucuy Club*, where he ladled hearty portions of purple prose atop fanciful musings concerning the folklore peculiar to South Texas, such as la llorona, lechuza, chupacabras, and the rest. Though I had not read anything specifically about talking dinosaurs in the middle of the Earth, such things hardly seemed beyond the scope of the topics he examined. I found it all entertaining, but I preferred not to fuel Johnny's ego over-much by letting him know I followed his journalistic efforts.

As we were getting in my truck, I realized the sun had burnt away the last of the fog. Johnny told me he didn't want to go home. "We're fighting again," he said, meaning him and his wife. "I said something unkind about her mother. And really, how could I not? I'm only human. So, could you drop me off at the puesto?" He meant the shop that his father runs downtown where Johnny helps out, selling south-of-the-border trinkets to the tourists.

That worked for me. It was already noon, and I had to head over to the Prometheus Performance Company to meet with Rachel, who would be directing my upcoming play. I also needed to turn on the charm and see if she'd help me write the script. All I had was that vague concept I submitted months ago. I hadn't expected it to be accepted. So now I had to slap something together for a March performance date—something which wouldn't embarrass me too much. I felt a slow slip into panic.

***

The Prometheus was in a state of chaos, but not the enjoyable kind associated with production work. The staff were engaged in the exhausting drudgery of moving the entire theater to its new home about half a mile away. Up in the mezzanine I heard some of the board members boxing up the racks of costumes. I could barely move through the lobby because of all the lighting instruments laid out—the thin Source 4s, stubby Parcans, miscellaneous LED panels. The hallway to the restrooms was crammed with coiled DMX cables piled in dusty mounds. In the offices workers from a moving company were cocooning filing cabinets in industrial strength plastic cling wrap.

Rachel led me to the darkened theater where we could sit on the front row and peacefully go over things such as rehearsal schedules and production timelines. The banal nature of those administrative details went a long way to help me dial down my nervousness. At some point, a noisy crew showed up with a scissor lift and some shop lights mounted on stands. They began dismantling the heavy pipes and battens of the lighting grid up in the ceiling. So we moved our meeting to Taqueria Guadalajara, where we could also enjoy a late lunch (or as it an early dinner?). When I nervously admitted to Rachel that I desperately needed help because I still hadn't written a complete script, she was unfazed.

"What we need this week is a title," she said. "Also the number of people in the cast. Write out a synopsis. Something longer than that sad proposal you submitted. But don't go crazy. Start with two or three

29

pages, and stick to the basic conceit you want to work with. And then next week we'll begin with the shape, theme, character work. You'll be surprised how fast it'll go."

If any one else had said those words to me, I would have only dropped deeper in despair. But I'd been around Rachel long enough to know her confidence was backed up by years of experience. She saw the work ahead as onerous, sure, but certainly not impossible. I trusted her completely. And when we parted ways, I felt a rising optimism.

However, as I sit here at my desk, putting off the work Rachel told me to do by writing my silly blog entry about washing machines and mushroom clouds, I feel my optimism failing me. *Basic conceit.* That sounds easy. But those two innocent words have suddenly chased away any creative thoughts that I would normally expect to find floating around in my head. What the hell is my basic conceit?

Maybe I can make the play about subterranean dinosaurs and their cunning political assassination plot. That sort of stuff just writes itself. Of course, because I now know that Johnny reads my blog, I'll probably have him demanding co-writing credits and a cut of the profits (as if the ticket sales of local experimental theater have ever lined anyone's pockets). Guess that means I need to ditch the dinosaur angle.

LAMENT IN THE TAQUERIA (DEC. 8)

In San Antonio, business gets done over tacos.

Which was the plan this morning. I met Ruben Villarreal for breakfast at El Rinconcito Taqueria over on Brazos Street. Ruben's in his seventies, one of the grand old men of the local art scene. As we were brainstorming on how best to fundraise for his lowrider festival, I realized someone was standing behind me. It wasn't the waitress come to refresh my coffee, but instead, a scruffy young guy clutching an oh-too-familiar book.

"Hey there, gentlemen," he said, placing the book on the table. "I don't know if you're familiar with Reggie Garza—may he rest in peace—and his Victory Chapel, but this incredible organization turned my life around." Ruben, who was clearly familiar with the spiel, shifted in his seat to reach his wallet. "Any donation would help," the man continued. "Also, I do have these woven keychains I made during the fellowship craft hour."

"I knew Pastor Reggie well," Ruben said, taking a keychain and giving the guy a five-dollar bill. "From back in the old days."

I picked up the book. *Lament in the Barrio, the Reggie Garza Story.* "That used bookstore in Dallas, the one my family ran?" I said to Ruben, waving the book in his direction. "I can't recall ever *not* seeing one of these on the shelf. I mean, copies of this book are everywhere. At least everywhere in Texas. I've always loved the cover design." I ran my hand over the artwork on the tattered dust jacket. There was a man with sunglasses who wore a bandana tied around his head. He guzzled from a bottle of booze. Seated on the ground beside him was another man shooting up dope. A weeping woman in a rebozo looked on, her eyes downcast. And there, in the middle of all that earthy squalor and sadness, was a Chicano Christ-figure, wrapped in both the American and the Mexican flags—he floated up heavenwards toward a glowing crucifix in the sky. "I mean, wow! You can't get more barrio lamentation than that!"

The young man shifted his weight, trying to figure out how to reclaim his property and move on to the next table. Ruben smiled at me. He took the book.

"I did this painting for Pastor Reggie. He paid me, I don't know, twenty dollars? Two hundred dollars? It was a long time ago." He looked fondly at the image.

"That's crazy," I said. "Why am I just now hearing this? I mean, this is your most famous painting. It's got to be. Hell, it's iconic." I craned my neck for a better view. "Where's your signature?"

"I think he mentioned me by name in here somewhere." Ruben flipped through the pages. He frowned, then turned to the back of the dust jacket flap. "I know I've seen it. Maybe it's only in the Spanish language edition."

The guy with the keychains waved to a passing waitress. He held up the five-dollar bill and pointed to the two tacos on Ruben's plate. "And some coffee," he added. He sat on the chair beside me.

"So, how would you do it today?" I asked Ruben. "Let's say someone came up and asked you to do the same thing, but 21st century style?"

"What are you saying?" Ruben looked at the cover. "Think it's too Cruz Candelaria?" he asked, referencing the artist character in the movie *Blood In Blood Out*. Pushing his plate aside, he put down the book. He removed a pen from his shirt pocket and began to sketch on a napkin. Then he looked toward the young man and moved the guy's baseball cap so the bill was askew. "Hold your chin up a bit." When the tacos arrived, the young man did his best to eat and model at the same time. He lifted his chin and raised his brows in an air of benevolent nobility, a tough look to maintain while eating a taco. "Okay," Ruben told him. "Now pretend you're holding a can of Lone Star beer, a tall boy." The young man did his best, but Ruben blinked. "What's that? You're holding a demitasse? With the pinky extended? This is a can. A *big* can. They're 16 ounces." Ruben rolled his eyes. "Kids," he muttered.

I'm very fond of Ruben's art. I'll admit to preferring his earlier work— that Cosmic Chicano style he reveled in back in his younger days. Way before my time. Feisty feathered serpents roiling up in the clouds as, below, blood-soaked jaguars slinking up the steps of pyramids. Stuff like that. That's not to say I don't care for his more recent historical canvases—deeply researched and meticulously painted scenes of life during the Mission period of San Antonio. There's a warm immediacy to all his work that lures me in close, compelling me to seek out all the unexpected details. Though I'd known Ruben for a decade, I don't often have a chance to see him working on his art. As I watched him lay down clean black lines from the chisel-edged art marker he'd removed from his pocket, I was pulled back to a summer eight years ago in Mexico.

***

The two of us, along with our friend Melinda, had secured a small humanities grant to research the Dia de los Locos parade in San Miguel de Allende where everyone dresses up in outrageous costumes and hides their identities with masks. It began as a lark. Wouldn't it be great to have a paid vacation in Mexico? That was what we had asked ourselves all those years ago. We'd been in a similar restaurant. Eating tacos.

And what do you know? The granting organization said yes. We ended up spending a month in the heart of that beautiful colonial city interviewing dozens of mask makers, as well as documenting all that went into the creation of that city's lavish, chaotic parade. The short documentary film that came out of that trip even picked up a few awards when it screened at various film festivals.

That first night in San Miguel, after checking into our roomy apartment, we drifted over to a dim bar off the main plaza and sipped brandy as a Cuban bolero band played with the reserved intensity of a yearning, passionate whisper. We each fell into the role of the Artist Abroad without even realizing it—retreating into our sketchbooks, our journals, engaged in private communion with this new romantic setting. At one point, I looked up from my notebook. Melinda was sketching the young man with the strong jaw who played the upright bass in the band. He stood out from the rest of the middle-aged, doughy band members. Ruben, his large sketchbook spread out across his knees, was creating an intricate vignette of the table across the dance floor from us. With masterful forced perspective, he drew the handsome bass player in the foreground, but managed to place the main emphasis on that table further back where an older elegant couple sat completely enraptured, she by the bass player, he by her.

God, I love that feeling. The first exciting days in a new city. Everything was all fresh in our minds and eyes—we were as ignorant as kittens. Around every corner, behind every door, a mystery. Our job for the next month was to become familiar with those mysterious spaces. And so, in the weeks ahead, as we interviewed the locals in the rough barrios beyond the tourist sectors, we found a city (like all cities), filled with passion, despair, conflict, and a profound appreciation for the little absurdities of life. Everyone we met, whether it was the Canadian expatriate gallery owner, immaculate in her white pantsuit, or the grease-stained mechanic who showed us the papier-mâché mask studio behind his body shop, they all had the same thing to say. Isn't it awful how this city has changed? True, not everyone agreed on *which* specific changes were so awful. But I knew each one would agree that those unwelcome changes (whatever they might be) happened without his or her consent.

I saw that when I recently visited San Francisco. It had been a quarter of a century since I had lived there, so there had been ample time for the city that once charmed me so deeply to change. So many of the things that caused me to fall in love with it were gone or had become so distorted and diluted as to be unrecognizable. The hippies had all but died out. The porno shops had transitioned into aromatherapy boutiques. Even the rat I spied skulking behind a dumpster seemed to be sporting hair product. It brought to mind my theater friend Rachel, and her deep love for New Orleans. Hurricane Katrina caused such heartbreak, even a decade in the past, which had caused her to put away a half-finished novel set in her beloved city. A place now sullied by avaricious developers who had exploited a disaster for profit.

I try not to fall into that stereotype, the grumbling malcontent opposed to all change. I blanch at the notion of becoming an aging reactionary raging for a return to some halcyon era back when I felt more secure with the world. What I yearn for is continuity. I want those indigenous and beautiful folkways I have stumbled upon throughout my life to remain intact. Perhaps it's selfish to wish that certain regions of the world will never change (just to appease my personal aesthetics). But the idea of setting off for a remote destination simply to arrive at the same cluster of fast-food joints and multiplexes is too ghastly to fathom. I see it happening in my own town. Without my consent. Often I succeed in escaping from it. In places like El Rinconcito.

***

I glanced over at Ruben. He had finished drawing and was scrutinizing his work with disdain. "Pretty much the same," he said. "But, you know, the barrio hasn't changed. The people are the same. And their problems. Well, there are more Walmarts. Some bicycle lanes. Places that'll buy your gold for pennies on the dollar. The boundaries are changing, I'll give you that. Closing in tighter. That fancy coffee shop across the street

35

wasn't there last year." He looked at the young man. "That where you're going now? For an espresso? A couple biscottis?"

Ruben handed the man his book. "Change is good. But you have to make sure you hold on to what is important." He nodded decisively and took a bite from his taco.

SIMIAN DREAMS (DEC. 18)

There is this choreographer I know. Eleanor. We worked together some years back on a large performance which was staged at the Lila Cockrell Theatre. A post-modern dance interpretation of Ovid's *Metamorphosis* with collaborative involvement from an Argentinian puppet group and a hip-hop collective from Port Arthur. I created a video design which was projected on the large scrim at the back of the stage. It turned out beautifully. No, really. In fact, it was instrumental in opening up for me new avenues of work providing video backdrops for dance and theater productions.

It helped Eleanor's professional career as well. She had been offered her current position teaching dance at an elite private school because of the buzz surrounding that performance. Of course, now, the only work she has time to create is with her students, who, no matter how precocious they may be, lack the rigorous focus needed to shine. These are rich girls who will be going off to get their MBAs, or marry further up the socioeconomic food chain. Not so much career track dancers or choreographers. But, still, Eleanor tries, every year, to recapture that triumph at the Lila Cockrell. There is always a video component which she needs me to provide for her school's annual dance showcase. I don't complain. The gig pays well and promptly. However, it exhausts me to see her put so much work and resources into another on-campus production for pampered, giggly rich girls and their distracted, unresponsive parents.

This year Eleanor wants an overall bird motif. I've already taken a few meetings at her office. The whole dance department is filled with feathered costumes and beaked masks. For the video, she wants images of birds flying, birds walking. Preening, floating on ponds, sleeping, socializing. So, that meant a trip to the San Antonio Zoo. It's not my favorite place. Zoos can be depressing. But because our zoo allows cameras and they have loads of birds, it was the obvious choice for today's camera safari.

After getting footage of some of the water birds—many who were free to move about the park—I headed to the avian house. The enclosed building was one of those older pavilions, where you peered through large glass windows into enclosures decorated to appear as various environments. There was the jungle, where sleepy-eyed toucans perched on artificial vines with glossy, plastic leaves. Or the prairie, with a morose bobwhite and two excitable plovers; the walls had been painted to show a thunderstorm sky, and spindly grass surrounded a pond made of brown-tinted glass, which might have resembled water were it not for the thick accumulation of dust on the surface.

I parked my tripod at one of the windows. If I shot straight on, I could avoid reflections. Fortunately, the cassowary continued to strut about the space as I reset my aperture and rotated the focusing ring. I smiled when I realized that the diorama was deep enough so that when I put the painted background out of focus, it looked like I had, indeed, captured images of a bird out in nature. The fake gum tree in the foreground didn't hurt the illusion at all. I knew this particular glass enclosure was supposed to depict the Australian outback, but it also resembled something closer to home. The parched, sun-blasted expanse of the Permian Basin, which was responsible for much of the heralded tedium of the Texas landscape. I recalled an excursion I made out there, decades ago.

***

It was the summer right out of high school, and my friend Claus had got a job at a roadside zoo. Intrigued, I knew I needed to make a visit. The dusty road off the highway took me under the curved metal sign for the Peterson's Snake Pit and Exotic Petting Zoo. It was a bit north of Abilene on the shores of Lake Fort Phantom Hill. The owners, two brothers who I only knew as the Petersons twins, scraped by, making just enough money to keep them in beer and frozen pizza. Ostensibly, one operated the snake house, while the other tended to the petting zoo. But in fact, Claus ran the whole show. The brothers would wake up around noon, and spend the rest of the day in the feed shed beyond the llama pen, steadily drinking while listening to sports on an old tinny RCA short-wave radio.

"This is the life," Claus told me toward the end of my visit. It took a second or so for it to sink in that he wasn't being sarcastic. When I had arrived at the zoo it was still early in the day, so I was able to give Claus a hand with many of his chores. Hosing down the peccaries, delousing the ostriches, and feeding the rattlesnakes, which was a grisly affair, as it involved live mice or rabbits, depending on the size of the snakes. We'd even had to mop up the patio in front of the box office when a toddler vomited. Too many Eskimo Pies, was my guess. Claus sold them out of a rusted, rattling freezer from another era, the era of roadside attractions.

Claus saw my confusion from his statement. He smiled and looked away across the lake. We were sitting on lawn chairs in the bed of my pickup truck drinking iced bottles of Dr Pepper fresh from the styrofoam cooler between us. A soft wind pushed in as the sun headed across the flat oil fields to a point beyond the horizon, beyond Merkel and Sweetwater. I peered over the rail of the truck, watching as dozens of large carpenter ants shuttled across the hard red earth, crisscrossing one another's paths, engaged in their archaic industry.

"It's this time of day," Claus clarified. "The hour after the mosquitoes have bedded down, but the bats haven't yet come out. Everything is simple, as though it's all come to a stop. Balanced just so."

We took a pull on our drinks. In the dying light, I saw what I at first mistook for a medium-sized dog loping our way. I leaned forward, squinting. It was a chimpanzee. As it came closer, I heard it breathing with a sort of asthmatic wheeze. It swung up onto the opened tailgate and squatted there, staring at Claus. The fur around its mouth was mostly white and its eyes were rimmed in red like a factory worker.

"This is Charlie," Claus said.

"Hi, Charlie," I said in that same voice I use for children, trying not to sound too patronizing. Charlie ignored me. He reached into the cooler to take out a bottle and handed it to Claus. Claus removed the cap and gave the bottle to Charlie. He swung over the side of the truck and was gone.

"He hates the crowds," Claus told me. "You know, the patrons. After breakfast, he lets himself out of his cage. Doesn't come back until sundown. I tried to follow him once, but he got mad." Claus lit a cigarette, the first one I'd seen him smoke that day. "Beats me where he goes. But he always returns and locks himself in his cage for the night."

The ostriches got into a noisy altercation, then they settled down. From the feed shed back toward the road, we could just make out the sound of a soccer game on the radio. We looked to the darkened western horizon and spotted a couple of satellites, tiny dots high enough to still catch the sunlight, as they glided untroubled across the sky.

That was the last time I saw Claus. I like to think he's still there, caring for each new generation of pythons and llamas. Maybe even cleaning the bedpans and changing out the catheters of the aging Peterson twins.

***

There in the bird house of the San Antonio Zoo I saw, in the reflection of the cassowary enclosure, a young man in an official olive jumpsuit behind me holding a mop and speaking to a young couple. Behind them, their daughter held her sandals in one hand, and a stuffed monkey in the other, as she stood barefoot and enraptured in front of a glass-fronted cage of some elongated water bird. When the bird moved, so did she, mimicking its decisive stiff-legged activity. It was one of those moments that occurs too often, when the action you feel you should be shooting is happening where you have not pointed the camera.

THE OFFERING (DEC. 22)

The new shirt was scratching me across the shoulders. I know better than to buy clothing at the Dollar General Store. However, this morning I was asked at the last minute to shoot some wedding portraits at Mission Espada and I didn't want to show up looking too shabby. The fabric was a synthetic blend; after a long afternoon, I was drenched in sweat. It was Hamid who had called. He's the best fine art photographer in town. But because a man's got to eat, he also shoots a lot of weddings. He explained over the phone that he had missed a connecting flight back from visiting family and he had a wedding portrait gig this very afternoon! Could I, please, help him out? Because I am known for shooting video rather than still images, it was clear to me that Hamid had already been turned down by several other camera colleagues before desperation forced him to contact me. Of course I said yes. I don't often get to be the hero. Besides, I'd be heading to New Orleans in a week for a creative get-away with Rachel—we needed to write a play. So, I could use the money.

I mostly avoid wedding work, whether photography or video. The whole thing seems so unpredictable. I imagine a nightmare scenario where an overwrought bride bursts into tears when shown the photos or video footage of the blessed event. How would I be able to shake off that realization I had *ruined* her wedding? You know, that whole till-death-do-us-part, and all she has to look at, forever, are pictures she finds unflattering.

Hamid gave me the details before I could change my mind. He told me the time and location of the shoot; however, as he began to describe the couple, I cut him off. "Don't worry," I said. "I'm sure to spot them. She'll be in white, he'll be in black." He thanked me and hung up.

And, indeed, she was in white, he in black. People don't much go in for non-traditional weddings these days. Leastwise, not in this town. It was an odd time of year to get married, as we were coming up on Christmas. You'd think folks would have enough anxiety. However, it was perfect weather. Sunny and in the 70s. I screwed on a polarizing filter to make the puffy clouds pop against the deep blue sky. The St. Augustine grass on the north side of the old stone building was lush and deep. With each shot I set up, I found myself distracted by their youth. And they, of course, were distracted by each other. They were just so amazed to be in one another's presence. Everything seemed to be their first time. I had him sit on a low stone wall so she could sit in his lap. She did, but she blushed.

"I've never done this," she said in a whisper.

"Honey," the groom-to-be said. He shook his head and looked at me. "Really, we're not so innocent."

"It's just that I've never sat in your lap before," she said. They kissed. I shot.

When we had wrapped things up, the bride and groom thanked me. They headed off. I decided to walk to a private graveyard nearby. I took a shortcut through a pasture.

At the edge of the cemetery, I stepped up on the thick trunk of a mesquite tree that grew at an angle over the fence, and I dropped down. I sat beside a small grave marker to take a few photos of a weathered stone carving of Mary, her head covered and her hands together. There were several plastic flowers which appeared old but still held a vibrant red pigment. I heard the metal gate creak open. Two young men entered. Each carried a votive candle to a grave near a live oak tree. They were speaking quietly, so I knew they had seen me.

One of them walked over. He said softly, "I hope we won't offend you." I watched, more perplexed than alarmed, as he unbuttoned his shirt, revealing a tattoo on his chest. "You know the Señora, Santa Muerte?" he asked. I nodded. The tattoo was a beautiful detailed image of a skeleton with long hair flowing from beneath the hood of her red robe. She held a scythe, as skeletons tend to do. "We're here to make an offering to Her," he said, touching his chest, "on behalf of our departed friend."

"I understand," I said. He buttoned his shirt as he rejoined his companion. I wished I had asked to photograph his chest. The two men burned candles and a bundle of sage as they said prayers in Spanish. I lingered longer than I normally would have near such a solemn service, but there's something about the smell of burning sage that makes a place seem intimate, welcoming.

Eventually I stood, making my way to the gate—the proper exit, not my irreverent fence climb. As I walked past the men, I was grateful that my new cheap shirt was appropriate for both weddings and funerals. I pushed through the gate and kept my head down, as though brooding upon the fleeting nature of mortality, all the way down the tree-lined path until I could no longer smell the incense.

THE TROUBLED TROUBADOUR (DEC. 23)

The holidays never sit well with me. It isn't about the nostalgia for that lost world of childhood when the hope for gifts held sway over the imagination. It's not even about the loneliness that comes from being single in a city in which you didn't grow up. What bothers me is the disruption of routine. Not *my* routine. No. I have crafted an amorphous lifestyle outside the whole work-a-day world and devoid of those cyclical obligations of the family man. I have no routines, so that means I rely on the routines of others. I want the majority of humanity to maintain predictable routines, so that I can more easily avoid them.

Let's say I'd like to get away from town on a Wednesday and drive out to Lost Maples State Park. Why not? I can head out the door right now. Have the whole park to myself. What if I want to go see a movie without the crush of people around me? A weekday matinee is perfect. How about a quiet meal out? Three o'clock lunch.

Which was what I did today. I do the three o'clock lunch often. Maybe I *am* driven by my own routines.

When I opened the door of Taqueria Guadalajara, I had to crab-walk my way around the portly owner who was up on a ladder placing a line of fake potted poinsettias on a shelf above the chalkboard which announced the daily specials—today's being pozole. I would have thought the place was already sufficiently decorated for Christmas, what with the images of snowmen, reindeer, and a large, laughing Santa painted on the windows. And the red and green tinsel hanging off of everything. And the multicolored lights. Was it like an advent calendar, each day requiring a new seasonal embellishment?

My usual booth in the back was free, so I sat there. When I decided what I wanted, I glanced up from my menu. Olivia held her pad and pencil poised, but she wasn't looking at me. Three musicians had just walked into the restaurant. She made a sound deep in her throat.

"I don't like that one," she said, without taking her eyes off of them. I'd never seen the men before, but I knew she meant the tall, sinewy guitarist with the clean-shaven face. The accordionist and the man with the upright bass were jovial, laughing. They adjusted their cowboy hats as they scanned the meager post-lunchtime crowd. The guitarist wore no hat. He was dressed all in black and had on a large silver belt buckle with a matching ring that caught the reflected sunlight for a blinding instant as the glass door to the parking lot closed behind him.

When I asked about the pozole, Olivia said they were all out. I glanced back at the menu. "He used to be a priest," Olivia said. I looked up at her. She said something that hinted of disgrace and then leaned down to tap at my menu with her pencil. "Get the gordita plate," she said. "You always do."

When the men sat down at a table by the jukebox, I felt cheated. I thought they were here to perform. I guess they'd been busy since noon, hitting restaurant after restaurant, performing for those customers. Finally, they'd settled on a place to eat lunch.

My desire for unscripted days has, at its core, an admittedly juvenile and romantic notion of the unfettered artist. A carefree spirit who can not only flit about at will but, whilst flitting, is also creating. I used to achieve this more often in my past. I'm thinking of my study-abroad year, when I'd wander the towns of coastal East Sussex, slipping into pubs for a couple of pints and a few hours scribbling in my notebook. Or my misspent years in San Francisco, when, on days off from a series of undependable temp jobs, I'd explore the gritty alleyways in the Mission and Tenderloin, taking candid portraits of the down-and-out.

Somehow, I thought I'd be able to do the same in San Antonio. In fact, a couple of years ago I went so far as to buy a lightweight netbook, so I could toss it in my messenger bag and ride my bike all over town, pausing at cafes or parks to type out chapters of my novel-in-progress. I did it for a week. I guess, as with so many other plans, I lacked the discipline. Or maybe I saw it as another routine. There's also the possibility that this just isn't a city suited for the peripatetic artist desiring to create on the fly.

I was doing my best today. I had opened my 3-ring binder and reviewed the notes I had so far for my upcoming play. There wasn't much. I had a title. *How's My Karma!* The concept was a game show set in the afterlife where everyone in the audience has died and is vying for a chance to be chosen as a contestant in a game of snakes and ladders, hoping to win a favorable rebirth. Rachel and I had outlined most of the action, though it was all still pretty vague. The only part cast so far was for the game show host, who would be played by my friend Samantha.

The more I looked at the notes, and the more I thought about the whole thing, the more pretentious it sounded. Rachel would direct, but just as important, I needed her to help me write something that wouldn't be an enormous embarrassment. I decided to play it optimistic by telling myself that our upcoming four-day writing retreat in New Orleans would result in an exciting, lively script. The Prometheus Performance Company was funded through several prestigious granting organizations, so my responsibility to deliver a smart and socially relevant play had my stomach churning. Perhaps a gordita plate wasn't the best idea. I tried to remind myself that, in addition to Rachel, there were other company members working on my behalf, people who believed in me. But I wasn't feeling it.

When Olivia returned with my food, I pointed to the table of musicians, where the guitarist leaned in close over a bowl with a spoon. "I thought you said you were out of pozole." I gazed down at the gorditas. They were always good, but I had wanted to break out of my routine. She laughed and walked away, humming a tune. I guess there's always enough pozole left for the fallen angels. And in Olivia's eyes, I was not yet one of those.

THE COVEN AT THE SIXTEENTH HOLE (JAN. 8)

Last year they tore down the old grain silos, a lovely row of squat iron structures with conical corrugated roofs that lined the river across from my neighborhood. When I moved to San Antonio, they were rented out as rough, simple artist studios. Many had such bad wiring that each month during the First Friday Arts Walk, the artists and musicians in the silos would overtax whatever type of electrical distribution network served the buildings. Brownouts and blackouts were common. On my maiden excursion over there for First Friday, a decade back, I stepped up to one of the silos and a fellow at the entrance handed me a flashlight. How wonderfully offbeat, I thought, assuming it was all intentional. I soon learned that the tiny gallery had lost power, and this was the only way I could view the paintings hung on the wall.

Over the years, most of the artists were pushed out, and the silos were fenced off, awaiting an urban renewal development. The silos were situated upon some sort of Superfund site, which needed to be cleaned of asbestos or arsenic, or whatever. But whether given over to impoverished artists or to the nettles and dandelions of neglect, those decaying reminders of a bygone industry were beautiful, particularly when viewed from the quaint pocket park across the San Antonio River.

I knew their demolition was bound to happen, eventually. Frank Maillard owned the land. He controlled so much property on the southern edge of downtown. Many people saw him as a great advocate of the arts, what with his seats on the boards of several museums. It was, however, in his real estate interests that it became apparent he had little concern for those humble artists he displaced with his developments. Still, the actual razing of the silos came as a shock to me one day when I walked to that little neighborhood park to look across at nothing. Nothing at all. I fancy myself as one who remains in the loop on such local matters. But that day, I learned otherwise. The silos had been flattened; the concrete foundations scraped clean. Nothing remained but a predatory bulldozer parked idle beside a mound of cracked timber and bent sheet metal.

Now, half a year later, they've begun constructing a huge concrete structure that brings to my mind a futuristic abattoir. As I stood in the little park this morning trying to figure out if the building was finished, or if I was just seeing the unadorned supporting elements, I wondered if my general disdain for the aesthetic paucity of contemporary architecture was simply that of a sour, out of touch middle-aged man.

"What do you think it's going to be?" a voice from beside me asked. I turned. It was a woman who I often see wandering the neighborhood. She always lugs around several shoulder bags. Her short graying hair lies close to her skull, as though she's never washed it. That, coupled with the outfits she favors that are decades out of date, had made me suspect she was homeless. But now, seeing her up close, she seemed not so desperate, not like one living so close to the edge. She must be in her mid-seventies. She told me her name was Mary.

"I know which house you live in," she added. Clearly she had noticed me, as well. "I used to live there too, years ago. Does Mario still own it?" That would be my landlady's husband. When I told her that he died some years back, Mary nodded. "The way he smoked and carried on, it's no surprise," she said. Then added: "That's awfully close to the river to put a parking garage. You know, if that's what it's supposed to be." I gathered she meant the building going up. I couldn't see how proximity to water had any bearing on a parking garage, but Mary was quite specific. "If they don't set their parking brakes, those cars will roll back and sail right through that opening." She pointed to what appeared to be a doorway halfway up the building. "They'll fall and fall and splash! That's how lawsuits happen."

Mary had a soothing manner about her. She seemed unconcerned about whether or not I contributed to the conversation. She explained that she grew up in this neighborhood and had, over the years, lived "on just about every street you could name." Her friends, the ones still alive, didn't get out much. So she made her daily rounds, checking up on *her ladies*. "I gotta get to Minerva's place today," Mary said, patting one of the canvas bags slung over her shoulder. "Got some tax forms she has to fill out. Don't want them taking her house away. You know Minerva?"

"Nope."

"She lives next door to Giovanni." She made the sign of the cross. "Well, where he *used* to live." I nodded, mentioning how his passing had been unexpected. "He will be missed," she said. "Giovanni was a good man."

"Yes, he was," I agreed.

She wanted me to understand that it used to be different around here. It used to be that the rich people lived on the *other* side of Alamo Street. You knew where you stood with someone because of where they lived. Now *they've* invaded, buying up everything. I suspect she meant newcomers arriving from out of town.

"Last week," she said, "I was standing in front of the Groos House over on King William Street. It used to belong to the Girl Scouts. Can you imagine that? The Girl Scouts had a mansion? They sold it to Charles Butt. Don't you wish you could sell a house to a billionaire?" She rambled on about how a tour group rolled up on Segways (which she referred to as "electric pogo sticks"). She edged in closer to hear what they had to say about the Groos House. "I already knew about the Girl Scouts and Charles Butt. But I didn't know how Mr. Butt built a tunnel from his mansion out to the garage—what I guess used to be the coach house.

51

Why he can't walk to his garage across the grass like everyone else? But, rich folks live by rules that make no sense to the rest of us. With all those billions, I can't imagine he'd stop with a hidden passageway to his garage. Where else you think he's built a tunnel to? Everywhere in town he's got to go, is my thinking. A whole maze down there. A bunch of those little circus cars zooming around under our feet to take him to the bank and the steakhouse and the golf course."

She veered off into talking about her older sister, who used to run with a coven of witches. "This was back before people called themselves pagans and such. They were witches, pure and simple. They kept secret about it. Every new moon they'd do their dark rites after sneaking onto the Riverside Golf Course. Naked? Probably. I was never invited. Not part of the coven. I should ask my sister. About the naked stuff. But she's got the dementia. These days I look after her in the mornings and the evenings." Mary explained that Teddy Roosevelt and his Rough Riders used to train in the park before it became the golf course. I wasn't able to hear her too well. At that point, a trash truck crept down the street toward us, making a racket. Perhaps Mary's sister is well-served by her dementia. She'll never know that the sleepy neighborhood surrounding the Riverside Golf Course is on an accelerated development schedule to be inundated by high-rise condominiums now that the quaint low-income trailer park has been bulldozed. It's hard for me to envision esoteric skyclad rituals secretly performed in the shadow of rooftop jacuzzis.

"I need to hoof it down the road," Mary said. She looked up with her head tilted, checking the angle of the sun. "Get some signatures from Minerva before too late. It'd be easier if she'd just give me power of attorney. But I'm not getting any younger. I'd have to get someone to be *my* power of attorney. And on and on. Turtles all the way down." She grinned up at me before setting back off on her rounds.

I walked down a footpath along the river, away from the new construction, and crossed over on the stone blocks placed there in lieu of a bridge. The water rushed by at my feet. I caught a glimpse of a catfish powering its way upriver. The sun came out earlier, but it was still chilly. I had wisely put on a knit cap and wound a scarf around my neck. I wished I had brought gloves as well. So it was with hands crammed deep in pockets, and shoulders hunched up, that I climbed the steps to the Blue Bird Arts Complex, another portion of Frank Maillard's domain, where the rents had so swiftly risen that it was impossible to spot an honest artist on the premises, unless he or she worked as a dishwasher in the expanding assemblage of artisan pizzerias or high-dollar cocktail bars.

This was where the Prometheus Performance Company rented space for two decades before Maillard refused to renew their lease and booted them out. As much as I'd like to paint the man as the villain, the theater was already struggling with funding difficulties just like all the other arts organizations I knew. And now that I was a company member I could attend the Prometheus Performance Company's board meetings and see the less glamorous side of show biz. I had a comprehensive lesson on the administrative responsibilities associated with a nonprofit organization that received a good chunk of its budget from the city's art funding office. In fact, they were already clamoring for all manner of paperwork connected to my upcoming play: detailed budgets, marketing plans, projected audience numbers, etc. With the shrinking staff at the theater, I suddenly found myself now responsible for much of those administrative duties.

I'd rather just work with Rachel on script work, casting, rehearsals, and performance. But paperwork? I need someone, like Mary, rushing around in the background, on her own initiative, filling out forms and interceding on my behalf with bureaucrats. I tried not to think of all that fiddly stuff as I walked through the Blue Bird complex, and watched, instead, all the new faces fluttering about. I had to admit a part of me enjoyed seeing the young people excitedly working their first jobs, rushing around the grounds in their valet parking-attendant jackets, or strapping on their aprons for their first shift at the new tapas bar (the space where the Pinhole Photo Gallery had been just last month). They were able to look at this place with fresh eyes, and they had no clue that the pale woman, blowing cigarette smoke at the sky beside the entrance to her art studio, received her eviction notice two days ago. In March, an Austin-based gelato chain will be moving in.

The downside to living in a place for a number of years is that you begin to see how things are run behind the scenes. Would it be better to just ignorantly drift through the world? As much as I enjoy collecting people's stories, there's something heartbreaking about possessing an overabundance of information. Try not to know people's business, I'd like to advise young people. Accept the clean veneer they show you; smile, and move on. But I find the lure of peeking behind people's curtains, so to speak, so seductive.

I tried not to look inside the door of the cavernous brew pub, which took over the space that the Prometheus Performance Company occupied for so many years. It was difficult for me to reconcile that the easiest path for me to take from my home to the new location of the Prometheus was to pass by this, the former location. Suddenly, I felt that the carefree young people milling about with their open, smiling faces couldn't help but sense the resentment and hostility radiating off of me as I created my own toxic Superfund site. And so, I took a deep breath, forcing a warm cloud of virtue to engulf my blackened heart. I made it a point to smile beneficently at them all.

Back on that final day of the Prometheus' tenancy at Blue Bird, as I scrambled to help my fellow company members move two decades' worth of paperwork, props, and racks upon racks of wardrobe, I made sure that I would be the final person out the door. Before I locked up for the last time, I took a red velvet heart-shaped pillow from our props collection and left it on the floor of the huge, empty, and now soulless space. Placed with loving care upon that cushion was a fresh mound of dog turds.

Enjoy my parting gift, Frank Maillard.

***

I have to pause. Think things through. To share such behavior through a public online journal seems unwise. However, there isn't anything inherently illegal in the casual utilization of dog poop. Or is there? Protected by the first amendment, I'd like to think. I *can* delete those words, but I don't think I will. Candor is an odd thing. It's beloved by both the courageous and the narcissistic. I'm not immediately sure where I fall. But because my blog seems to have a readership very close to zero, it's more likely that this candor is related to my frustration of being under-appreciated by the world at large, forcing me to keep upping the stakes until finally someone confronts me on the street. "I read what you think of me, you smug jackass!" And *then* I'll know someone is reading my words.

So, narcissist it is.

Of course, typing in the glow of a laptop and a desk covered with flickering candles creates an unreal, liminal realm free of the fear of consequences. And, frankly, I'm too cold to worry much about such things. It took over an hour, but finally I've got the place warm enough so I no longer see my breath in the air. I just now closed the door to the oven and turned it off. My little space heater can probably keep me comfortable until I go to sleep. Another bit of unwise disclosure. If my elderly landlady stumbled upon this entry, she'd be unhappy to learn I heat this property with the gas range. In all likelihood I'm breaking some rule embedded in the massive lease agreement I signed all those years ago without ever reading it.

Lawyers must hate having clients who blog. Especially if those clients also drink.

***

So, where was I?

Ah, right. Walking past the old location of the Prometheus on my way to the new location. In theory, they were not far apart at all. In reality, considering the weather, it turned into quite the hike. Halfway to Flores Street, with the wind kicking up, I realized I should have driven. Maybe after our meeting, I could cadge a ride back home from Rachel. It was hard for me to process the fact that tomorrow we would be driving to New Orleans to work on the play.

The two of us, we worked well together. I was excited (and a little overwhelmed) with the prospect of a deeper collaboration with her on this new project. Our upcoming play would be the first Prometheus performance staged in the new building. I wondered if there would really be enough time for the place to be made ready. The lights hung, the sound system installed, the rickety loft turned into a functioning tech booth.

I stopped for the light at the crosswalk, looking across the street at the building. It used to be a lumber yard for as long as I had lived in town. A heavy rain, I felt certain, would bring the whole thing down. When the light changed, I crossed the street and rushed around the building. When I opened the back door to the theater, a gust of wind took hold of it. Only with difficulty was I able to drag it shut behind me.

Rachel was there, laughing. "Your ears are so red," she said to me. "You don't handle the cold well at all, do you?" She sat alone in the cozy office lit only by a gooseneck desk lamp and the glowing mesh element of an electrical heater. The clutter of dozens of unopened boxes, still unattended to since the big move, were half-hidden in the shadows. It was too early for any of the staff to show up for work yet. We had the place to ourselves.

"I made you hot chocolate," she said. "I even found marshmallows." I walked toward her and that warm circle of light.

ESCAPE (JAN. 13)

The bullet was the color of an overcast sky. It had caught my eye when the sun glinted off it, revealing where it hid in the grass. I got off my bike, picked it up, and took a seat at a picnic table in a park pavilion near Mission Espada. It was a beautiful day, and I was treating myself to a leisurely bike ride on my first day back from New Orleans.

I placed the bullet so that it stood on the table, pointing up.

It guess it's inaccurate to call it a bullet. It was an intact and unfired .45 ACP cartridge, stubby and fat. I leaned my chin on the picnic table and looked at it up close. It was like being a kid again. Seeing not a round of ammo but a huge rocket on the launchpad, ready for takeoff.

I grew up with images of spacecraft poised to hurl the brave and the brilliant into realms of extraordinary adventure. I had hoped to be one of those young explorers whose quick wit and bookish habits would make me an obvious candidate for early adventures to the stars. While I flipped through pulp magazines with their lurid covers, there was a whole world of misery being pumped out of muzzles and turrets. Right here, on Planet Earth. I could have kept up with *those* stories on TV or in the newspapers. But the horror of the real world couldn't compete. Not when planets full of lizard people were waiting to be discovered by a crew of nebbish young spacefarers.

The world of fiction is so often where hope resides. In the real world, we watch with sadness how the science of ballistics concerns itself with muzzle velocity more often than escape velocity. How retrograde it all seems. Guns are an old, clunky technology, without even the ability to fling a bullet at a fraction of the speed needed to escape the gravitational influence of Earth. I looked closer at the cartridge. The bullet and the shell casing displayed a couple of shallow dents. Someone had chewed on it. A dog? A kid? I rolled it about in my palm, feeling its weight. That's the thing. Weapons are heavy. And if we insist on taking them in the cargo holds up to the stars with us, they will continue to drag us back down to the surface, down here with all these fear-ridden simpletons, fumbling and obsessing over their primitive appetites.

The worst seems to be how customary it has become, this notion of giving in to our appetites without any real consideration of the consequences. This hunger for wealth and comfort and novelty is resulting in an increasingly inhospitable planet. I'm afraid the science fiction written for the kids of tomorrow won't be so much about the wonder of exploration, but the sad necessity of dragging ourselves away from a ravaged, lifeless cinder.

Lifeless cinder? Lord, where did that come from?

I should be happy. Overjoyed. Buoyant, even. I mean, I wrote a play. Well, *we* wrote a play. Rachel and I. The product of a four-day weekend in New Orleans. Between the occasional excursions in search of po' boys, or short jaunts to historic cemeteries, we kept a busy schedule seated at our laptops. It helped that neither of us were drinking. And that we weren't romantically involved. Although I held onto that fantasy all the way through our final night in that tiny, drafty bungalow we rented in the Garden District. Of course, wistful hope rarely results in anything tangible.

Anyway, a play. That's great, right? Yes. In fact, *it* is something tangible. I mean, a play is almost literature. I'll admit I often dismiss the work of screenwriters and playwrights, particularly those with literary pretensions. Anyone can write dialogue, I'll say with a sneer. Sure, there's more to it than that. However, dialogue comes easy when you're writing for an actor who you know well—in this case, Samantha. Let's be honest, the playwright provides the basic ideas. The actors do most (if not all) of the heavy lifting. So don't be giving me the side eye when I'm not wearing linen gloves whilst reading your precious script. You've done your job, now get out of the way. Let the director and the actors finish the work you started.

With us, things will be a bit different. Rachel will direct. And we agreed that I will perform a character who functions as sidekick to Samantha's character. That made things much less stressful. We won't have to worry about some sensitive writer looking over our shoulders. And if we need to make changes in the moment, we can do it without any consultation.

We're happy with our results. Most of our drive back yesterday was spent discussing who to bring in for art design, wardrobe, lighting, and who should be cast as the three other characters. I know Kat will be upset when she learns there isn't a part for her. The fact is, Rachel can't stand her, and production work is tough enough without *that* sort of drama. But by the time we were about an hour out of San Antonio, we had each drifted into our own thoughts.

I was struck by the number of trucks getting on and off the highway. Then I realized most were hauling the heavy machinery of the fracking industry. Like so many folks living in San Antonio, I have remained shockingly oblivious to the growing oil and gas extraction in the area. Over the years, I've heard mention of the Eagle Ford Shale, and the active drilling fields covering an arc from Hallettsville all the way down to Carrizo Springs. But it was just one of many troubling environmental indignities happening somewhere out of my line of sight. Another of those things I'll become more involved with one of these days, I'll tell myself. If you hop on the internet and call up a recent nighttime satellite image of Texas, you'll see a crescent of light between San Antonio and the Gulf Coast. It is pure industry. Not towns, but utility lights from thousands of drilling and pumping pads, as well as the flames of ignited gas off the flare stacks.

Not everyone's happy about this. No surprise there. What *does* surprise me, is hearing rural Texans speak with such open hostility toward the oil business. What used to be a respected pillar of our state's economic stability has become an unwelcome cancer tearing through the farm and ranch lands of the Texas coastal plains. Heavy machinery chewing up country roads. Methane belching into the atmosphere. Benzene poisoning the well water. Prostitution. Meth labs. Moral turpitude! It used to be that in towns like Tilden and Dilly, the biggest scandal was when the high school quarterback got caught smoking weed. Those innocent days are long gone.

All these workers in the fracking fields need housing. Many of them prefer living close to a sizable city and commuting out to their work sites. This is part of the development of the southern portion of the county—former farmlands bought up for the construction of dense stands of cookie-cutter homes and apartment complexes. I should be more aware of this. I claim to know well the southside neighborhoods of San Antonio.

I often take lengthy bike rides all the way out to Mission Espada, and beyond. Just as I did today. My preferred path is a bike trail that follows the river. But because it is a linear park, and thus all protected public land, I have remained blind to much of the encroaching developments. The sloping floodplain crowded with mulberry groves and mesquite thickets hides the spread of tract homes and strip malls. Of course, you can still find farms out around Mission Espada, though I expect this is the last generation for them. The folkways of rural America are almost gone. As a city boy, I used to envy kids from the country. Skinny-dipping in creeks. Blasting dirt clods with hand-me-down rifles. Riding into town in the back of a pickup with a dog or two as stray rounds of ammo roll around in the bed. An innocent and mostly untroubled life.

ONE LUNG AND A PONYTAIL (JAN. 22)

"Cut!" cried the assistant director. This he followed up with: "And let's all take a meal break. That'll be—" he looked over at the camera crew "—thirty-five?" The director of photography shook his head and held up one hand with all fingers and thumb spread. "Be back in fifty minutes, guys," the assistant director bellowed with final authority.

The team of grips, in their steel-toed boots and baggy shorts, hustled around to shut off the lights. The equipment needed to cool down before it could be moved for the next camera set-up. Our talent—a young fresh-faced actress—was steered back toward the makeup tables for her face to be refreshened. And, finally, two humorless women descended upon the real star of this commercial, a plate of latex-molded fried chicken. Latex, because real chicken fell apart under the hot lights and long hours of a commercial shoot. It wasn't just any fake chicken over which these women fussed. This was El Pollo Fuerte, the fastest growing chicken chain in California, now making its debut in the South Texas market.

When I moved to town, I kept busy working on any film or video project I could find. Usually in the camera department, but also some post-production work. San Antonio is not a town where this sort of freelance worker can make a living, but I've honed well my frugality over the decades. I don't need much to get by. Besides, I had this grand notion that if I made myself available to everyone in town, they would also help me with my own projects. I guess I eventually burned out when I realized how little people cared for films that weren't their own. I got sick of the personalities. Also, I bitched too often around the wrong people. The phone stopped ringing. The only reason I landed today's El Pollo Fuerte gig was because the guy they contracted to do sound flaked and Vincent, who'd been hired to shoot this commercial, recommended me. It seemed not everyone considered me a jerk.

The boundary microphone hidden on the table next to the plate of chicken was still hot. I was bored, so I cranked up the headphone output on my Fostex deck so I could eavesdrop.

"Dab it some more," one of the art department women hissed to the other. "That breast is all sweaty."

"Just work on your thigh, Linnie. I'm on top of it."

Linnie saw me laughing. She leaned in toward the microphone and spoke in a clear voice. "This is our time to work and your time to slack off—got it?" The other woman shot me an ugly look. I removed my headphones, shut off the Fostex. I wasn't in the mood to visit the craft service table to see what was for lunch, so I rummaged in my backpack for the two extra breakfast tacos I had grabbed earlier in the day.

"Hey," a voice said. I looked up. It was Mari, the script supervisor. She held up my phone which had been resting beside the mixing console. "You missed a call." I liked her. And I liked that she was nosy. "Fernando De Leon," she added, reading the screen. "I like the name."

I reached out to retrieve my phone. "Don't let that impress you. I'm not even sure it's his real name."

"Yeah?" she said, shifting her weight to lean a hip against my sound cart.

"There are about five people I never want to speak to again," I told her. "But I still keep them on my phone."

"Of course," she said. "So you know not to answer."

"If you ever see an incoming call from Fernando De Leon, do not feel compelled to answer my phone. Some of the others are more obvious, such as the one listed simply as Unhinged Actress."

"So, this Fernando? He's also in this business?"

"Yeah. More or less."

"I'm getting a sense there's a story here." Mari looked across the set. "But our illustrious director is all panicky and trying to make eye-contact with me. El Pollo Fuerte waits for no man." And she was gone, leaving me alone with my cold egg and chorizo tacos. Mari was right. There was a story there. Although maybe not a grand story.

***

I only ever saw Fernando twice. Last year, he phoned me up. I forget now who gave him my phone number. He told me he was finally prepared to launch into production for a feature film. In fact, he said, he had emailed me a copy of the script just before calling. So, that someone had given him my email as well. He explained that he had directed a low-budget feature film fifteen years ago that starred Hector Baltierra, one of the more prominent actors to have come out of San Antonio.

"Yeah," I said, interrupting him. "*Silver Nightshade Dreams*. I've seen it. Great stuff." He became excited that I knew his work, and he insisted we meet. So I agreed to lunch the following Tuesday. I suggested Taco Junction, a restaurant in my neighborhood. The truth is, I was intrigued, but not enough to drive.

At Taco Junction, I ordered a coffee and waited. Fernando had said I wouldn't be able to miss him. "I'm an old hippie. I'll be the guy with the gray ponytail." As I sat in a booth facing the door, I wondered if I should give him the copy of the script I had printed up. All 115 pages. It was riddled with misspellings and poor grammar; I'd filled it with red notations. However, the writing was enjoyable. Fresh, playful. So many unexpected turns of phrase. Interesting characters. Thick on story, thin on plot. All fine by me, but far from having any commercial appeal.

When Fernando came through the door, there was no mistaking him. I suddenly decided not to let him see my notes. He'd either be miffed at my liberties, or thrilled that I had already put several hours into this project. Either way, I was not yet ready to move into a deeper relationship with a man I did not know. So, before he spotted me, I slipped his script off the table and put it in my backpack. I stood up, we shook hands, and he took a seat across the table from me.

Before we could take our introductions any further, the waitress arrived. Fernando ordered a coffee. After scanning the menu, he chose a bean and cheese taco. I looked over at the bus transfer peeking out of his wallet.

"Get whatever you want," he said. "It's on me." I muttered something about having had a late breakfast and ordered a small serving of the capirotada.

Fernando was a small man of indeterminate ethnicity. He buzzed with a warm, nervous energy that had you leaning in, listening. He sported a pointy beard, long hair, and an easy smile. When he asked what I thought of his script, I had to take a breath and reevaluate what I had planned to say.

"There are a lot of kids in this script—"

"It's my homage to *The Goonies*! You know, had it been directed by Pasolini."

"I see." I wanted to convey the problems of working with children, but if he saw them as a central feature, I continued to the next issue. "Then there's this dog who gets into all this mischief. You're going to need a very well-trained dog."

"Oh, I have the dog. My dog. Murphy. He's just as cute as the dog in the script. He *is* that dog. I have this old tennis ball. Murphy loves that ball. I'm out in the park every day. Me and Murphy, we're coming up with new tricks constantly!"

"Well, that's good. I'm glad you've taken into consideration all the variables."

Fernando took a sip of his coffee. "Look," he said, with a soft smile.

"I'm not getting any younger. But I've found that there's one thing that I do well. And that's writing screenplays. I'm a writing machine. This one you love so much is one of many. I wrote *Junkyard Kids* in only four days. I'm on fire. And I've been in contact with some serious investors. I'm honest with them. I tell them that even after that last operation brought me down to just this one lung—though I don't smoke anymore, well, not tobacco—I'm doing great for a man in his sixties. I'm on top of my diabetes, the sight's coming back to my right eye, and I'm feisty and ready for action!"

"That's good," I said cautiously. "You know, investors."

"I have a commitment for eighty thousand so far," Fernando said. "I've budgeted this cheap at a quarter of a million dollars."

"Sounds like a plan. You can make a good film for that amount."

"It will star, of course, Hector Baltierra."

"Great," I said. Maybe this wasn't so crazy. "I'm glad to hear he's on board."

"Well, I'm not even going to mention this to him until I get the full budget."

"Wait," I said, setting down my coffee. "On the phone you said that shooting starts next month."

"Yep! I've got most of my actors lined up. My locations are locked."

"And your crew?"

"Well, I have you."

"Anyone else?" I asked, starting to feel rather dizzy.

"Well, I hired Vincent Lopez—"

"Oh, wow," I said, impressed. "He's hell with a camera. Congrats! I know a lot of people who will want to work with him."

"I said *hired,* as in the past tense. We had a difference of opinion. He had some problems with the script. If he can't see the beauty of the story, we don't want him, do we? I had to tear up his contract." I managed a weird medley of nodding and shrugging, probably with a whimper thrown in for good measure. "We'll build our crew fast, I tell you. You're my ace in the hole. Once that money comes in, we'll, by god, show them how real movies are made!"

The rhetoric softened once our lunch arrived. Fernando never asked about my film-making production credits; however, he spent considerable time talking about the films on which he had worked, chiefly in the art department.

"You remember that remake of *The Seven Year Itch* shot here, in San Antonio? I worked on that film. The props people wanted a Cubist painting in the background for a museum scene. They were going to use a famous painting, but word came down that the artist's estate or some museum or whatever was asking for too much money. I said, look guys, I can give you Cubism, Abstract Expressionism, Rococo, what the fuck ever. I know you need this in twenty-four hours. Pay me time and a half, deliver catered meals, and give me a bag of grass." Fernando gave me a wink, to which I responded with a weak smile. "They gave me what I asked. I love Hollywood. You need to rent that DVD. That horrible remake of *The Seven Year Itch*. The Georges Braque pastiche painting on the wall behind those B-list actors, that's me. That's fucking me!"

At the moment, my phone rang. I looked down. It was Unhinged Actress calling. I grabbed it. "Holly, how are you doing?" I had no idea why she was calling me, but clearly Holly was thrilled to hear my actual voice. I assume she was confused when, before she could utter a single word, I blurted out: "Oh, no! I forgot about our meeting this afternoon. I'm on my way. See you soon."

I hung up, letting Fernando know I'd pay for the meal. I got out of there fast. We'd talk later, I insisted.

***

The second time I saw Fernando, I was riding my bike on the trail though Mission Park. I zipped by, with the wind at my back, but I couldn't ignore the little man with the gray ponytail and the pointy beard who was tossing an old chewed up tennis ball to a wire terrier. I don't know what's sadder. The old man with one lung, one dog, a ragged tennis ball, and a big dream, or a guy with no dream, running audio on a chicken commercial. But I hadn't time to dwell on such matters. The women from the art department had finished primping the latex chicken, and the lights and camera had been repositioned. As Mari had said, "El Pollo Fuerte waits for no man."

ANGEL MONEY (JAN. 30)

It had been a hard winter. Cold, yes, but I was also watching my bank balance dip more each day with no hope of replenishment. I had three invoices out for work completed. One was a music video for a heavy metal band that, if I believed the gossip, was about to break up. Then there was that company history I had ghostwritten for my neighbor's chain of pizza parlors. He was ignoring my calls, and, in all honesty, I was at the point where I'd be happy if he'd pay me with food. And finally, there was the audio work I'd done on that chicken commercial. I wasn't too optimistic there, either. Vincent emailed me a link to a *Wall Street Journal* article explaining that El Pollo Fuerte filed Chapter 11.

That was just the financial stuff. There was also Gerald. My fellow company member at Prometheus. He had been a quadriplegic since before I met him. Though, amazingly, he remained productive in the theater world as a director, writer, and set designer, he often struggled with health problems not unusual for people in his situation. Last week, while in the hospital for a routine procedure, he stopped breathing and passed away. The damp, gray days had stacked up so deep that I had forgotten what blue skies and sharp shadows looked like.

And then, fortunately, today happened. A sunny afternoon in the 70s in January was too enticing to ignore. I pumped up the tires on my bike and hit the road. I had found a twenty-dollar bill yesterday blowing across the parking lot of the Dollar General Store. It's what my friend Kat likes to call "Angel Money." Seemed rather heartless, as that poor bastard who lost the money obviously wasn't being blessed by a heavenly being. Nothing I could do but put it to good use. So I cycled over to La Barca and got four tacos to go. I rode down Mission Road, across Steves, under Highway 90, and pulled off onto a patch of brown grass near the railroad crossing. I laid my bike down and sat on the ground with my back against a wire fence. The sun warmed me up. As I unpacked my tacos, I watched the wild parakeets that nest up in the transformer gantry towers of the electrical substation. This feral colony had become quite large; they flew in groups across Mission Road to perch on the telephone lines along the river.

Before I started eating, I eyed the homeless man emerging from the deep shadows cast by the highway overpass. He was a man of about my age, dressed in layers of tattered clothes. I remembered noticing him over the weeks, camped out with his bedding neatly arranged alongside a stand of mesquite. It was painful to see him limping along the sidewalk. His shoes were too large, but there also seemed to be something physically wrong with his leg or foot. He stood over me, swaying. "I don't mean to trouble you," he said. "But if you could help me out? A dollar? Or whatever you can spare."

I was feeling compassionate, which, I admit, isn't my default. I fished out a five dollar bill from my taco change and held it up for him. "I'm also happy to share my breakfast," I said. I gave him two tacos, a bean and cheese, and a potato and egg. He smiled and sat down beside me.

"I'm Billy," he said.

I told him my name. He muttered about how, years ago, when he left home to ride the rails, he called himself Billy the Kid. "Back then, I was on an adventure. Or so I liked to think. Now it's just Billy." He slipped off his knit cap and raked his hand through his hair. He caught me looking. "I cut it myself. I hoped it might help me get a job. I don't know how to cut hair. I don't always do things that make sense, not since my medication ran out." He put his hat back on and began to unwrap his tacos. "Even when it warms up, I'll keep this hat on. The hair makes me look crazy. Yesterday, I knocked on the door of that building up ahead." He pointed. "Thought I'd offer to clean around the man's place. Whatever. But you know what? He turned the hose on me. I was drenched. It was a cold day yesterday." I passed him a plastic container of salsa verde and two salt packets. "Can't hardly call that an adventure," he said, managing a thin chuckle before he started to eat.

I knew the man with the hose. His name's Garth. A photographer who used to teach at the community college. His work runs toward the cheesecake end of the spectrum. I met him through my friend Melinda. She's a photographer, and she used to be one of Garth's students years ago. Also, I believe she modeled for him back in her younger years. That's the way it usually is. People know Garth either because they had him as a photography teacher, or, during a lean time, they worked some as a model for his internet soft porn business.

About five years ago, Garth came into a substantial sum of money. He decided to travel the world. He left his little warehouse studio in the charge of a model who had, at that time, been staying with him. Sierra, however, was far from dependable. Garth began to worry that the money he sent Sierra every week wasn't going toward groceries and the care of his beloved cats. He was right. It went to drugs, booze, dining out.

So he called up Melinda from a beach cottage in Corfu and arranged for her to stay in his guest room to make sure things didn't get out of control. This worked out well for Melinda. After an argument with her boyfriend, she had been camping out in her tiny studio in the Blue Bird Arts Complex, trying to keep a low profile, because the management didn't want people living there. What Gerald offered had all the promise of a peaceful setting, there in the bend of the San Antonio River where the wild parakeets found sanctuary. It had bordered on the idyllic for a short while. Melinda took care of the place with Garth's periodic money orders, making sure to pay the utilities, keep the cats well fed, and even hand out Sierra's weekly stipend.

Melinda found herself with a domestic southside refuge which was, at first, made even more charmingly offbeat by the introduction into the household of Yonten, a Tibetan monk, traveling the country in exile. Melinda had managed to secure a grant from the local arts council to allow the monk to run a series of workshops on Buddhist painting. She let Yonten use Garth's darkroom as a combination monastic cell and meditation studio.

I'm not sure when things started to unravel; however, I remember one day when I stopped by to help Melinda change a flat tire on her VW bug. She was quite distraught. Sierra, who was strung out on Fentanyl, often disappeared for two or three days. One of the cats had developed an abscessed tooth. And the monk had overstayed his visa. Immigration agents were sniffing around the San Antonio Museum of Art, where she had arranged for him to give a series of lectures.

After I tightened the lug nuts and stowed away the jack, Melinda gave me a tight hug. She began sobbing. "Thank you. I need my car today. I have to drive up to the Himalayan Market on the northside to get Yonten some yak ghee for his butter lamp. You know, for his rituals." Before I could suggest what Yonten should do with his yak butter, she sped off.

It was a stressful summer for Melinda. Even though she managed to get Sierra into an inpatient rehab center, the girl fled on the second night and died of an overdose in a Corpus Christi motel. Yonten was nabbed by ICE agents during a lecture he gave at the Institute of Texan Cultures—during the Q and A session, which struck me as acutely uncouth. He was to be deported back to Tibet, but somehow found his way to Canada. The cat recovered, which was all Garth cared about. And when Garth returned from his grand tour, dressed in a silk kurta and a bejeweled Rolex knockoff, rattling off tales of amoebic dysentery and jazz concerts in Peruvian ice caves, Melinda eased out the door with her little canvas bag and yoga mat and retreated to the solitude of her art studio.

So, I rather think that Billy the Kid came out fairly well with only getting hosed down in January. I guess it's all relative, isn't it? Some days you get a soaking. Other days, an angel gives you a break.

LOCKJAW AND RATTLESNAKES (FEB. 9)

Johnny's been lying low for a while now. He and his wife have been fighting, so he moved in with his father until things settle down. No concern of mine. Well, other than the fact that with him gone, the duplex is quieter. His wife's so silent, I feel like I'm on a peaceful vacation.

When I bumped into Johnny last week, I was taken aback at how quickly and completely he'd fallen away from my life. I'd been strolling along the River Walk, dodging the tourists as I idly snapped pictures with a little point and shoot camera I recently bought. As I was about to walk under the Augusta Street bridge near the downtown library, I heard someone call my name. It was Johnny. He and an elderly man were sitting on a bench eating hot dogs and drinking sodas. I headed over. Johnny introduced me to Mr. Wilkins. I shook the man's hand. He wore scuffed Army boots, a moth-eaten pea coat, and an orange knit cap.

"He's staying over at the SAMM shelter until he gets on his feet," Johnny told me. After the man finished the final bite of his hot dog, he wiped his fingers and mouth with a paper napkin. It was still winter, but as was often the case in San Antonio, quite warm if you stayed in the sun. I thought the man must be roasting in that coat.

"Mr. Wilkins played drums for Lightnin' Hopkins," Johnny explained, turning to Wilkins with a smile of respect.

"Weren't nothing more than three months at best," Wilkins said with a slow East Texas drawl. "Back in 1953. I know the year, 'cause that's when I joined up with the Army." Wilkins pulled a half-smoked plastic-tipped cigarillo from a shirt pocket and fired it up with a butane lighter.

Johnny asked what I'd been doing. I began my current patter about not being able to land a decent gig, but I faltered mid-sentence just before I uttered the word "poverty." I changed the subject when I saw Mr. Wilkins screwing the cap back on his soda. He slipped the bottle into his coat pocket to be enjoyed later.

I guess Johnny must have registered my unfortunate financial state, because a few days later, I got a call from him asking if I'd like to help him tear down a barn on his brother's land out in the country. "It pays a hundred dollars a day. We're thinking it's a three-day job." That sounded like two days more than I was capable of putting up with Johnny's manic moods, and I could tell from his voice that he was running turbo-charged at the moment. "Hey," he added, "we get free room and board."

When he paused for breath, I said, yes, I would do it. He laughed as though that last bit of sweetening the pot had won me over. The fact was, I had no other idea of how to get enough cash to make my landlady happy. The end of the month had already come and gone. Besides, the people at the theater were driving me nuts, asking me to help on the upcoming NEA grant, wondering why I wasn't pushing harder to promote my upcoming show, and bickering over the plans for a memorial performance honoring the passing of Gerald. Oh, and someone had told Kat that there was no role for her in my play, so she was not speaking to me. I was more than ready to bug out of town for a while.

***

The next day, I swung by Johnny's dad's place across from Roosevelt Park to pick him up. He looked hungover as hell, which was fine by me. It kept him subdued. And I like subdued in the morning. I'd already prepared a thermos of sweet black coffee, which sat on the seat between us.

"We're going to Uvalde," Johnny said. "Take the highway to Castroville, and keep going." As I got onto Highway 90 and headed west, Johnny made his way gratefully through two cups of my coffee. It put life back into him. In fact, it chiseled off enough of the rough edges of his hangover so that he could get some sleep. He curled up like a baby, clutching the pillow he'd brought along. He ducked his head under the shoulder strap of his seat belt so that it brushed his ear, but he seemed not to notice. I found his soft snores soothing as I sipped coffee and headed into the scrub brush barrens of the lowest reaches of the Texas Hill Country.

Johnny's brother, Francisco, is a doctor, but I have never talked to him long enough to find out what sort of medicine he practices. He'd bought a ranch along the Nueces River, about thirty miles north of Uvalde. The property fronts the river. It's situated a mile and a half into the low hills up from the river valley. Lovely and lonely. Prickly pear cactus, low mesquite trees, and a charming clump of squat cedars surrounded by a field of prairie grass. When I pulled off Highway 55 and rolled over the cattle guard at the entrance to the property, Johnny awoke. He pointed to a doublewide trailer at the end of a caliche road. A gleaming SUV sat out front. When I rolled up beside the trailer, the door opened. Francisco, his Italian wife, and their five-year-old daughter, Martina, all came out smiling.

Johnny had told me that his brother bought the property a year ago. He wanted to build a proper house as a vacation home. "All they've got is that doublewide right now. He's too embarrassed to invite his friends to come out and stay in a trailer. Can you beat that?"

Francisco, Lena, and Martina invited us inside for lunch. We all had pasta salad and seafood bisque. Francisco and his wife were playfully dismissive of Johnny, he being the black sheep of the family, but Martina adored him. In fact, the little girl was crushed when her parents announced that they were all heading out on a day trip to explore the ruins at Fort Lancaster. But Johnny and I, Francisco asked in the form of a statement, we would know what we were supposed to do. Correct?

Johnny nodded, of course. He told them not to worry. "Enjoy your family outing—we got this." As the family went about loading picnic items into their SUV, I followed Johnny down a path and over a hill. We came upon a humble shack. Not a barn, nor a cabin. Something in between. It possessed a rustic beauty and I couldn't understand why anyone would want to destroy it.

"Well," Johnny explained, "they say it's infested with black widows, rattlesnakes, and rusty nails infected with tetanus. They worry about Martina. You know how it is." He led me to a pile of tools. He handed me a twenty-pound sledgehammer, and he took the largest crowbar I had ever seen.

"Where do you think we should begin?"

"What?" I asked. "But haven't you done this before?"

"No experience necessary, man," he said with a grin. "We're tearing down, not building up."

I entered to see what we were up against. There was no foundation, and that was good. A dirt floor. One entrance. Inside there were three rooms. The timber truss of the pitched A-frame roof was visible, as there was no proper ceiling. Two wooden pillars helped to support the central beam. They were fixed into the ground with concrete, as were the four wooden corner posts. Johnny seemed under the impression that we'd hook up my truck to these posts and pull the whole place down. Then we'd smash the boards into small pieces with the sledgehammer.

"You think we could stretch it out to three days?" he asked.

"Why don't we just douse it with gas and torch it?" I mused.

"No way," he gasped, looking around like someone might have heard me. "That's the obvious, of course. But we'd be out of here tomorrow. It's a hundred dollars a day, man. A day!"

I told him we'd need to remove every board from the outer and inner walls, and every board on the roof. At the end of each day, we could make a bonfire from the scrap boards. "If your brother's afraid of spiders and snakes, a big pile of lumber is just as bad. Probably worse." Then, and only then, we'd drag down the supports.

Johnny placed a hand on his chest and nodded. "That's why I brought you along. You see the big picture. This is exactly what we need to do. And now you're making it into a four-day job. Maybe five! Brilliant!"

***

Johnny was wrong. It was a three-day job. Well, three and a half, if you count our first day. It was quite an ordeal. And, indeed, we found a few rattlesnakes (one buried his fangs in the toe-leather of my left boot, and I dispatched the poor creature with a small ball-peen hammer). However, that little piece of Uvalde County history, that humble cedar board abode, was, as agreed by all parties, stripped down and burned.

Last night ended our final day at the ranch. Johnny and I fed the last of the roof slats into the bonfire. We were both exhausted. Johnny was drinking beer that he had managed to sneak past Francisco, who was puritanical in these matters. I was impressing myself with abstemious restraint, sticking with an RC Cola.

I turned to Johnny. "Remember that guy, Mr. Wilkins?" I asked.

"Who?"

"Lightnin' Hopkins."

"Oh, yeah. A righteous guy. Ends up homeless. Chewed up and spat out by the country he served."

"His one claim to fame," I said. "Playing with Lightnin' Hopkins. I can't help but wonder if there was more to his life?"

"He was in the military. Must have killed some Nazis."

"Joined in the 1950s, so he said."

"Maybe saw action in Korea," Johnny said. Then he lowered his beer so he could look at me. "What are you getting at?"

"What is your Lightnin' Hopkins story?"

"Um, I guess that's it. That Mr. Wilkins guy."

"No," I said, shaking my head. "What is it that makes your life important? You know, your mark on the world?"

"Whoa, man," Johnny said, forcing a smile, but I could see his lips tightening on the edge of irritation. "That old fool was probably lying. And what do I care? I hate the blues!"

When the sun came up this morning, we got back on the highway and headed home to San Antonio. And much like on the drive out, Johnny kept silent. He was dozing from the quart of Carta Blanca he'd picked up at the Shell station in Uvalde, where we gassed up for the ride. It was the one time I wished Johnny was awake and chattering and full of his own brand of excitable giddy nonsense, because all I was left with was the chatter of my own mind, asking again and again, what have I done with my life? I'm not even a bit player in the successful life of another.

As we passed Lackland Air Force Base, Johnny roused himself. "I might not be Lightnin' Hopkins' drummer, but in a couple of weeks, me and Alfie Montoya are planning a guerrilla performance art piece at the Alamo." Johnny leaned closer. "You want in on the action?"

"Is anyone gonna get hurt?"

"Naw," he said. He fluffed his pillow and twisted around to get comfy again. "But they might arrest us. I mean, it *is* the Alamo. Those litigious biddies who make up the Daughters of the Republic of Texas!"

"Sounds fun," I told him. He was turned away from me. "I'll check my schedule." I'm not sure, but I thought I could hear his soft snoring.

REMAINS IN THE RANGE (FEB. 15)

I had priced and arranged as many items as I could out on the back deck by the time I heard the front door open at nine a.m. As Gerald's estate sale was being held at his house in Lavaca—a neighborhood which was filled with bohemians and other manner of discerning oddballs—I expected a huge crush of people over the next three days.

Most of the members of the Prometheus ensemble were helping out as well. Kelton was up in the attic, handing down dusty boxes of holiday decorations to Toby, who was too stoned to be of much use. Kat fled to the porch, once I showed up, and busied herself arranging gardening items on a couple of folding tables. Rachel and Samantha were in the dining room arranging Gerald's books and art, and generally getting on each other's nerves.

Connie and Nathan, Gerald's closest friends, were running the sale. Whenever I was uncertain about what price to put on an item, I'd search through the bungalow until I located Connie. Connie had an opinion about such things. Nathan, for the most part, did not. However, because Nathan was the official executor of Gerald's estate, when I found a rosewood box in the kitchen, I thought I should talk to him about it. The simple, darkly varnished box had a lid with small brass hinges. It was half the size of a shoe box. When I opened it, I immediately recognized human cremains. The ashes were packaged just as my father's had been. Gerald was a big guy, even when he wasn't in his mammoth electric wheelchair, but now I found myself holding all of him in one hand. I slid it into the oven and shut the door.

I walked into the dining room and squeezed behind the card table where Nathan sat writing up receipts and making change for a group of people. "Nathan," I said softly, leaning down, my mouth close to his ear. "Is there a good place to put Gerald's ashes? They were sitting on the stove beside a set of CorningWare. I was afraid someone would buy them by mistake."

Nathan sighed. Not at me, but at the woman haggling with him over a Venetian mask. "I'm sorry," he told her. "It's priced as marked. My friend traveled all the way to Italy for that. If you don't want it, please put it back, because I'm sure someone else will." The woman stepped back to examine the mask closer. "Where are they now?" Nathan whispered to me.

"In the oven, which, well, might seem appropriate, but—"

"Seal the door shut with masking tape and put an NFS sign on it."

"NFS?"

Nathan tilted up his head. He looked pained. Then he laughed. "I thought everyone knew that. *Not For Sale.*"

"Do you take checks?" asked the woman, placing the mask on the table.

I returned to the kitchen to tape up the oven.

I didn't know Gerald that well. True, he belonged to the same theater company as did I, but he'd been a member for over twenty years, and I was a newcomer. Most people seemed to know him from well before he fell off the stage at the high school where he taught theater. That was about ten years ago, and during those years as a quadriplegic, he continued making art, writing, directing, and creating theatrical stage designs. We shared the stage in a rather unorthodox version of Hamlet. I played King Claudius, and he, the Ghost. He'd even been in a short film I made. But my intrinsic introversion had been compounded with a sense of awkwardness around those with such noticeable handicaps. Not an unusual response, but still, I felt like an idiot that I never got to know him better.

There was a lull around noon. I was outside straightening up some items on the round patio table when Connie came out with two bottles of Topo Chico. She used an opener screwed to the wooden railing to uncap them. She handed one to me and then took a perch on the deck railing. Nathan emerged from the house, wiping his brow with a red bandana. "Kat's handling things inside," he said. He arched a brow my way. "She's still pissed off at you for not writing her a big juicy part in your snakes and ladder show." I shrugged as I helped Nathan clear some stacks of DVDs off of a folding canvas chair.

"Lordy," Connie said. "There sure is a lot of stuff."

Nathan took a seat in the chair and I sat down, too, on a wooden crate.

"I guess this is the last time I have to clean up after Gerald," he said. Connie offered Nathan a sip from her drink, but he shook his head. "I was at the hospital after Gerald's fall," he explained to me. "Just before he went in for the first of a series of surgeries. He asked me to go to his apartment and clear out all his pornography."

"That was an adventure I was not invited on," Connie said.

"I believe you were with Gerald's sisters," said Nathan. "Making canapés, no doubt."

"Canapés? Nothing more than peanut butter and jelly sandwiches, as I recollect."

"I counted seven big black trash bags that I hauled out. He had that stuff all over the place."

"What does one do with seven trash bags of gay porn?" Connie looked down for a moment and then shrugged. "Donate it to a senior center, I suppose," she said with a sigh.

"Hadn't occurred to me," Nathan said. "It was nighttime, and I tossed them all into a dumpster behind Panchito's."

"Oh, I love their flautas!"

"We didn't know if Gerald would live or die, but we damn well made sure his place was appropriate for the family to come in and deal with his effects, if need be."

"It's like cleaning up for the maid," Connie added.

We looked up as Cheryl emerged from the house. She'd been Gerald's chief nurse for years. She was smiling and wiping at tears with a tissue. "I had to come out for air," she said. "It's nice to see so many people happy to take a bit of Gerald away, but, well, it's just so…"

"Yeah," Nathan said, nodding. "So impersonal."

I stepped away to straighten up the DVDs and reposition a rack of t-shirts. Connie and Nathan consoled Cheryl.

When I moved here from Dallas a decade ago, everything I owned fit in the bed of my pickup truck. It took me half an hour to unpack. My little East Guenther Street home was spartan with a futon, a chair, some books and CDs, my computer, a box of clothes, an old battered oak table that used to sit in the back room of my father's bookstore, and an electric guitar I promised myself I'd one day learn to play. Of course, that was then. I've since managed to acquire more and more.

All those years ago when I had decided to leave Dallas, I had to purge like mad. Stuff just accumulates. My apartment is now the antithesis of spartan. I feel anxious and responsible for all those things. What if I want to cut away from it all and disappear again? I won't be able to manage a graceful, mysterious vanishing. There will be garage sales. Trips to the dump and resale shops. Or what happens if I go to bed one night and don't wake up? I don't have any Connies or Nathans to take time from their lives and come to dispose of my sad excuse of an estate. Who's going to spirit away my more unsavory possessions?

***

I met this guy once. Ross. No, Russ. It was back when my father was still alive and one of my jobs helping out at the family bookstore was to do rare book appraisals. Russ lived in this ultra-modern condo complex in a formerly seedy enclave adjacent to Deep Ellum, the artsy region of Dallas. The building was a row of minimalist townhouses. Five units, side by side. Each had an enclosed garage on the ground floor, living space above. I parked on the street and rang the bell. Russ buzzed me in. He was about fifty. Fit, shaved head, and still dressed from his morning run. The place was one huge room. Windows along the front. One door at the back, to a restroom, I assumed. There was a counter along one wall with a sink, refrigerator, and stove. One king-sized bed. A table with one chair. And a bicycle. A laptop was open on the table. Beside it, a book. That was it. I couldn't even see where he kept his clothes.

"Just moved in?" I asked.

"What? Oh, no. I travel a lot. For work. I keep it simple."

"That the book?" I asked, pointing.

"That's it. I'm all digital these days. Music, movies, books. All on my computer. Except *that* one."

I found that rather appalling. And yet, I was more than a little envious.

The book had been left to him by an uncle. It was a first edition of Nathaniel Hawthorne's first book, *Fanshawe*. A scarce book, indeed. Hawthorne hadn't been fond of it and supposedly destroyed any copy he encountered. It was a bright copy, in a contemporaneous leather binding. Russ told me that he wanted to sell it. It wasn't so much about him needing the money—and he could get ten to fifteen thousand with little trouble—but it didn't fit into his lifestyle. "Frankly," he admitted, "I don't want the responsibility." I explained that our shop couldn't afford to purchase it. We'd be happy to take it on consignment, but that sounded too fussy for him. I was hard pressed to think of any other book dealer in town with the resources to buy it outright, so I got out a little notebook and scribbled the contact information of a friend who worked at a high-end shop in Philadelphia. "These folks would be thrilled to make you an offer," I told him, ripping out the page and handing it over. He thanked me.

Back on his porch, I turned as he pulled the door shut, getting one last glimpse of that pristine space, uncluttered, and undemanding.

***

So different from the significant remains of Gerald's life.

"How much is this?" asked a man in grease-stained coveralls. He held up a tool chest without a price.

I found some white price stickers in my pocket and stuck one on the side of the box. With a felt marker, I priced it at six dollars.

"There's a hammer and two screwdrivers inside," he said.

I added, with the marker, *contents included.*

ELASTICITY (FEB. 18)

I'll admit to getting misty now and then. A song, a movie. It hits just so, and I'll wipe back a tear. A minor, poignant leakage. I almost never find myself crying, you know, full-on sobbing. But then there was last night.

I wanted to use the word "profanate" for a short story, but I wasn't sure if I was using it right. Normally I'd go online to research usage, but my internet was dead for some reason. So I went to the bookcase for my copy of the *OED*. It's the "compact" edition, where the entire work has been reproduced with four pages on one, crammed into two mammoth volumes. My father gave it to me for Christmas twenty years ago.

The print is tiny, and I suppose my vision isn't what it once was. I realized I would have to use the magnifying glass. For those unfamiliar with this particular edition of the *Oxford English Dictionary*, it was published in a large slipcase with three compartments. One for each of the two volumes, and a skinny drawer at the top that held a magnifying glass. As I opened it, I saw there was something else in there, pushed to the back.

I pulled the drawer all the way out. There, behind the magnifying glass, was a miniature book. A tiny dictionary, measuring about two inches by one inch. It was printed in 1903 and bound in a leather chemise with a metal snap to keep it closed.

It was exactly the kind of thing my father would do and not tell me about. Hide a second gift inside the main one. He liked surprises, and thought everyone else should as well.

It was Christmas all over again. An old gift, but new to me. I held it as tears made their way down my face.

For some reason, the memory that first surfaced was of a time when I was seventeen. I was at our family's bookstore in Dallas, sitting across from my father's desk, reading a book. He put down his newspaper, sipped his coffee, and then he caught my eye. He lifted his left hand, fingers out with the palm down. I watched as he used the other hand to pinch a bit of skin, just a little fold back where the bones of the thumb and the forefinger joined at the wrist. When he released the pinched skin, it took a moment for it to lie back flat. He nodded for me to do the same. I did. My skin fell back as fast as my thumb and finger moved away.

"I'm not so supple with age," he said, with little concern. He returned to the newspaper. I assumed it was some sort of life lesson. I too would age.

And I have.

Next, I remembered that road trip I took a decade ago, not long after he died. Back then, I was older than he was when he pinched his hand. The third day out, I pulled into the unpaved parking lot of a bar in Tularosa, New Mexico. It was mentioned in the dusty oblong notebook I found at the back of my father's desk when I finally shut down the bookstore. It was a journal of a road trip he took decades ago, right after graduating from college. It served as the guidebook to *my* road trip.

The entry for Tularosa was the first—several pages before had been torn out. It was short.

The Vinegaroon Bar, my father wrote, *has only one beer on tap. Schlitz. The stucco ceiling is the color of flypaper, and it appears as though it'd be tacky to the touch from decades of cigarette smoke. If there was a window to look out at the mountains, I might have stayed for a second beer.*

There it was, the bar. It still had the same name: Vinegaroon. It was filthy inside, and it was so dark I couldn't even see the ceiling. The three men playing dominos never looked up. There were now two beers on tap, but I asked the man behind the bar for a cup of coffee. He asked if instant was okay. I nodded. Even with milk and sugar, it was awful. I opened the notebook, impatient to learn what would be the next stop on my tour.

I don't know what I was looking for on that trip, so I don't know if I found it.

But last night I found the word I was looking for. The *OED* had it, the miniature dictionary did not. I chose not to use it. I mean, really. Profanate? What was I thinking?

REBELLIOUS DRIBBLES (FEB. 19)

I'm not sure when Alfie Montoya filed the non-profit incorporation paperwork for his Alamo Urination Appreciation Society, but he's been soliciting donations as long as I've known him. Every year, on February 19, Alfie closes the doors of Across the Alley Records, his music shop in the basement of the Kress Building. He carries a camp chair and a folding table. He sets up in Alamo Plaza within spitting distance of that historic Texas shrine. Or, as he might put it, within pissing distance.

For years Alfie has been trying to get the city of San Antonio to commemorate that famous day, February 19, 1982, when Ozzy Osbourne peed on the Alamo. Or, as Alfie makes a point of clarifying, "on the Cenotaph, that grand sculpture in Alamo Plaza." I have to think that, when he was younger, Alfie was much more colorful. But these days he maintains a sedate vigil through the early afternoon, handing out his brochures there in the shade cast by the Cenotaph, which is a sort of stubby obelisk with figures carved into the stone who represent some of the individuals who were inside the Alamo during the famous battle.

As I walked up to his table today, Alfie was holding forth to a couple of curious tourists. "It was only after much research and interviews with primary sources," he said, slumping back in his chair and adjusting his straw Stetson, "that led me to ascertain *exactly* where Mr. Osbourne's rebellious stream and dribbles landed. He might have been drunk, and who knows what else, but that golden torrent served as a warning shot across the bow of the DTR, demonstrating that they can't control everything in this town!"

One of the tourists asked what was the DTR.

Alfie immediately responded.

"A scourge is what they are! Those sanctimonious harridans at the Daughters of the Republic of Texas, with their ceaseless sycophancy for a bunch of slave-owning filibusters claiming ownership of sovereign Mexican soil…those bluenose biddies have usurped well-documented facts and bent them to fit their vile, Anglo-centric narrative." The tourists exchanged puzzled glances. Then they turned away.

When Alfie noticed me, he smiled and waved me over.

"I heard Johnny was doing something with you this year," I said, watching as the two tourists walked toward the Alamo.

"Who?" He rubbed his chin for a moment before chuckling. "Oh, right. Johnny. Check this out. He wanted us to throw water balloons at people. Performance art, he called it. Water tinted with yellow food coloring. Get it? Pee-colored? I thought it was puerile, and I let him know he'd have to do it without me. Of course it's a free country, and the plaza *is* a public space. But the cops *will* get you, I warned him. That's for sure. If not for littering, then for battery. You can't go around blindsiding folks like that." Alfie laughed. "Oh, that Johnny. But, no, I haven't seen him yet. He's still in bed, is my guess. Wait, doesn't he live next door to you?"

"He's been at his dad's house the last couple of months, sleeping on the couch."

"Trouble with the wife, again? Leave it to Johnny to mess up a good thing."

A kid on a skateboard rolled up. He read Alfie's sign. He grinned. "That's so hardcore! But the way I heard it, Ozzy whizzed right on the front door."

"Nope," Alfie said.

"Guess that's how Hollywood will do it," the kid said. He looked at the arrow on the sidewalk Alfie had drawn with chalk pointing at the location of Ozzy's pee. "Maybe he just didn't care for this cheesy sculpture." The kid tapped at the Cenotaph.

Alfie bristled. "Cheesy? Pompeo Coppini, the sculptor, was a greater man than you'll ever be."

The kid laughed, and he skated away.

I've never come right out and asked Alfie if this whole Alamo Urination Appreciation Society is just a silly joke. Could it be that Alfie sees himself as providing serious social satire? Johnny says he's a zen trickster. Alfie's sister says he's a low-wattage savant. Me? I dunno.

***

Alfie reminds me of one of my father's friends. A Dallas journalist named Clay Bigelow, who insisted people call him Daddy-O, which, surprisingly, many people did. I remember back when I was in my twenties. It was November 22, and I spent the day wandering around downtown Dallas. There's always something interesting going on around Dealey Plaza on the anniversary of JFK's death. There's this old woman—and I have to assume she's dead by now—who used to pace up and down Elm Street. Rain or shine, she'd be flogging her self-published book detailing her theory of an unlikely partnership between Fidel Castro and the Birch Society. You know, to assassinate Kennedy. I walked up to the crowd gathered around to listen as she pitched her thesis.

I spotted Bigelow at the edge of the crowd. At well over 300 pounds, sporting a wild beard and a porkpie hat, he was far from inconspicuous. I made my way toward him. He was listening intently and scribbling in his notebook. Slowly, he inched his way off the pavement and onto the grass, seemingly engrossed in his note-taking. I was the only one who noticed as he slipped his hand into the pocket of his raincoat, pulled out a rifle shell casing, and dropped it on the ground. His eyes flashed across the top of his reading glasses and he looked directly at me.

"You didn't see that," he said.

"See what?"

We walked up the hill and took a seat on a cement bench.

"One of my yearly rituals," he told me, fishing out a pack of cigarettes from his breast pocket. He offered me one. We smoked and watched the people milling about the small park which faced the infamous triple underpass. "Puts color in folks' lives," he said. "They look down and… My goodness, what's this? Today I scattered three rifle shells up around the grassy knoll. I always make sure that they are old and rusty. Then four more down that slope of grass to the sidewalk. And now? Now we wait." It took no more than ten minutes to get results. We both saw the slim young man in a fringed leather jacket pause by the light pole. He bent down to pick up something small from the grass. He held it up to his face before glancing about nervously. He put the object in his pants pocket and hurried off. Bigelow grunted. "Good, good." He began writing in his notebook, so lost in his musings that he didn't react when I excused myself and walked away.

***

Dallasites have Dealey Plaza. San Antonians have the Alamo.

Alfie patiently waited as a man in a crisp, dark suit studied the AUAS brochure. A lanyard hanging from his neck identified him as an attendee of the *Texas Association of Music Educators* convention. "This is hilarious," the man finally said. "So, if I make a donation, and I'm not saying I will, how will my money be spent?"

"Two action items sit at the top of the list for the AUAS." Alfie pointed to the rear panel of the brochure. The man turned it over, and Alfie recited from memory. "First, we need to commission the design and casting of the commemorative bronze plaque which will be placed adjacent to the *anointed* spot." Alfie placed a hand on the marble flank of the Cenotaph. "Second, we need to hire our legal team to help navigate the labyrinthian array of regulations presently keeping us from affixing said plaque to said location."

"You should think bigger," the man said. "You could do up a whole festival. Call it, Legends of Rock and Roll at the Alamo. I heard Phil Collins donated his collection of Alamo artifacts to the museum over there. What a fantastic gesture!"

"Phil Collins?" Alfie's voice had risen an octave. "Good lord! One of the Four Horsemen of Prog Rock."

"Isn't he about to receive some sort of recognition up in Austin?"

"Yeah." Alfie sighed, his ire flattened. "Honorary Texan. Another dark cloud on our horizon."

"Well, keep the faith," said the conventioneer as he returned the brochure to the stack on the table. We watched him walk into the Alamo.

"In a perfect world," Alfie said with a wistful smile, "this is when Johnny would appear and lob one of his urine balloons at that philistine."

"Don't worry," I told him, "that's how Hollywood will do it."

CROSSING ASYLUM CREEK (MARCH 3)

It was a day of contrasts. I had gotten up before the sun to make it to the downtown TV studios of KTBX. I was on their morning show, *Fresh Start.* They interviewed me and Rachel about our upcoming play at Prometheus. How did it creep up? We're opening in ten days!

The hostess was named Megan or Melanie. She allowed Rachel to give the basic patter about what the audience might expect, and the important information about the times and the location, and how to purchase advance tickets. Then Megan or Melanie turned to me with her frightful, toothy grin. "I believe you've brought along one of your cast members to give us a taste?"

"Indeed, we have," I said, pivoting my gaze to the camera pointed at me. "Samantha Rogers is all set to perform a short monologue from *How's My Karma!*"

"Well, then, take it away, Samantha Rogers!"

Samantha had been told to stand on the other side of the television studio, with the meteorologist's green screen behind her. She launched into the short snippet from the play that we had all deemed inoffensive enough for morning television. Rachel shifted in her seat to watch Samantha on the studio monitor. I did the same, and was delighted that they had used the green screen so as to composite the logo for the Prometheus Performance Company behind Samantha.

I'd never seen *Fresh Start,* and likely never would. The blond hair and bleached teeth of the hostess were too strident for such an early hour.

But everyone working with the show was pleasant and professional, and the team had the three of us in and out so smoothly that our segment was over before we knew it. And then, just like that, we were back out on the street, blinking in the morning sun. Samantha suggested we all head out for breakfast.

"Sorry," I said. "I've got an appointment."

***

I transitioned straight from that harshly lit and chaotic studio that smelled of vinyl upholstery and hairspray into a more sedate milieu, the peaceful expanse of the southside, where clusters of live oaks grew along the river, and rusting strands of barbed wire surrounded fields that were no longer tended. Over these bucolic trappings raced the low clouds of uncertain weather.

I made it inside before the rain began. When I stood at the high bay windows, facing the gravel road I had just driven on, I was able to see South Presa Street, the railroad tracks, and the creek. Three parallel lines. "It's called Asylum Creek," said the woman, Irma, who handed me a glass of iced tea. "On account of, you know, the State Hospital up the road." Irma turned and pointed at the pale, older woman with braids who sat on the sofa leafing through a coloring book. "Maisie here used to live at the hospital. Isn't that right, Maisie?"

"C'est un peu vrai," Maisie said, her eyes remaining on her book.

"Oh, child," Irma said, "No one understands you when you play these games." She smiled and walked over to adjust Maisie's braids so that they fell behind her shoulders. It was a hairstyle that might have worked on a child or a younger woman, but was not so effective on hair streaked with gray. Maisie kept her attention focused on her coloring book. "Well," Irma said to me with a sigh, "I'll leave you to it. Don't mind Maisie. She's a quiet one."

I watched a sly smile flit across Maisie's lips as Irma left. She turned a page and, without looking up, mouthed those same words again, "C'est un peu vrai."

There was a desk in the corner; it was clearly set up for me. The gooseneck lamp was switched on, and a large Royal manual typewriter had been pushed aside. I placed my shoulder bag on the floor and set my laptop on the desk. I'm not sure how Irma found my contact information. I've been out of the rare book appraisal business for a decade. But I needed the money, and well, South Presa Street was not too far from home, so I said yes. I walked up to the five bookcases, each with five shelves. It soon became obvious there wasn't much of value—standard reprints of classic novels, mid-century fiction in book club editions, later printings of art books. All in all, the sort of stuff one can find secondhand on the internet for a few dollars each. There was one, however, that stood out. I instantly knew what it was, but I kept combing through the shelves, saving it for last.

When I was done with the rest, I moved toward the middle bookcase and bent down to the bottom shelf. As I lifted up the large, slim volume, and placed it on the desk beside my computer, I heard Maisie clear her throat.

"Eh bien, c'était rapide," Maisie said, placing her coloring book in her lap. "Nothing of interest, right?" she continued in English, with a French accent. "Just that one. The obvious one."

At that moment, Irma walked in. "Don't let her throw you off," Irma said, patting Maisie on the head. "Our little girl here grew up in a tiny town outside of Beaumont. She has an East Texas accent thick enough to march an alligator across. Poor child. Grew up in the bayous of Jefferson County, and then off to the San Antonio State Hospital after her daddy died. All the while her momma was waltzing across Europe, Hawaii, Cuba."

Though Irma was surprisingly candid, I'm sure the juiciest parts of the family history were left out. But from what I gathered, the mother came into some money, returned from her travels, and bought this little house so she could be close to her daughter. One day, she moved Maisie out of the hospital and hired Irma to help out. Irma eventually found herself taking care of both mother and daughter. When the mother died, Irma stayed on. They'd been scraping by, barely making the monthly mortgage payments. Nothing much left, just a lot of furniture and kitchen appliances that were purchased back when avocado was a color. And, of course, the library.

Irma had errands to run, but she insisted that Maisie would be no trouble. Normally this was when I'd explain that there was nothing of value, waive my consultation fee, give the names of a few local book dealers who might buy the lot on the cheap—and then make good my escape. However, there was the matter of that lone, slim volume.

I sat down at the desk. As I waited for my laptop to warm up, I saw Irma drive away across the little bridge over Asylum Creek in an old rusty Impala. The book was a collection of poems by Charles d'Orleans. He was a 15th century French nobleman. The book's value has little to do with the poetry of this man, this Duke of Orléans. In fact, the selected poems are not even in their original state. The illustrator took it upon himself to rewrite the poetry into a more modern French. The book is notable because of the *illustrator*. Henri Matisse. He provided 54 color lithographs, as well as additional illustrations. The edition was limited to 1,200 copies, each signed by Matisse. I knew the book well. I had been working at an auction house some years back and wrote a description of a copy consigned by an elderly man from Pauls Valley.

Maisie pulled a chair next to mine. She sat down. She leaned over and ran her fingers across the cover of the book. This collection of poems is not what everyone would recognize as a proper book. It is what is often referred to as a "livre d'artiste," that is, an artist's book. The publisher, printer, typesetter, designer, bookbinder, all of them, came together to showcase the work of the artist—the text was usually the least relevant element. *Poèmes de Charles d'Orléans* resembles an unbound portfolio. The front and back covers are stiff pasteboard, with an illustration on the front. This unattached cover (often referred to as a chemise) was wrapped in the publisher's original glassine paper. The pages inside were loose gatherings, never bound by the publisher. Strictly speaking, it was not a *rare* book. If all the plates were present, and lacking any notable flaws, it was worth four to six thousand dollars. Not enough for Irma and Maisie to make it through more than a couple of months, was my guess.

"I love this cover illustration," Maisie said. "It looks like it was done by a child with crayons. I think Irma believes it's one of my coloring books from when I was a girl." She placed her hand palm down on the book and gazed into my eyes. "Charles d'Orleans was imprisoned by the English for 25 years. For me it's been longer. Well, not by the English. The doctors."

I opened the book. On the preliminary limitation page, I saw Matisse's familiar signature. But there was no printed number to identify this copy. When a limited edition lacks that number, it's considered an out-of-series copy. Sometimes these were test copies so that the printer could check various types of paper, or maybe experiment with different inks. However, in this copy, the place where there should be a number wasn't blank. Instead of a number, there was a small red heart inked by a pen with a broad nib.

"It's a heart," Maisie said. "You know, for love." She pushed back her chair and left the room. I heard her rustling around back in the kitchen.

I checked some reference material on my computer to see the proper pagination of the book, as well as all the important information concerning the various illustrations. I began the process of collating, making sure that the book was complete. It didn't take long. All was as it should be. And then I turned my attention to three envelopes that were placed between pages at the back. I love finding stuff like that. It was when things could get interesting. But before I could dig deeper, I heard Maisie return.

She wore an apron. She set down a chipped Wedgwood platter containing several artfully arranged celery stalks stuffed with peanut butter and topped with green olives.

"I would have brought the jam," she said. "But there were ants. So many ants." She wiped her hands on the apron, sat back down beside me, and gathered up the envelopes. "There's a story that goes with these. And I thought you'd like a snack." She waited, leaning in toward me, her eyes wide and expectant. When I finally took a bite of one of the celery sticks, she began.

"My mother's name was Lilly, short for Lillian. It was 1943, and she was young, traveling alone through France. This was during the war. I think she was a spy. Irma says she was just a loose woman. I don't know why she couldn't have been both. But she was my mother, so I was never able to get the whole truth. Anyway, this is before I came into the picture."

Maisie lifted up one of the envelopes. She removed a crisp sheet of paper folded into thirds. She handed me the envelope and read from the letter. "Mon cher monsieur Tériade…" Maisie glanced up. "How's your French?" I shrugged and shook my head. "Pity," she said. "It's from Matisse. You can recognize his handwriting. He and my mother were lovers. It's all in the letter. You have to read it right. Matisse quotes some of Charles d'Orleans' steamier couplets. Anyway, the letter is written to Tériade, who my mother said was a snake. Tériade published this book. He also created *Verve* magazine. That's a sexy word in any language, isn't it? Verve. Anyway, in this letter, Matisse is instructing monsieur Tériade to track down my mother and deliver *this* copy to her, heart and all. The book took a couple of years to get published and my mother had left in search of new adventures."

Maisie opened the book to an illustrated page. We looked at a nude woman seated with her knees to her chest. "That's my mama, Lilly. She would have been 19 when this was done. Here's another picture of her." She handed me the larger envelope. I pulled out Matisse's original charcoal drawing, identical to the lithograph in the book. It was signed and dated by Matisse. Maisie tapped the back of the drawing. I flipped it over. Even with my poor French, I translated "ma fleur préférée, Lilly" as "my favorite flower, Lilly." I noticed there was something else in the envelope. I pulled out a slip of pale blue paper with a one hundred franc note pinned to it. There was a short paragraph in ink on the paper. "It's Matisse explaining that he'd forgotten to pay Lilly for the sitting," Maisie explained. "One hundred francs? In the 1940s? What a cheapskate!"

Maisie handed me the final envelope. It was thicker than the others. I removed a folded panel of brown butcher paper, which had clearly been used to wrap up the book for mailing. It had French stamps, a return address for a M. Tériade, in Paris, and was addressed to Lillian Calhoun, 7300 South Presa Street. "I don't know why the book took so long to find Mama. I like to think detectives were employed. It arrived in the post while she was living here, throwing what money she had at cheap wine, palm readers, and therapists. One day she cleaned out a little room in back and moved me out of my prison across the road at the State Hospital into this new prison here, on the creek."

We heard Irma come in the back door. Maisie put each piece of paper back into its envelope and tucked everything into the book. She returned to her sofa, taking the book with her.

"Nothing of interest?" Irma asked, pointing to the wall of books. "I use her mother's cookbooks now and then." She glanced over at Maisie. "I hope she wasn't a pest. She's good one-on-one, but put two people or more in a room with her and she shuts down. It's not that hard to imagine. Some of us can't take too much stimulation. The doctors don't have a name for her condition. As for all her talk about being in prison…" Irma shot Maisie a look. "Yes, Maisie, I'm aware of what you get up to when I'm not around. Anyway, don't believe a word of it. She comes and goes whenever she wants, but she refuses to cross that creek."

Irma sighed and ran a hand over the spines of the books on one shelf. "I was hoping that these would get us some money. I work when I can. Maisie helps out, too. She cooks at least one meal a day for us. Isn't that right, Maisie?" And then, quieter, but still loud enough for Maisie to hear. "And it's awful."

Irma stepped into the kitchen. I heard water running and glasses clinking. I closed my computer, gathered up my things. I told Maisie that she had a wonderful book. I thanked her for telling me about her mother and Matisse.

"It belongs to me," Maisie said, holding the book tight against her chest.

"I know," I said.

"I kept it safe all these years, protected it from the roaches and the mildew."

"You're doing an excellent job of it," I said. "You really are." I placed one of my business cards on the table beside the gooseneck lamp.

Maisie got up and walked over. She picked up the business card and returned it to me. Then she handed the book over. I looked at her, but she lowered her head and shrugged.

So I walked into the kitchen to tell Irma that her life had changed. I wrote out a description of the book, the letters, and the original drawing by Matisse. I gave her the phone number of a friend who worked at a major auction house. "Tell him everything I've written. Mention my name. He'll fly out and take it from there. He can call me if he needs to." I added that she didn't owe me anything. My friend would send me a finder's fee.

I walked out. Maisie didn't look up from the sofa. I got in my truck, drove across Asylum Creek, over the railroad tracks, and then I turned left on South Presa Street.

I never did learn what Maisie's affliction might have been. Certainly something more than just being "French."

WINDOWS ONTO MADNESS (MARCH 6)

Pandora Salazar—though I doubt that's her real name—dropped me an email a few days ago wanting to talk about making a music video for her band, Chingolandia. They play what she referred to as "death cumbia." I was intrigued, so I looked up her band on the internet. I found a few videos of live performances. All were shot on cheap handheld cameras or smartphones and the audio was too horrible for me to get a sense of the band's sound. But Pandora definitely had stage presence. Goth makeup, Betty Page bangs. She projected pure charisma as she played her accordion and screamed into a microphone.

She taught Introduction to Accordion classes downtown at the Alamo Music Center on Friday mornings, so we planned to meet for lunch today at the Oasis Cafe. In person she was quiet, mousey even, with no makeup and wearing a pink sweater. But I recognized her by her hair and that sort of naive intensity I see in many performers who only seem comfortable on stage. I'd place her at about thirty. When she wasn't teaching accordion or performing, she worked as a freelance full-stack developer. I pretended to know what that meant.

"Mainly on the backend," she clarified. "PHP and Python."

I nodded. Of course. We began with the basic getting-to-know you session, common among people in the arts. You start off picking around the edges, identifying mutual friends and acquaintanceships. Who do you like, who do you hate? If you're lucky, you'll find shared values to bond over.

I had agreed to meet her because I was bored, and I had fallen into a dull slump where I wasn't leaving the house most days. When I did leave the house, it was to go to the theater where we were running rehearsals for my show, a process which was becoming more stressful than I had anticipated. There was an additional enticement. I found Pandora's intensity very sexy. Though I had no expectations that this would lead to anything along those lines. At best, I'd have some respite from my tedium and stress while doing another pro bono video project. So, I was surprised when she told me she had a budget. That was encouraging. The band would be releasing their first album in May and wanted a promotional video for their song "Una Locura Privada."

She described a storyline for the video in which she, the protagonist, has made a blood pact with an evil entity by bargaining her soul for… What, exactly? That wasn't so clear. Rock and roll fame, I suppose. So this devil or pestilent alien or whatever has taken over her life. It's everywhere. In the audience at gigs, skulking in the dog park when she's playing with her chihuahua. It's at the hair salon. At traffic court. She was specific when describing the creature. Tentacled, scaly. Very Lovecraftian.

I like to think I'm the type of person drawn to macabre stories of malignant inter-dimensional beings, unholy possessions, and dark intentions; however, I thought that her ideas were trite. I guess I've grown out of being interested in those tropes. So I found myself drifting, listening as she talked without really listening at all—my mind on a sort of cognitive autopilot. I idly looked out onto Main Street. I watched through the window as the owner of the bicycle shop next door appeared on the sidewalk. He reached into a coffee can and scooped out a fistful of birdseed, which he threw down on the ground. A huge flock of pigeons, who seemed to know the routine, dropped down, aflutter, from the ledge above. They fell to work cleaning up the seeds.

Pandora Salazar thought our meeting went well. We left with a couple of action items. I'd create a list of possible locations for the shooting.

And she'd work with her friend who made costumes for the shows out at Sea World. "He'll construct the perfect demon costume!" She was sure of it. She paid for lunch, so I left feeling I was already ahead of the game. I decided to wander over to the downtown library, as it was just a couple of blocks away.

***

Soon I was sitting at a table on the third floor reading Korzybski's *Science and Sanity*. The view out the window was the clock tower of the old Ursuline Academy, and I could catch a glimpse of the River Walk through the trees. Two kids dropped their backpacks on the floor and sat at the table next to mine. I hoped they were ditching school.

The girl pointed to a locked door past the row of bookcases and asked the boy if he knew what was in that room. Clearly the boy didn't. She launched into a story that she'd heard from one of the librarians, or so she claimed. That room was no bigger than a closet, she said. But it had a window. Nothing fancy, three feet by three feet. And through that window, you can see into another dimension. Anyone who looks through that window goes crazy, the girl said with a straight face. The only people allowed close to the window are the window washers, and only from outside. They are paid double and have to wear special polarized goggles.

I thought the girl had overplayed her hand with that bit about the goggles, but I watched as the boy walked over to the door. It did appear odd. A huge brass hasp had been bolted to the doorframe. The boy delicately touched the padlock. He turned back toward the girl, telling her he didn't believe her. She walked over and leaned close. I heard her whisper to him. "Ricardo Legorreta, the architect for this building, was a member of a secret occult lodge." She increased her dramatic tone by adding: "He died in an insane asylum." Stepping back, she shrugged. "Don't believe me? Look it up. We *are* in a library." She walked back to the table and grabbed her bag.

The boy was left standing, staring at the door.

103

"You hear it too, don't you?" I asked just loud enough for him to make out my words. He looked at me, confused. "That weird sound in there," I continued. "Don't tell me you can't hear it." His eyes got big, and he almost forgot his bag as he rushed to the elevators.

Yeah, the stuff you can't see is the scariest. The mind fills in the gaps. It's all about the gentle touch. Be subtle. Let the audience provide the bulk of the imagery. Pandora's desire to show the creature would result in something more comic than terrifying. Didn't she know the horror movie mantra? Never show the monster. At least not all of it.

THE EXHIBITIONIST'S JOURNEY (MARCH 8)

I have this thing about shooting wedding videos. I avoid them. It's not a pride thing. Lord knows I don't think they're beneath me. I just don't want to deal with the families. They never get what they want. And I would rather not navigate through such expectations, particularly at an event that is so emotionally charged. However, if I'm brought in as a supplemental shooter, subcontracted by a company that does client hand-holding all the time, I can find myself enjoying myself. In these instances, the potential heated entanglements are someone else's problems.

Morton and his wife run one of the city's preeminent one-stop wedding shops. The wife manages all the planning. Morton does the photographs and contracts for additional shooters, both still images and video. I rather enjoy working the occasional gig with them. It seems I was still on their list as a backup shooter because this morning I received a last-minute call.

I needed the money, so it was easy to say yes. Besides, I welcomed the distraction from the theater. Toby had done his usual brilliant job with the lighting design. He'd just finished hanging and focusing the instruments when he came down with appendicitis. We were counting on him to handle the job of the light board operator for the run of the show, but that wasn't going to happen. Tomorrow began Hell Week, the final days before opening night, and Rachel and I had spent most of yesterday training an intern on all the lighting cues. So, a wedding and reception, with white lace, pink cakes, fuzzy-headed inebriates, and sentimental music, promised to chase all that clutter from my head.

Tonight's shoot did just that.

After the ceremony at the Basilica of the Little Flower, the wedding party moved to a French restaurant downtown, overlooking the River Walk. I can't remember the names of the bride or groom, but I can't forget the smiles on everyone's faces from just-enough-but-not-too-much wine at the reception. While the wedding party and their guests ate, I sat at a table in a far corner with Morton, and his niece, who were both shooting still photography. We three were also enjoying the food. As a rule, one doesn't photograph people eating, unless it's the wedding cake. The cake would be soon, followed by dancing, speeches, and so on. Until then, we kicked back and recharged the batteries for our cameras using an outlet behind a potted ficus.

That's when I saw Ron walk by in a waiter's outfit. Ron! I'd completely forgotten about him.

***

It was back in November, when the recent shift into Daylight Saving Time still had me confounded. I had just finished a late lunch—late, even for me. It was starting to get dark as I rode my bike home from Norma's Cafe. When I turned onto South Alamo, I saw one of those tourist bicycle rickshaw things. The sign printed on the side identified it as belonging to the Mission Pedicab Service. The operator was parked at the curb. He squatted down shaking his head. I pulled up.

"What's wrong?" I asked, leaning my bike against a phone pole.

"Check it out, man," he said pointing at the broken chain. "And I gotta get it back to the office so the guy riding the night shift can head out." He was a Latino, maybe thirty. Shaved head and goatee. He had sunglasses on a neck strap dangling at his chest.

"Hey," I said. "I think I have a chain tool." I'm in no way a mechanically inclined type, but I'd replaced the chain on my bike back in the summer, and I had bought this special chain-breaking tool. I dug around in the little tool bag that hangs from below my seat and got it out.

"Please tell me you know what to do with that gizmo," he said, "because—and this is just between the two of us—I don't know jack about bikes." His jittery laugh was almost a giggle. I tried to remember where I had heard that laugh before. He stood up, wiping sweat from the back of his neck with a neatly folded bandana. He was a head shorter than me, but solid, stocky, with broad shoulders.

"It's tricky," I said, looking down at the device. "But I'll give it a shot." The sun had dropped down so that even the top of the flour mill tower over on Probandt was in shadows. I sat down on the curb and turned the lever on the tool through thirteen full rotations. Perfect. I tossed the two twisted links down a storm drain and reattached the chain. I got up. The guy raised his eyebrows, impressed. He handed me a towel. I did my best to wipe the grease from my hands. "You're riding a fixed gear bike," I said. "I don't know anything about them. I probably made the chain too tight by not replacing the broken link. It'll at least get you where you're going."

"You saved my ass, man! The name's Ron." He slapped me on the back. "You follow me back to the shop, I'll buy you a beer." He got back in the saddle and began pedaling. I gave him a half a minute. Without a gear system, it takes awhile to get a contraption that size, even without passengers, up to speed. I followed him, nervous, because I wasn't sure my repair would hold. We crossed over the San Antonio River, turned left on Probandt, and pulled into a gravel-strewn beer garden with about a dozen picnic tables just down the block from the Nopalito Bar and Grill. I'd heard about this place. It was a combination pedicab service and bar. I guess it catered to the downtown alcoholic hipster bicycling community. This was the home of the Mission Pedicab Service, as well as the Derailleur Beer Garden. There were a few patrons seated about. I followed their lead and sat at a picnic table, leaning my bike against it. Ron left his pedicab at the curb, behind another one. He walked inside the only structure on the property, a corrugated steel Quonset hut. I watched a third pedicab roll up, parking behind Ron's. The operator got off and headed inside.

Soon Ron came out and took a seat across from me. A waitress walked up. She wore a hoodie and cut-off shorts. Her left calf was covered with a tattoo of pink and black floral designs.

"Hey, Ronny," she said, leaning down to kiss his cheek. "How are the tourists treating you?"

"My tips today came to forty-seven dollars and a bag of weed. All I can say is, they're showing me love and respect. Get me a strawberry soda, please. And give my friend the finest Texas beer from your cellars."

The waitress nodded and walked off. As she approached the hut, she waved at three guys who left the building and got onto the pedicabs. They slowly u-turned and rolled their way off toward downtown.

"Let me guess," I said, watching the pedicabs depart. "You never mentioned the broken chain."

He gave me that jittery laugh again. And that's when I knew who he was.

"That guy on my bike? He's douchier than a high school quarterback."

"Hey," I said, pointing at him with a grin. "Aren't you Casanova Mendoza, the Chicano Chick Magnet?"

His eyes bugged, and he hissed at me to keep quiet.

"Lone Star tallboy for the gentleman," the waitress said, placing the beer in front of me. "And a fruity Topo Chico for, what was your name again, sir? Casanova?"

"My friend's just messing," Ron said.

The waitress laughed and walked away.

"I didn't take you for a Lucha Libre fan," Ron said, keeping his voice low. "I hardly ever see white guys at my matches." I explained that I saw him in a student film—a short documentary about the San Antonio Luchador scene. Ron, AKA, Casanova Mendoza, the Chicano Chick Magnet, was the best part of the film. He's muscular, but a bit pudgy. And even in a mask, he's still kind of goofy-looking. He exploits all this, playing his Lothario character for laughs.

"So, the people here don't know that you wrestle?" I asked.

"Hell no they don't! I'm like a superhero with dual identities." He laughed again. "How'd you crack my secret?"

"Your voice—your laugh, really. From that film."

"Those kids finished it?"

"You bet. It played at the San Antonio Film Festival."

"What do you know?" He sipped his soda. "I hope Lone Star's okay," he said, pointing to my beer.

"Just fine," I said, taking a drink. "So, you're not drinking? You in training?"

"Something like that. Actually, I need to drive to Junction tomorrow morning for a match."

"Junction? Junction, Texas? They have wrestling there?"

Ron gave that signature laugh of his. He had to catch his breath before he could talk.

"There's wrestling all over the place, man. Think of some place that's got nowhere written all over it. Chances are, there's wrestling there."

"Well," I said, "your secret's safe with me. So, do you pedal under an alias?"

"Nope. This is all me. The real me. Whoever that is." Ron bought me another beer. He became intrigued when he learned I made movies. What he really wanted to do, he told me, was to use his wrestling as a launch pad into acting. He was convinced he'd be perfect in commercials. "Hey, what time you got?" he asked.

I pulled out my cell phone. "It's ten after seven."

"Oh, wow," he said. His grin was so wide I could see his back teeth. "There's something I've gotta show you. But we only have ten minutes."

"Sure," I said, draining my beer.

"Follow me." I stood up and paused, looking at my bike. "Dude," he said with a sigh and a patronizing smile. "This is a bicycle bar. Your ride couldn't be in a safer place." He had me convinced, and so I followed Ron down a dirt path behind the Quonset hut. He was moving fast, and I fell into a trot to keep up. We headed along the railroad track for about a block. Then he grabbed my arm and pulled me through a tear in a wire fence. We were on the grounds of an old factory. We stopped at the base of a low water tower. He pointed up. I shrugged. Why not? The ladder felt firm, and I made a point not to look down. We went up about thirty feet to an iron catwalk which circled the water tower. Ron took a seat on this platform. I sat down beside him.

"Seven-twenty the Amtrak comes through," he told me. "You see that building over there?" I followed his finger. He pointed to a warehouse across from us which had been gentrified into upscale lofts. There was a light in the huge floor-to-ceiling window of the third floor. It was well lit—I mean, they might have been making a movie in there. There was a naked man in that large room. Slim body. Fit. Middle-aged. Long brown hair. He was pale as a grub worm. We watched as he worked out with two dumbbells.

"This guy's my hero," Ron whispered to me. "I've even seen him dancing, wearing nothing but leg warmers. Nothing but motherfucking leg warmers!" He sucked in his breath. "Wow!"

I was beginning to get uncomfortable. "Okay, um. I guess if you love the human form and, well—"

"What?" he yelped so loud that his voice bounced off the metal skin of the water tower. "No. That's not... No!" Ron took a deep breath. "Let me start over. At seven-twenty, every night, the Amtrak comes down this track." As Ron said this, I felt a slight vibration and heard a distant rumble. "And this guy, he's giving a free show to any curious fellow or gal from Poteet to Mumbai, who is lucky enough to be seated at the window on the starboard side of the Amtrak carriage."

We watched in silence as the train trundled by. From our perch, we saw the whole performance. "He presents well," Ron said thoughtfully. "A solid performer." It occurred to me that, for Ron, everything was a staged event. Not just the well-lit workout exhibitionist. But the two of us, as well, seated up on our perch. We were playing the role of audience members.

The man in the window strained with the weights until his hair and flesh dripped with sweat. It was frustrating not being able to see the faces of the passengers on the train as he came into view. It was definitely a sight which lingered in my mind. Whether I wanted it to or not. Once the train disappeared down the tracks, we returned to our table. My bike was still there. I thanked Ron for the beer, and we parted company. I wished him luck on his match the next day in Junction.

***

And tonight, there at that swanky River Walk eatery, I saw Ron involved in another performance. Because, as any actor will tell you, it takes some serious acting chops to be a waiter. Good for Ron. This was a high-dollar joint, and he had to be making more money waiting on tables here than working for a bicycle taxi service. I headed over, but before I managed to get his attention, a young woman stopped to ask him directions to the ladies' room. Ron answered in a thick French accent, perhaps more Pepé Le Pew than Charles Boyer; but he sold it all with his natural charm and his smooth delivery.

"Through those doors, to the left, ma chère." His words were followed by a wink. The girl thanked him and blushed. I decided not to bother him. He was in the middle of a grand performance, playing the role with as much heart and gusto as he put into his portrayal of that mythic figure, the Chicano Chick Magnet. For now, he was right where he needed to be. Well, at least until someone tried to talk to him in French. Besides, I had my own work waiting for me. I could hear the band starting up in the event room and I grabbed my camera with a fresh battery and headed in to shoot the cutting of the cake and the dancing.

Near the end of the night, I remember watching Morton place his camera around the neck of his niece. He took off his shoes and socks and slipped into the crowd on the dance floor and joined in. I'm not sure what Ron would think of this lack of commitment to his assigned role, but I envied Morton's ability to move so fluidly between both sides of that line, shifting freely from backstage to front of stage, and back again. He was truly in his element. Natural. Not so much like the rest of us who are constantly putting on a show or playing a role. How liberating it must be to take off the costume and just let the music pull you in.

MESMERIZED (MARCH 20)

My show at the Prometheus was heading into its second weekend. We received two reviews, neither glowing nor dismissive. All our names were spelled right. So that was good. I guess. I went over my lines for an hour or so this morning. I should be happy that Johnny finally moved out. His wife went back to Mexico, and he got a little apartment over on the westside. My life is already much quieter. No shouting. No stomping. No unexpected knocks on my door, which led to unplanned and occasionally unrewarding adventures—though I'll probably begin to miss those.

Actually, I have to admit, the silence is already starting to get to me. Today, all I've heard is a mockingbird in the pecan tree and the barely noticeable sounds of Nora doing yard work along the side of the house. They don't come any quieter than Nora. She stopped talking when she was 14. That's what my landlady told me. Elective mutism, they call it. She's capable of speaking. Just doesn't do it. She's maybe forty and is around the place often to take care of the yard. She also attends to assorted maintenance for the tenants in this duplex. I always see a spiral-bound notebook in her back pocket, which I assume she uses when she wants to communicate with other people. But she's never used it with me. If I need the air conditioner serviced or a drain snaked out, I'll call the landlady, and Nora will come by the next day. She'll knock. I'll let her in. She'll do what is needed.

This afternoon, when I stepped out on my porch to check my mailbox, I saw Nora standing under the carport. She was removing a sandwich from waxed paper. She turned to me and pointed, with her chin, to something overhead. I walked out, past the lawn mower and the rake, until I was standing beside her beneath the corrugated aluminum canopy. We watched an enormous spider construct a web up there. With its legs spread out, it was as large as Nora's hand. The silk threads were anchored to the wooden support beams. Now that the radial lines were set, the spider began the work of laying out the laddered mesh to snag the hapless prey. The tedious work was mesmerizing.

The mountain laurels recently began blooming all over the neighborhood, and their fruity scent came in on the wind. I leaned back in such a way as to see not the carport behind the spider, but the cloudless sky. Just the way I would compose a photograph. The spider was suspended up there, in all that blue, working tirelessly.

***

There's an old story about an enormous spider who lived in the desert, in the valley where the Rio Conchos empties into the Rio Grande. They call it La Junta de los Rios, where the rivers join. High above the pueblos, this spider built a web that was anchored to Chinati Peak and Sierra La Santa Cruz. This menacing creature would lower itself from its web, usually at night, to feed upon the native people. When the missionaries arrived, local lore shifted, and the spider became the Devil.

The missionary priests, in an attempt to be seen as useful to their parishioners, banished the Devil to a cave high atop Sierra La Santa Cruz. Or so it was claimed. Every year, the faithful climbed up a dusty trail to recite prayers in front of the cave. This ritual that kept the Devil imprisoned had been going on for generations. So, if you want to know where the Devil is, drive to the outskirts of the Mexican frontier town of Ojinaga. Up on that long and low mountain look for a little tooth, the highest point of the upper ridge. At the base of the tooth is the cave. And if you don't believe me, trudge your way up the path. It's well marked. At the top you'll find, at the mouth of the cave, a cross sunk in the rocky soil, surrounded by votive candles and the piles of ash from generations of burnt incense.

I made that climb once. It was in the winter and the wind bit and stung. At the top, I was alone. I took shelter in the shallow cave, but if the Devil was home, he did not reveal himself. I settled down on the ground and blew into my hands to warm them. That's when I saw the spider. Well, *a* spider. It seemed untroubled by the cold or the wind. I sat there and watched it, silhouetted against the deep blue sky, wrapping and wrapping an ashen moth in its silk.

***

I never even heard Nora crumple up her sandwich wrapper and walk away from me. When I noticed the sound of her raking leaves, I realized she'd been working for some time. I looked around to give Nora a sheepish smile, but she was lost in her task, pulling on the rake in long, double strokes. I decided to leave them both to their jobs. Nora, and the spider. I went back inside and took a shower before walking to the theater for tonight's show.

THE GREAT PEACOCK MASSACRE (APRIL 8)

Huge cottonwood trees shaded the garden, with scattered light stabbing in from the morning sun. I positioned my camera to get some video images of Salvador painting on a large canvas. He wore a black t-shirt and dark gray chinos. He was working in the shade. The shot looked great. The problem was the alpaca wandering around. Normally an adorable and fluffy exotic animal would be a perfect addition to some b-roll of the "artist at work." However, the alpaca was white, and it kept wandering into the light, becoming overexposed to the camera. It wasn't easy to collect useful footage with both Salvador and the alpaca harmoniously lit in the same frame. Annette had been sitting at the picnic table nearby, but she soon grew bored and walked to a low-fenced enclosure where several chickens roamed about. They ignored her wiggling fingers.

Annette had arranged the video shoot. She's an artist who comes from old Texas ranching stock, tough and self-sufficient, the sort of person who has no concern for other people's opinions about her. Recently, she wrangled a grant to produce a series of video interviews with famous Texas artists. Salvador, ever since he won the prestigious Linnea Muskgrove Prize, has enjoyed a degree of international acclaim, and Annette wanted him for her first interview session. I had been hired to shoot and edit the interview.

Because of Salvador's love of larger-than-life drama, we'd had to reschedule the shoot three times already. Something always came up, and taking into account Salvador's particular notoriety, I assumed drugs were involved. But, finally, we made it into his westside compound, an estate of three small houses clustered together in the barrio. The place was surrounded by a chaotic garden, charmingly rustic, with exotic birds, chickens, goats, and everywhere a clutter of hundreds of art projects in various stages of completion, or, even, abandoned altogether.

When Annette and I showed up, we were dismayed to learn that the previous night a pack of dogs had gotten onto the property and killed all five of Salvador's peacocks. While I set up my equipment, Salvador pointed over the back fence to the city workers who had been called to dispose of the bodies. They were lowering the tailgate of a pickup truck to collect the remains. I was surprised at how prompt they were. Salvador explained that Miguel, a sullen neighborhood boy sitting in the adjacent lot atop a of pile of discarded tires and drinking an orange soda, had done an admirable job wrapping up all the peacock carcasses in white sheets which he had then tied up with red flocked velvet ribbon left over from one of Salvador's projects.

"Beautiful work on those bundles," Salvador said. "And he's heartbroken. The boy loved those birds."

I thought it best to shoot Salvador working on his art for about an hour or so before we moved on to the interview. I wanted to give him time to decompress after what must have been a stressful night and an unpleasant morning. As I stood beside my camera, I realized that there's a kind of phony intimacy in watching an artist at work. Can anything resembling truth emerge when a painter working at an easel is allowed to be treated as a performer? As I repositioned the camera to record Salvador's expressions while he painted, I remembered back to when I lived in Fort Worth.

***

I must have been about 33. I worked at a record store near the university. One of my coworkers was an art student. I wish I could recall her name, but I can't. For some reason, I think it was the same as a liqueur or cordial made by monks in one of those charming mountain monasteries. Sambuca? Campari? No.

When she discovered that I fancied myself a writer, she began pestering me to let her paint my portrait. By the time I finally agreed, it was less romantic than my imagination had allowed. I had fantasized, of course, that I would pose for several days in her disheveled studio. There, adjacent to her unmade bed, I would maintain the studious scowl of an overlooked genius. Actually, what happened was that she came to my place and took a series of photographs of me at my desk, sitting in front of my old manual typewriter.

She would paint me from a photograph. How unromantic.

She confided that she often left art work for people when they least expected it, and in strange places. Under their windshield wipers, or at their favorite table of a local coffee shop. I never expected to find a rolled-up canvas tucked behind my screen door or anonymously placed atop the dashboard of my truck, but I did enjoy the attention of that young art student as she focused more energy on my work than anyone else ever had. I even considered giving her the story I had been typing while she photographed me but, when I read it later, it was horrible.

***

"You know what?" Salvador announced to me and Annette. "This isn't feeling so much like a bouquet of white flowers," and he rotated the large canvas 180 degrees, "as it does a wedding dress." As he made a few fast embellishments with a can of white spray paint, he shouted out: "Boys!" Two young men appeared. "These are my most trusted house boys," Salvador said with a laugh. "I try to help out the local youth. I need assistance in the studio, you understand. Maybe in the kitchen or the garden. With the animals. Always with the animals. I pay my boys and they keep me comfortable. Isn't that right, Leo? Rudy?"

The two men stood at the ready.

"Boys, these two good people will be wanting a snack soon. I know I will. Why don't you drive over to Taco Cabana and get as many chalupas and sopapillas as this will cover." He pulled a wad of cash from his pocket and held it out. One of the men reached for it. "No, Rudy. Not you. Leo, you take the money." The other did so. "Rudolfo's a sociopath, aren't you, dear boy?" Rudy smiled and shrugged. "What a charmer he is, but don't you trust him! Well, off you boys go."

Salvador returned to the painting. Annette sat back down at the picnic table and I kept shooting. We watched as Salvador transformed the flowers into a detailed wedding dress, with just a hint of a slim young woman inside it. A soft wind caused the delicate petals of the crape myrtles surrounding us to scatter across the camera, and a rooster crowed a couple of times back in his enclosure. Then all fell silent, but for the soft whoosh of Salvador's brush as he applied long aggressive strokes of black to the outer edges of the painting.

When Leo and Rudy returned with the food, Salvador provided them with instructions as he cleaned his brushes. "Set the table up on the deck. Cut a few leaves off the banana tree for a festive tablecloth. And you could even tear off little squares to use as rustic plates, you know. Whatever. Use your judgement." The final bit of advice was spoken to Rudy, who responded with rakish solemnity, well conveyed with a wink and pursed lips.

After Salvador put away his brushes, we climbed the rickety steps up to the deck, which resembled a tree house built by a precocious child, fashioned from scavenged doors and masonite panels, and covered by a roof of window casements with the glass still intact. The large carved banquet table, surrounded by wrought-iron chairs, had been decorated with a spread of huge banana leaves. All the Taco Cabana bags and foam to-go containers had been removed. About a dozen each of chalupas and sopapillas had been arranged in the center, with salsa verde and honey dipping sauce transferred into small stone molcajetes. A large clump of marigolds tied with yellow twine had been dropped onto the table with careless attention.

"Rudy sets a lovely table," Salvador said, as Rudy moved to pull back a chair for Annette to sit. Leo came up the stairs carrying a bucket of iced Mexican beer. We enjoyed a long, leisurely lunch, with Salvador and Annette gossiping about mutual friends. Eventually, the food and drink were consumed, and Salvador's "boys" cleaned up.

I had not been drinking, but by the time we climbed down from the deck and entered the cluttered kitchen for the interview, Salvador and Annette were more wobbly and groggy than I would have liked. It was hell to get them focused on the task at hand, which was to get the lights set, the microphones clipped on, and the camera set up; also, Salvador had to go through a series of sports coats and dinner jackets in search of the right look. A fair amount of mascara and face powder was also required. Or so Salvador insisted. During all this, I was glad to have Leo and Rudy helping out. They proved to be the more dependable adults around. Once the camera began rolling, it all fell into place. The interview went well. We got about an hour of Salvador talking about his life and his work. Annette performed admirably as the two traded artist-to-artist pleasantries. They ended the exchange with a warm memory of a road trip they'd taken together many years ago all the way down to the tip of Baja California.

Salvador, now in good spirits, offered to do portraits of the both of us on little 8 by 10 framed canvases. He pulled out tubes of acrylic paint and brushes and quickly knocked out a painting of me. After ten minutes, he was done. I took Salvador's portrait of me and sat down, waiting for him to finish with Annette. It was a good likeness. He managed to flatter me by removing what I would guess to be about thirty pounds. I have to admit that although Salvador is an accomplished and renowned artist, the Fort Worth art student all those years ago managed to capture me much better.

***

I did indeed see her finished painting of me. A couple of years back, out of curiosity, I looked her up on the internet. That was when I still remembered her name. Amaretto? No. Anyway, it was there, featured on her home page. It was awesome. It was me. From behind. But there was enough of a slight profile to recognize my chin, the downward swoop of my eyebrow, and the onyx stud I wore in my left ear at the time. There was my trusted Remington Rand typewriter. And she had placed me and my desk on a bleak, dusty plain. The sky was pure apocalypse. An undulating tornado had just touched down, and, as it tore up the dry and naked earth, it bore down on me. I kept my head down, typing away. Chartreuse? Drambuie? No.

But I do remember the name of the painting. *Portrait of Jerome Hollister.* Who the hell is Jerome Hollister? No doubt a man who made a greater impression than I upon young Cointreau. Or was it Frangelico? Frangelica?

***

Annette sat down beside me, blowing on her portrait. "Isn't it delightful!" It was. She looked like a slightly out-of-focus Audrey Hepburn, circa Holly Golightly. I began collecting all my equipment. Salvador waved us off when we made to help him return his home to the state in which it was before we arrived. "I have my retinue," he said, indicating Leo and Rudy. At that moment, the two young men stepped forward and began gathering up all my equipment cases, light stands, and tripod. We followed them outside. I was surprised the sun was still up. Just barely.

Salvador gave us each a warm embrace before withdrawing back into his home. Leo placed my tripod and camera case in the bed of my truck. Rudolfo kissed the back of Annette's hand, and he plucked a hibiscus

121

flower from the tree beside him and placed it behind her ear.

We drove off, just as the sun was setting, making our way down an unpaved, overgrown alleyway. In the empty lot adjacent to Salvador's garden, I noticed the little boy, Miguel, was still on top of his pile of tires. He now had, slung over his shoulder, a menacing compound bow with a lime green grip. He gave us a dismissive glance as we rolled along, before he lifted up a pair of military binoculars and began a slow, sweeping scan of the creek.

TUNNELS UNDER SOUTHTOWN (APRIL 13)

I angled the chair so I could better look out the kitchen window and see the downtown skyline. Johnny placed a scorched moka coffee pot on his stove. He opened a cupboard to pull out two mugs and a woven basket that overflowed with creamer and sugar packets taken from various restaurants. This was the first time I'd been in his new place since his wife returned to Mexico and he moved out of the other half of my duplex. It was a small apartment over a defunct bar on the westside.

"I'm sorry it's so hot in here," Johnny muttered.

I said something about how summer seemed to have come early.

"The landlord promised to bring in a couple of window units," he said. "Don't know when that'll happen. I'd open the windows, but they're all painted shut. I need to take a utility knife to them."

"Shouldn't the landlord do that too?"

"Yeah, well, it's *my* paint job."

That had been obvious to me, but I kept my mouth shut. Every wall was a different shade of red, and the ceiling was mottled in blue and white, which I assumed was meant to convey the appearance of clouds.

"Probably should get on that soon," he added. "Before he brings those air conditioners over."

I shrugged, waiting for Johnny to explain why he'd called me. Since he left my neighborhood, I wondered if we'd ever find a reason to do anything together. The fact is, we didn't have a lot in common. It was likely, I thought, that he needed my truck to help haul a big piece of crap from one place to another.

Johnny poured out the coffee. We both added cream and sugar. When I suggested we go sit out on the balcony, where it was cooler, Johnny shook his head, explaining it'd be too windy. "Wouldn't want *this* to get carried off." He placed a roll of blueprints on the long, homemade kitchen table. He rolled out a portion. He weighed it down with salt and pepper shakers. There was a date on a lower edge. 1939. "The Yanaguana," Johnny said wistfully, using the Indian name for the San Antonio River. "Recognize your neighborhood?" It looked like a portion of the plans for the WPA flood control project that eventually became the San Antonio River Walk. "You do know that most of the river water passing through your neighborhood has its origins in several artesian springs, right?" he asked me. "Most people know about the San Pedro Springs and the San Antonio Springs."

"These are great," I said, trying to lift up the pages and see what other blueprints were there. "Where did you get them?"

"Garage sale," Johnny said, pushing my hand away. "Some dead architect." He placed a finger at a point on the river. "Know where this is?"

"Um, yeah." It was on the banks of the San Antonio River, just two blocks from my home. "There's that big cypress tree there. And a tiny pond."

"And the water in that pond?"

"Comes from a culvert. Runoff from the streets, I guess. It pools up and trickles into the river."

"No," he said in an authoritative tone. "Before the streets were paved, it used to be a little creek. The creek was later contained in a cement channel. And years later they buried it all in a tunnel, so it could continue to flow." He dragged his finger along a dotted line. "This is the tunnel.

You see, right here? Weird, isn't it?" I admit I got a chill when I noticed that the tunnel went directly under my house. "It travels underground all the way from Hackberry Street. The creek is fed by the old San Flores Springs, which is now buried under the AT&T Center."

"You've done a lot of research."

"Well, the real research came out of this book you gave me." Johnny reached behind him and retrieved a paperback book from the counter. It was a copy of *La relación of Álvar Núñez Cabeza de Vaca* I'd found at a used bookstore. A couple of years ago, Johnny expressed interest in Cabeza de Vaca, and as I didn't care for that particular translation, I gave the book to him.

"Oh, yeah?"

"Well, it was in a footnote," he said, handing me the book. I didn't recall that edition being academic enough to have footnotes. I flipped it over to read the name and address of the publisher. Top Chakra Press, Taos, New Mexico. Now I remembered why I got rid of the book. It had all the hallmarks of new age pseudo-history. I turned back to the page Johnny had marked. The passage concerned the time Cabeza de Vaca and his men were held captive in a region identified by most scholars as present day San Antonio. The footnote at the bottom of the page quoted an obscure report by one of Domingo Terán de los Ríos' men during an expedition of 1691. The passage described a spring that emptied into a small creek which itself drained into the San Antonio River.

The spring flowed from the mouth of a little cavern sacred to the Indians. It was just wide enough for a man's shoulders to fit through. A great treasure was purported to be cached inside the cave. The words from the native tongue were roughly translated by one of the Indians with a smattering of Spanish as "gold and jewels." The governor [Terán de los Ríos], however, had little interest in Indian legends, and so on the following morning, we decamped for territory further north and east.

"So," I said, mildly intrigued, "this is a treasure hunt?"

"If this underground creek is the one in the book, then there must be a place along the tunnel where there's, like, a conduit, an opening, to accommodate the added flow from this little sacred spring." He looked up with a grin. "Interested?"

"When?"

"What are you doing today?"

"Let's do it," I said, because if I thought about it too long, I'd remember how almost everything I did at Johnny's insistence had turned into disaster or ordeal.

"You still have those bolt cutters?" he asked.

***

Forty-five minutes later we pushed through the tall grass along the banks of the San Antonio River until we arrived at a smooth cement retaining wall. A trickle of water came out of a five-foot-diameter tunnel and dribbled into a pool green with algae. Little fish darted about. The whole area was shaded by a massive cypress tree. Johnny was dressed in a pair of sandals, shorts, and a red hoodie. I'd changed into heavy boots, work gloves, and jeans. I had a backpack with two flashlights, a folding shovel, and a portable GPS device, in case my phone wouldn't work underground. Johnny's contribution had been a half a dozen tacos and two quarts of beer. We met up at my house, just around the corner, and since I'd be carrying all the stuff in my pack, I swapped out the beer for bottled water when Johnny wasn't looking.

I heard a loud pop. Johnny had just cut the padlock that kept the hinged grating into the tunnel shut. "Come on, before we're spotted," Johnny hissed. I followed him inside, closing the grate and positioning the lock in such a way that it would appear to be still fastened. We didn't want to lug the bolt cutters with us, nor did we want anyone seeing them, so we carried them a bit deeper into the tunnel. I handed Johnny one of the flashlights, and we set forth. The cramped space forced Johnny to walk with a slight bend to his knees, and because I was taller, I had to move along in an unnatural stoop, which I knew would become painful before too long.

***

The last time I used a pair of bolt cutters to sneak into some place I wasn't supposed to be was twenty years ago, back when I lived in the Big Bend region of Texas, in the tiny town of Vado Rojo.

Chuck Stevens, a school teacher over in the town of Presidio, had agreed to buy a rifle I'd inherited from my father. A Winchester lever action chambered for .44 magnum. When Chuck wasn't living in town, he was at his little ranch near La Plata, an isolated community in the rugged wasteland between the Bofecillos and the Cienega Mountains, which is only accessible by a jeep trail. His chickens had recently been killed by feral hogs. He wanted a good varmint gun. And I needed the money.

It was early on a Saturday morning when I drove to Presidio. Chuck greeted me at his door. He gave me cash. I gave him the gun. "So, what are you doing today?" he asked me, just as I was turning to leave. In retrospect, it seems this question is often asked of me and, more often than I'd care to admit, has led me into stupid and uncomfortable situations. But it sounded straightforward enough. Chuck said he needed to drive to his ranch to pick something up. I assumed he wanted company. I'd never been to his ranch, and a road trip up into the mountains along gravel roads was always a nice way to spend the day.

The unpaved road we took toward Chuck's ranch had no sign to give it a name. If you didn't know what to look for, you'd never see it. But it was an official county road, and as rutted and unkempt as it might appear, it was repaired when it fell too far into ruin. There were dozens of such roads ahead of us. Few were marked or on maps. You'd best know where you were heading, or you'd be fumbling about the desert for quite some time. Chuck knew to turn off onto a smaller road when we passed the cluster of adobe buildings where the train used to stop a couple of generations ago. We followed Alamito Creek for about twelve more miles, through the scrub of mesquite and tamarisk, until we came to a sad line of short posts which used to hold up barbed wire. We pulled into Chuck's property.

Not much. Just two buildings. A squat adobe house, missing the front door, and a wooden shack covered with tarpaper. When he drove up to the buildings, he set the brake but left the engine running. He hopped out and went inside the shack. I thought I'd walk around exploring, but Chuck came right back out lugging an oxyacetylene torch. Before I could help him, he heaved it into the back of the jeep. He told me to get the tow chain out of the adobe and then he went to lock up the little shack. The chain had links the size of my fist. It was twenty feet long, and once I'd looped it over my shoulder, I reckoned it to be about sixty pounds. By the time I had it in the jeep, my breathing was heavy.

"Let's head back by way of Pinto Canyon," Chuck said, and he shot me a grin. He cut the wheel to the right. We headed north. After a short stop in Marfa to gas up, we took Ranch Road 2810 back toward the border. The paved county road soon gave way to gravel as we climbed up into the Chinati Mountains. Half an hour later, bouncing and heaving, never getting over twenty miles per hour, Chuck angled off the road, coming to a halt beside a sign. There were two rusted iron poles, one on each side of the road, and about ten feet overhead was a huge rectangular sign spelling out *Haas Ranch*, in letters fashioned from bent rebar.

"That motherfucker and his goddamn sign," Chuck said, his eyes wild, and grinning like a madman. "This is still a county road. His ranch entrance is over two miles away. That's where this sign should be. On his property, not the county's." I realized he was talking about Manferd Haas, the artist who owned considerable property in Marfa, as well as ranch land out here in the Chinatis.

Chuck got out and removed the torch from the back. I watched in amused disbelief as he set it up near one of the posts and lit it with a butane lighter. He began cutting through the metal. I hadn't known I'd been invited out on a vendetta. I was glad, though, that he'd not brought along the rifle. He cut clear through one post, and the structure stood. Chuck warned me to "look lively," as the thing might fall anywhere. I moved back about fifteen feet. When he was almost completely through the second support, it slumped, leaning forward. Chuck leapt back, staring up with fierce excitement. The whole thing lurched forward. The pole which was cut clean through finally separated. This allowed for an ugly torque. The frame spun sideways, with the free leg plowing a deep arc on the caliche road. There was a high-pitched squeal, like a hawk spotting a rabbit, and the other pole finally broke apart. When the metal frame hit the ground, I didn't hear it. I felt it, from my feet up to the base of my skull.

"Easy-peasy," Chuck said, standing up straight with hands on his hips. Then he fell into convulsive laughter, slapping at his thighs. "Take that, you carpetbagger!"

Chuck tossed me two huge carabiners and told me to use the chain to hook the metal sign to the jeep's trailer hitch. I was afraid someone would be coming down the road soon. Maybe the Border Patrol. I moved quickly. Chuck was busy breaking down the torch and stowing it away in the back of the jeep.

"Ready?" he asked.

"Don't know what your plan is," I said. "But it'll hold."

We dragged that chunk of metal for what seemed like ten minutes before we reached Haas' property line. That was where we used Chuck's bolt cutters to snap the chain on the entrance gate. Chuck drove onto the property, dragging the metal sign a short distance along Haas' little road, and stopped where an arroyo dropped off into a steep canyon about forty feet below. We manhandled the sign over the edge and watched it crash down into the gravel wash, crushing a tall shrub of catclaw.

"Wow!" Chuck said. "You have no idea how cathartic that felt." He took a deep breath as he looked up into the deep blue sky with delicate dots of clouds. He exhaled slowly, as though he'd never taken such a sweet breath.

On the return journey down to the river, Chuck found a radio station broadcasting from over in Ojinaga. We listened to Norteño songs and split a six-pack of beer that Chuck kept on ice in a cooler under his seat. It was a beautiful day, the sort that reminded me why I once sold everything I owned so I could afford to live out in the desert. I felt we had accomplished something important that day. I wasn't exactly sure what, though, and I guess I still don't know. But I have to confess, even years later, our behavior still sits well with me. It does.

***

In a dark and cramped culvert under the streets of San Antonio's King William neighborhood, I followed behind Johnny. I put my flashlight in my pocket. His was bright enough. We kept at a slow pace. Mostly because I was too tall for the tunnel and had to stoop and shuffle along. After fifteen minutes, Johnny asked me to check the GPS. I pulled the little device from my pocket and switched it on. It came to life, sought a signal, and then I found myself looking at a street map of my neighborhood. It took another moment for our location to be confirmed.

"Okay, we're under Stieren," I told him. "Almost to where it crosses Cedar."

"It's like we've been walking forever," he said. We pressed on for another five minutes or so, splashing our way through the scant flow of water at our feet. "What's this?" Johnny asked. He shifted aside and played his light on a region of the tunnel about four feet up the wall. I got out my compact LED flashlight and leaned in close. It was a smaller pipe, connected to the bigger one we were in. Water trickled out, joining the meager flow at our feet. "This is it," he said, his voice quavering with a touch of reverence. "The sacred spring." He turned to me. "Where are we?"

I checked the GPS. "We're under a house at 246 Cedar Street." I opened up a little notebook and wrote it out. I added the full coordinates. It should be accurate to several feet.

"Well, that little shovel in your bag won't be getting through this," Johnny said, sticking his arm into the opening. It was big enough to accommodate a basketball. Johnny put his entire arm in there, up to his shoulder. He shivered.

"Cold water coming out," he said, removing his arm. "I bet it's a spring."

"Maybe it's a storm drain," I countered.

"It's not raining."

"Could be from a cracked water main."

"Give me a break. They'd fix it, not install a drain."

"Maybe it's raw sewage," I added quietly, looking for a reaction.

"Let's collect some," Johnny said with excitement. I reached into my backpack, removed one of the water bottles, emptied it, and handed it over. Johnny filled it with the water that seeped out of the opening. He screwed on the top and stuffed the bottle back in my pack. "We've made history today," he announced with a big smile. "Now let's get out of here!" I followed him back toward the pool under the cypress. As we came closer and closer to the light spilling in from the opening, I was anticipating that liberating moment when I could stand up straight. Suddenly, Johnny shrieked and stumbled.

"What a couple of idiots," he said, leaning down. "We should have tagged this guy with a bit of glow-in-the-dark tape." He got up, holding the bolt cutters. We continued up to the grating, pushed it open, and emerged into the light.

"It's celebration time," Johnny said. "We've, maybe, discovered a treasure trove. Stage One is complete! Let's crack open those beers." He rummaged through my backpack. I explained I had swapped them out for water. "You did what?"

"Calm down," I said. "We still have the beer. It's in my fridge. Two blocks away. You can walk two blocks, eh?"

"Yeah. It's just that, well, I wanted a celebration."

I fished out a bean and cheese taco and handed it to Johnny. I headed home. Johnny padded along behind. I glanced over my shoulder to see him eating the taco, somewhat pacified. "This is all falling into place," he said as he chewed. "Stage Two will take time. I have to call in a few favors. Save up some money to rent the backhoe. First, I need to get that water sample analyzed."

"Sounds like you got it all figured out."

"And keep your mouth shut about this. It's a secret. Don't put this in your blog. Hey, I'm serious. Don't forget, we used *your* bolt cutters." That fact was hardly lost on me. Especially because I was carrying the bulky cutting tool slung over my shoulder. And Johnny can see my full transparency as I publicly post it right here that, yes indeed, they were *my* bolt cutters. Though I doubt anyone will read my description of our little adventure. Oh, and let me just add, for the record, there's something warm and so transgressive in openly carrying a set of bolt cutters through a residential neighborhood. I highly recommend it to anyone. It's like smoking a cigarette in the back of a bus. No. Strike that. In the front of the bus, standing there, next to the driver. It's hard to express how, sometimes, a pointless adventure can feel like a hard day's work, well done.

PALETAS AND BEER (APRIL 16)

I landed this gig from a guy named Randell. He's one of those artsy guys with a finger in every pie in town. Music, dance, theater, film. He had been hired by the San Antonio CVB (that's the Convention and Visitor's Bureau) to create a twenty-minute performance spectacle for the opening breakfast of the annual Americans for the Arts convention happening this year in San Antonio. Randell wanted me to provide all the video, which would be screened as a mammoth backdrop for the all-singing, all-dancing extravaganza at the downtown Hyatt Hotel. Give those jaded art snobs from the big cities something to gape their jaws over. Randell insisted that the video needed to be spread across four rear-projection screens. It promised to be, by far, the most ambitious project I've yet to deliver.

Yesterday, in the morning and early afternoon, I shot all of the scenes with our humble "tour guide" who was to travel through neighborhoods all over the city, introducing out-of-town arts administrators to San Antonio's local color. Even though the concept was not mine, I was thankful that Randell had enough faith to allow me to choose the locations. He, however, had chosen the actor. Which was fine. I'd worked with Lorenzo before and quite liked him—he was sensitive, patient, and always made interesting decisions when the camera rolled. Randell's concept for the video was that Lorenzo's non-speaking character, a humble paleta vendor, would be seen pushing his rolling cart filled with frozen treats through a wide variety of San Antonio's neighborhoods. We rented the cart, which came preloaded with an assortment of the Mexican popsicles along with a block of dry ice, and lifted it into my truck.

The shooting went smoothly. Lorenzo pushed that cart past diverse locations: libraries, cemeteries, tire shops, commemorative statues, even the obligatory downtown vista with the Alamo in the background. Some of my favorite shots were of Lorenzo handing out free paletas to grateful kids.

After I returned the cart and dropped Lorenzo off at his place, I headed home. My next task was to cut all the footage down to a manageable run-time. That was the plan for the remainder of the day. As I was reviewing the clips, I heard footsteps on my porch, followed by the sound of a key in the lock and the door opening. Someone walked into the kitchen. I knew it was Kat.

She'd had a falling out with her fiancé—he skipped town on her—and because she couldn't stay another night in her *dismal den of heartbreak* (as she called her apartment), she asked to crash on my sofa. She had apparently forgiven me for not casting her in my show last month; or, perhaps, this was how she thought I should do penance for my unspeakable transgression. As I'm not too found of having house guests, I hoped that she had just returned from talking things out with what's-his-name and was coming to collect her pink Hello Kitty overnight bag. But I doubted I'd be so lucky. I could make out the sound of her rummaging around in the refrigerator.

"Hey, you're home," she said, walking into my office. "You must have been up early and cleared out. I woke to an empty house." I noticed she was eating a paleta. She had another one, which she handed to me. "What's up with all these popsicles in the freezer?" Before I could answer her, she reached out and tapped the screen of my monitor. "Is this what you were doing today? Wait! I know that guy!" It was a closeup of Lorenzo, looking benevolently toward the camera with the downtown skyline behind him. His gray hair, thick mustache, and the crinkled lines around his eyes gave him an air of distinguished wisdom.

"That's Lorenzo! He's so handsome. Wasn't he in that lowrider movie with Danny De La Paz?"

I shrugged. I continued to work, placing the paleta, still in its wrapper, on the desktop. I ran the playhead of the editing software through the montage of shots from the day. "Hey, I recognize that overpass," Kat said, leaning over me. "Right by the County Jail." A few more video clips came and went, while Kat added scraps of commentary. "Wait!" she said, clamping a hand on my shoulder. "Go back. No. The one before that. There! Stop!" Kat leaned in closer to the monitor. In this clip, Lorenzo was rolling the cart alongside a dusty red sports car. "I know that car," she said. "Where'd you shoot this? Can you remember?"

"Um, yeah," I said. "I do. A side street off South Presa, near Che's Chicken. What's the big deal?"

"This dude, he owes me, like, three hundred dollars."

"I see. Well, I think it's one block south of— "

Before I could finish, she grabbed up my car keys from beside the computer. "This is faster," she said. "I'm driving, you're navigating."

"Now, wait." I tried to sound firm. "I have to get this stuff edited."

"Look at it this way. Guy owes me 300, and I owe you 100. Everyone wins."

"Except you owe me 200."

"Even better." She grinned. "I win, and you win more. Come on! Don't forget your paleta." She hustled out to the porch. I followed. I don't have an issue with other people driving my truck, but things would have gone a lot faster if Kat hadn't spent so much time adjusting the driver's seat so she could reach the pedals.

Once we were underway, I got a call on my cell phone. It was Randell. "Yeah. The shoot went great," I told him, while waving my hand at Kat, indicating that she keep driving south. "It all looks good. I'm working with the footage right now." He wanted to know when he could see the cut. "Early tomorrow," I told him. "I'll have a rough edit for you. I'm planning to pull an all-nighter. So, yeah, I'll give you a call tomorrow." I slipped my phone back into my pocket, but before I could instruct Kat on when to turn off Presa, she violently cut the wheel and we rolled into the parking lot of a liquor store.

"Ha," Kat said, parking next to a familiar red sports car. "He's here buying booze. How typical!" She flung open the door and ran off to confront a man who was stepping out of the store. Then I realized we weren't just tracking down some "dude" who owed Kat money. Nope. This guy was her wayward fiancé. I wasn't sure what to do as I sat in the passenger seat of my truck and watched as Kat tussled with a surprised and nebbish-y young man clutching a bottle in a paper bag, so I unwrapped my paleta, and enjoyed the show. Kat threw a roundhouse kick at the guy that would have impressed me had she not missed his head by about three feet. She fell to the gravel. The guy scrambled into his car and drove off. Kat rolled over onto her side, fist raised. She shouted at the departing sports car.

After that, I guess I fell into the role of Consoling Friend. We drove to a barbecue joint over on Hackberry and had a couple of beers. I had been doing a good job of avoiding all things alcoholic for several weeks. Now I seemed to have begun to backslide. Eventually, we headed out to a few other places. I have a vague recollection, sometime during the night, of switching from beer to tequila.

I woke this morning burrowed beneath a sheet on my sofa, with a hangover. I didn't remember what happened after we left Kike's Ice House, but I picked up my cell phone from the floor beside me, and I was able to piece things together by clicking over to Kat's Instagram feed. I scrolled through photo after photo, each tagged with my name. It sure looked like the both of us were having a good time. The ubiquitous double-selfies, drunken and foolish scenarios of a raucous night on the town. Doing shots, hitting the dance floor, salaciously licking lime wedges. The usual embarrassment.

Then I noticed I had a voice message. From Randell. The edit! I pressed play.

"What gives?" Randell's voice echoed like he was in a cave somewhere. Maybe it was just because he was shouting. "I wake up this morning to see you all over Facebook and Twitter. God dammit! I thought you were supposed to be working last night? Not getting drunk in a bar with some floozy. Those are NOT billable hours!"

I turned it off. Floozy? There's a word I don't hear often. But I guess it's all perspective. Someone looking at those photos could well build a narrative about a hot and heavy and unfolding assignation. I make my living with a camera, so sometimes I take them for granted. I mean, we're surrounded by them. Cameras, that is. There's no place to hide from the accumulation of photographic evidence. I guarantee you, there's someone taking your picture or videotaping you whenever you think you're safe. As much as we crave attention, we often get it in the wrong ways or from the wrong people. Even the most innocent snapshot can convey all kinds of unintended information.

I heard a door open at the back of the house. Kat walked in, sipping a cup of coffee. She wore a t-shirt of mine, and from what I could tell, nothing else. I found myself wondering what else I didn't remember from last night. And hadn't Kat been sleeping on the sofa?

"Um," I began. Kat stopped and looked at me, blowing across the coffee cup. "Last night." I paused. "We didn't...?"

A slow smile began spreading over her face. "We didn't what?" she asked, taking a sip of coffee.

"It's just, you know. The shirt...?"

"You thought, what?" She dipped a finger in the coffee and sucked a moment on it. "That because I'm wearing your shirt, you thought that we spent an evening of long passionate lovemaking? First, I don't want to brag or anything, but you'd remember it. Second, well, I mean… Me and *you?*" She fell to laughing as she walked away.

MACKEREL SKY (APRIL 23)

The clouds seemed so low, but I knew it to be a trick of the setting sun. They were altocumulus, and they formed high above, in that region where the airliners fly. These clouds had a splotchy and smeary iridescent quality, what is often referred to as a Mackerel Sky, because they resemble the underside of that fish.

I looked not up at the sky, but across the still surface of the San Antonio River. The reflection of those clouds was enhanced by the subtle heaving up of the surface as waves moved downstream, so gentle as to make no impact on the cattails growing along the banks. I was sprawled on my belly, my face pressed to the viewfinder of my camera, which was on a tripod with all three legs deep in the mud of the river. I had an egret lined up. With my zoom lens, I was able to get him in close first, and then wide; wading, preening, and poking his bill into the water.

Vincent had hired me to collect video clips of the river for a short documentary he was making for a local nature conservancy. They liked his edit, but wanted some birds and maybe turtles. Because he was attending a conference in Chicago for the week, he needed me to shoot the footage and email him a download link so he could finish the piece. Easy enough for me. This river location, across from Roosevelt Park, was a short distance from my house. That's one of the perks of living in Southtown. Nature is always only a few blocks away. In fact, if you're assiduous in composing your shot, framing out the joggers, the dog walkers, and the trash, you can make this urban area along the river look like pristine wilderness. My own little backlot.

Of course, in my idealized fantasy world I'd be hitting the gym every day to prepare for a trek up a glacier or into the jungle with a couple of cameras, half a dozen lenses, and a badass tripod, just to get those perfect nature shots. So, I guess this felt like cheating. But was it? I wonder how many exciting, dynamic photographs of noble eagles or playful foxes had been shot, in actuality, using a long lens from the sliding side door of a Toyota 4Runner. I imagine that if we could turn some of those shots around, we'd see a parking lot full of tourists hefting up binoculars and bottles of cream soda.

***

I remember, some years back, I treated myself to a few days adventuring around New Mexico for my birthday. When I was done with my visit to the Very Large Array, I gave my road atlas an arbitrary stab and decided my next destination would be Mount Taylor, outside the town of Grants.

After driving three hours, I parked at a trailhead deep in the Cibola National Forest. It was at the tail end of winter, so I bundled up. Stuffed a good-sized day pack with plenty of water, snacks, a rain jacket, and my chunky DSLR with three lenses. I was headed along a trail to the upper portion of the eastward flank of Mount Taylor. The complimentary contour map provided in a little box where the trail began let me know that after a few miles, I'd reach a scenic overlook where the mountain dropped away. I expected some striking photographs, which would be of even greater value to me because of the work involved to get them.

It took me about two hours trudging up a steep winding path that sometimes was hard to discern. There were a few scree fields where the shifting rubble underfoot had me inching along with caution. I was glad I brought along my hiking pole. Once I made it to the end of the trail, the view went on forever. It was as though I could see half the mountain ranges in the state. Perhaps I could. I got up on a boulder and took about a dozen shots, switching between a couple of lenses. I climbed back down and was pulling a sandwich from my pack when I

140

heard voices. I craned my neck and peered around the boulder. There was a little red hatchback in a gravel parking lot. A young woman in flip-flops headed toward me.

"How's it going?" she said when she spotted me. "Nice hike?"

I nodded as she scrambled up on the boulder to shoot a few pictures with her little automatic camera. Then she returned to the picnic table where her husband had finished laying out their picnic. When I finished my sandwich, I walked to my truck by way of the paved road the hatchback couple had obviously driven up.

***

When you're perched on the side of a mountain, it's easy to slip into the fantasy of being deep into a raw adventure that tests the very limits of your strength and resolve. But it's harder to generate the same level of self-deception when the plot of land you're crouched upon is more easily defined by zip code than GPS.

I tried my best to block out the sounds of the city today, as I leaned in close to watch the egret through the camera's viewfinder, but I wasn't able to ignore the kids playing basketball on a court just up the bank. They could see neither me nor the bird, and I found myself watching them from my other eye—the one not pressed against the viewfinder. It was girls playing boys. And the girls were crushing, mercilessly, the boys. Their taunts, in both English and Spanish, had left the boys dispirited. The egret, however, was unfazed by the game above. I was hoping to get a shot of it taking off, but the bird seemed quite content where he was, not even turning to look at the nutria which swam placidly by.

CONDOMS AND SARAPES (MAY 5)

It was a quiet afternoon in May. I sat on the second-floor balcony of Johnny's apartment above the shuttered Michoacán Bar on the western fringe of downtown. On the thrift shop table between us lay scattered a dozen tubes of oil paint Johnny claimed to have stolen from the Southwest School of Art. His place was along the railroad tracks between a light industrial area and an impoverished neighborhood of wooden cottages. There were two apartments above the bar. He had a kitchen, bathroom, and two other rooms, all arranged in a row from the front balcony back to the rickety stairs down to the alley. Across the central corridor was the other apartment where four undocumented Guatemalan laborers lived. Polite young men, all from the same town high in the sierras. We were painting on one-foot squares of Masonite that Johnny had cut earlier in the day with a Stanley blade. I was painting my impressions of the downtown skyline, trying my best to incorporate into the foreground a coffee can with rosemary growing from it that I had balanced on the railing. Johnny was working on a new piece for his Modern Lotería series—this one featured crack pipes, sex toys, and former Governor Rick Perry.

"You should come over here at dawn," Johnny said, adding shadow to a butt plug. "The sun rises up over the Alamodome and the light is alive! The whole porch glows. You can hear the doves, the ones nesting under the eaves over there." He waved his brush at the abandoned shop across the street. "I make a pot of cafe de olla and sit out here watching the city." Johnny stopped and leaned in close to his painting. He muttered a bit in Spanish as he over-painted the cartoon fart emanating from Perry's rump so that it became an enormous mushroom cloud. He smiled in satisfaction.

We heard someone moving along the inside corridor. The door opened. Wesley stepped onto the balcony with Johnny's nephew, Abel. Johnny, Wesley, and I are all in our forties. Wesley is the product of an Anglo father and a dark-skinned Mexican mother; he grew up blond and blue-eyed in the barrio and, no doubt because of that, he can be a fairly tough customer. Abel was just a couple of years out of high school. He rarely added much to the conversation. He followed behind Wesley, tottering out onto the balcony in flip-flops, cut-off jeans, and a denim vest with no shirt. He sat on the floor and placed a twelve-pack of Lone Star beer beside him. He tore the box open and cracked a can for himself. It was clear he'd already had a few.

Wesley fished out drinks for the rest of us. He squinted at Johnny's painting. "Still doing that Lotería stuff? The condoms and sarapes?" Johnny chose to not respond. The two men have known each since they were children. Late in life, both decided to become artists. A competitive streak began to grow.

Johnny opened his beer and looked up at Wesley. "Compliments of the loco check?" he asked, raising the can and one eyebrow.

Wesley collects a disability check. Something to do with mental illness.

"Naw. I've been getting money painting apartments over on Zarzamora."

Abel turned his moist eyes in my direction. He tapped on my boots.

"That your bike?" he asked. "The one in the hallway?"

"Yeah," I said. I squeezed out some light blue onto the pizza box I was using as a palette.

"I used to have a bike. Rode it everywhere. But I'm diabetic, and I can't do it anymore."

Johnny shifted his attention from Wesley. He glared at his nephew.

"Then you shouldn't drink, doofus."

Eventually the painting supplies went back into boxes, and we drank and watched the traffic over on Frio Street. As dusk began to fall over the neighborhood, the Guatemalans walked onto the balcony with a six-pack of beer, a bag of charcoal, and a package of frankfurters. They nodded to us and turned toward the little hibachi on their side. Johnny bounced over and, after a quick exchange that had the men laughing, he returned to us and reached into his pocket, pulling out a couple of twenties.

"Wesley, go with one of these guys to the Culebra Meat Market over on Flores. Get some good meat and more beer."

"Fuck," Wesley grumbled, crossing his arms and looking away. "I just got here. I'm not going anywhere."

At that moment, Renaldo Jiménez flung open the door and came out to join us. He's an established local artist with a flair for the dramatic.

Johnny beamed. "Naldo! It's officially a party now!"

Wesley made a sour face. He didn't care for Renaldo. "Okay, I'll go to the meat market," he said.

"What's this?" Renaldo asked, ignoring Wesley and turning to Johnny. "Meat market?" After Johnny filled him in, Renaldo grinned. "No one knows the subtle code of the barbecue better than I," he said with gleeful electricity. He snatched away Johnny's money and pulled Abel to his feet. "You're coming along, wallflower." With Abel in a state of mute inebriation and securely in tow, Renaldo next separated the smallest Guatemalan from his people and spoke soft words into the man's ear. When Renaldo Jiménez finally departed, it was with a baffled yet committed entourage. A man on a mission of barbecue bacchanalia.

***

I suddenly remembered a similar night, years ago in Dallas, during another time in my life where I played at being an artist. I was living in a drafty loft in an old downtown warehouse. It was the Fourth of July and I was out on the roof with friends. There were maybe five of us, passing around a big jug of wine. As the fireworks began going off about a mile away at the Cotton Bowl, Keith wandered to the far end of the roof and began to fire off rounds from a tiny Italian .25 automatic I had given him earlier in the day in trade for some hash. I wasn't too concerned. The clip only had four rounds in it and I hardly saw what sort of trouble he could get into shooting down into the railroad tracks at night between two mostly abandoned warehouses.

Giving the matter no more thought, I returned to the explosions in the sky. Moments later, Keith tugged on my sleeve. He pulled me aside and placed the gun in my hands. He whispered to me in a panic that he thought he had shot a homeless man sleeping beside the tracks. The first shot, he said, was to see if what he saw was, in fact, a person. "It moved. I think it was a man. I don't know why I shot three more times." I checked the chamber. It was empty. There were no more rounds in the clip. Keith looked at his shoes and said something to himself. I slipped the gun into my back pocket, took the fire escape down to the loading dock, jumped off, and walked back and forth along the tracks. There wasn't anyone there. Nothing that remotely resembled a sleeping person. When I got back to the rooftop, Keith was gone. We drifted apart after that.

***

Strange, I had forgotten all about that night so many years ago. The beers on the balcony brought it back, along with the fireworks display from the direction of Woodlawn Lake commemorating Cinco de Mayo. I had been oblivious to the date, and I was as surprised as the Guatemalans when the colorful flashes began throwing quivering shadows on the walls behind us. Johnny and Wesley provided a running critical commentary, comparing the display to previous years. Renaldo returned while the fireworks were in progress. As the rest of us watched the sky, fascinated, he fired up a joint, examined the coals in the hibachi which the Guatemalans had been tending, and busied himself with food preparation.

Just beyond midnight, after I'd lost count of beers and barbecue tacos, I realized I had been nodding off in Johnny's lawn chair. I glanced around. The stereo inside played Lila Downs. Johnny and Wesley were arguing about a girl who died fifteen years ago. Renaldo was dancing with one of the Guatemalans, while the other three looked on uncomfortably. I eased up and walked inside. I rolled my bike along the hallway and carried it down the back stairs, almost falling over Abel who was snoring, slumped on the bottom step. The moonlight struck a streamer of saliva from his mouth and it glowed blue like a fiber optic cable.

I rode south down Colorado Street and paused for a few minutes to watch a couple of kids throwing lit firecrackers at each other in their front yard until their father yelled for them to shut up. I continued through peaceful neighborhoods reeking of ripe blossoms of mountain laurel and huisache marinating with the odor of barbecued meat. The measured thump of norteño music drifting through open windows followed me all the way home.

BACKTRACKING (MAY 17)

San Antonio's Tower of the Americas dominates the downtown skyline. Its shape is right up there in local iconography alongside the facade of the Alamo and the outline of the famous Rose Window at Mission San José. When I moved here, I immediately found comfort in looking up, and there it was. It isn't just its usefulness as a compass, pointing the way to downtown—it also exudes a nonjudgmental benevolence over us all. What it represents to me is the public nature of this city. The Tower of the Americas rises from the spacious grounds of Hemisfair, the site of the 1968 international exposition. Just on the edge of the bustle of downtown, its grassy slopes, hidden gardens, and quirky buildings offer a place of respite and exploration.

The first time I went up the Tower—the exciting ride on the glass-fronted elevator—I was showing off my new city to friends visiting from out of town. At that point, I'd been a resident for two years. "I can't believe it took me this long," I remember telling them. "I should be coming up here all the time." Actually, I love playing the tourist in my own city. Especially when I live in a tourist town. Back when San Francisco was my home, I'd take the tour out to Alcatraz at least once a month.

In truth, that was *not* my first trip up the tower. It came back to me when I stood with those friends on the observation deck, looking not, as they were doing, out at the expanse of Texas landscape falling away to the horizon, but rather back at the curved wall behind us. I knew there used to be ashtrays placed along that wall. Square metal trays filled with white sand perched atop waist-high pebble-encrusted cement plinths. Back before public smoking marked one as a social pariah. God. I couldn't have been more than eight years old when I saw those ashtrays. It was during a family mini vacation. We'd made the short trip from Dallas. We stayed in the Crockett Hotel, toured the Alamo, floated on a river barge. And we went to the top of the Tower. I had my little Kodak Instamatic camera with me the whole time. I knew I had it with me atop the Tower because when I went to the restroom I placed it behind one of those ashtrays. Even back then, I considered it unseemly to be spotted carrying a camera into a public bathroom. Being eight and in a strange town, I should be excused for forgetting the camera. It wasn't until we were back at the hotel that I realized my blunder. My parents were unconcerned. We'd go back and search for it tomorrow before heading home, they said. If we didn't have time, I wasn't to worry. They'd buy me another one.

They did nothing of the kind on either account. It wasn't until I was sixteen and made enough money delivering newspapers before I bought my first real camera. A Nikon FM.

Nowadays, I make my money, my meager income, with a camera. Maybe it's all connected. Maybe I had been eyeing that tower, wondering when I was going back up to retrieve my long-lost camera. A little unresolved bit of business whispering for my attention. For many people, this is comforting. This returning to parts of their past. I often find myself at odds with this, though. When the past pops back into my life, I have a habit of thinking myself stuck, like a rocket ship going around and around the Earth, not quite able to break from the gravity and head out to the beckoning unknown.

***

Yesterday, driving back from the bank, I saw a black Cadillac on East Guenther Street parked in front of a house two blocks from my home. It was a 1969 Coupe de Ville. I knew this not because I'm a car guy. Far from it. I don't know a Hemi from a semi. And, in all candor, I consider it a good day when I remember which side my gas cap is on. This bit of specific auto lore comes from my having owned a caddy like that one. The same color, even. And today, as I returned from a morning run, I was able to examine it better. I slowly circled around the car. It wasn't just the same model. It was the exact same *car*. There, on the rear bumper, was the dent from when I backed into a live oak tree in the parking lot of the unfortunately named Koffee Kup Kafe in Hico, Texas. And there was the pale, faded green interior, which hinted at the original exterior color which I had paid to have painted over for seventy-five dollars. The imitation brown leather steering wheel cover from the previous owner, which I never took off, was still there. The only noticeable difference was that the rear wheel skirts were missing. Not a good look for this particular model.

The car had a For Sale sign on it. I was not tempted. Though I was a bit freaked out. The last time I set eyes on my black Cadillac was a decade ago, when I left Dallas and moved to San Antonio. I didn't sell it. I paid a salvage company to haul it off. It had been sitting idle for over a year in front of my Elm Street loft, and I couldn't afford to fix it. I stood there, watching them load it onto the flatbed tow truck and then take it away.

We'd been through a lot, me and that car. I'd owned it for ten years. The first week I had it, I took it to a lonely stretch of Noodle Dome Road out past Abilene, and got it up to 120 miles per hour. The car made no complaints. In fact, over the years, I don't know how I avoided getting a speeding ticket. I have never gone above the speed limit in any other car. That Cadillac, though, seemed happiest traveling around ninety miles per hour. That car and I were together when I moved out to the Big Bend. I knew I wanted to disappear into the desert, but I didn't have a specific location. The little town of Valentine looked promising on the map. It was small and maybe I could find a cheap place to live. I hit town a couple of hours after midnight. I slowed down along the main street, hoping for an empty, dusty store front with a For Rent sign. I didn't see anything promising, but I circled back and drove through town again, slower. Perhaps because I was driving a long black car which appeared as though it belonged to a crime boss from a 1970s Mafia movie, on that second pass an old woman came padding out of her brick cottage in her slippers and robe. She eyed my car suspiciously. Probably she was clutching a gun and trying to decide whether to call the sheriff or just start shooting.

To hell with Valentine and its paranoid citizenry. I headed to my second choice. The town of Vado Rojo, desolate and dusty. The people there were more welcoming. And I soon found myself part of a community. Whenever I'd head across the river to the Mexican town of Ojinaga to shop, I was never met with the contemptuous suspicion of that slippered woman from Valentine. Instead, I encountered people grinning and waving at the crazy Texan in the big black car. Sometimes the prostitutes hanging out in the Bikini Bar near the Zócalo saw me through the windows as I rolled through town, and they'd come running out, shouting and laughing. Maybe they thought I was a celebrity. The car, when it had a good washing, did give me a general air of prosperity. Unless you looked too closely. At me or the car.

But, again, I'm not a car guy by any stretch. I should have taken better care of it. By the time I moved back to Dallas, it had become a second car, living a static life, almost never taken out because of fluid leaks and an unpredictable electrical system. Until, of course, the day I realized I didn't want to lug it along with me on my next big adventure.

Why it came back to me—so to speak—I don't know. I don't believe in fate. It's just a coincidence. A rather improbable coincidence, in that I might send a car off to a scrapyard in Dallas, only to have it reappear in San Antonio, just down the block from where I live. It managed to cross half the state and an entire decade to find me. Or maybe I found *it.* No matter how much we—meaning human beings—think we're searching for the new, we are more likely on a constant lookout for the familiar. It is often remarked upon that our brains seem wired to seek patterns. And how better to construct a pattern than by scanning our environment, trying to find something we already know well enough to easily recognize? I tell myself I have free will, agency over my decisions, but, still, I'll always pause for closer inspection when I see an older model Coupe de Ville parked at the curb; always take the elevator to the observation deck atop a tower; always walk into an establishment called the Bikini Bar. It'll be automatic. I won't even think about it. I'll just head that way, looking for something I don't even remember that I lost. And each time I begin this dysfunctional dance of nostalgia, I'll cringe and try to stop. And I will always fail.

WEIGHT OF THE YEARS (MAY 22)

I realized recently that I've stopped thinking of myself as a filmmaker. Sure, I've accumulated a sizable body of work, though it's more amateur than I care to admit. I've even won awards in regional festivals. And I manage to pay my bills—barely—while occasionally upgrading my equipment. At some point, though, I drifted into the world of the hired camera guy—a person who is rarely asked for his creative input. I guess, on a subconscious level, I've decided I no longer want to face the shame of dragging actors and crew members into my unpaid personal projects anymore. A decade of this work—this paying of dues—should have elevated me to a more professional status. Right? Well, it hasn't.

When I began working with the Prometheus Performance Company, however, I was able to produce my own work. Even pay cast and crew. Strange, because film work is supposed to be more financially rewarding than theater. The fact was that the Prometheus had spent three decades cultivating stable relationships with a whole raft of philanthropic foundations. I was well aware of my good fortune to be welcomed into their company.

That was until recently. Because of the restructuring of a couple of granting organizations, as well as the Prometheus' internal bickering, things are now floundering. The eviction and relocation of the theater space didn't help. I learned that my show back in March was the last Prometheus production which could pay the cast and crew a respectable rate, at least for the time being. And though it's not about the money for me, I feel weird cajoling friends and colleagues to work for some paltry honorarium on a theater project in which they have no large creative stake. The situation places me right back where my filmmaking failure had left me. I don't enjoy having that constant reminder that I am stagnating in this world of amateur productions without even having the vague semblance of a dependable day job.

So, as I was riding my bike to the restaurant, I was trying to find the words to tell Rachel I needed to extricate myself from the company. She sent an email inviting me to lunch. Because Rachel wasn't particularly adept at socializing outside of the world of devising and producing theater, I assumed she had a plan for a new show. Maybe I didn't want to give up just yet. I *did* enjoy working with her. No. No, I had to stand firm. I locked my bike to the gas meter in front of Maria's Cafe, entered, and slid into a booth across from Rachel.

After ordering, we exchanged pleasantries and light gossip. We had our rhythm, which we'd developed over the years, and just when I expected her to launch into a pitch about an idea she'd like to develop, she presented to me a completely different proposition. "I'm done with this city," she said. "It's too tedious. The people are petty. And poor work receives more attention than good work." I nodded, waiting to see where she was headed. "I've hired a realtor to put my condo up for sale," she added. "As soon as I find a buyer, I'm off to New Orleans." She had desired to live there for years, so I couldn't fault her.

"I'll miss you," I told her. Which was true enough. As I said it, it struck me how few folks I knew ever moved away. This city has a weird hold on people. They so rarely leave. And the ones who do, do so only after having lingered well past their freshness date.

"I have a proposal," she said, shifting in her seat. She wanted me to come with her. And before I could think of anything to say, she laid out a comprehensive scenario where she'd take the money from the sale of her condo, buy a small house in an older neighborhood, and I could have a couple of rooms. Pay what I could, if I could. No strings.

"That's quite an offer," was all I said. My mind had gone blank.

We sat in silence. She fidgeted. Then she explained that there was a vibrant theater and film scene in that city. A refreshing adventure. We did a good job sharing a small place during our writing vacation back in January. We were good creative partners. It made sense. I told her it all sounded exciting, but to give me time to think about it.

"Of course." She smiled. I knew her well enough to realize how difficult it had been to ask me this. I also knew myself well enough to realize how it would end. I'd had women roommates before. I invariably develop these neurotic infatuations, begin acting immature, and ruin everything. I didn't want to do that with Rachel. I should have told her no. But I needed time to fashion a well-considered email that wouldn't jeopardize our friendship.

Our meals arrived, and we shifted gears to talk about other projects we were each working on.

Afterwards, I decided to ride around for a while, doing what I do when I want to clear my head. I don't know how effective it is as therapy, but when my mind begins to gnaw on itself, usually about matters of money, but often enough about other things as well, I hop on my bike and take to the side streets, with no real destination in mind. I was turning onto Probandt near a new brew pub when the rains hit. It was a wall that just came down; the noise was absolute, like a train screaming through a crossing. I angled across a gravel parking lot and coasted through a giant doorway into an enormous corrugated steel building. Against the back wall were several windows, but with the clouds and the rain, it was too dark to make much out. There were no lights on, and the place was empty. I wasn't sure if I'd stumbled into an abandoned building or a factory during the lunch break. I leaned my bike against the sliding metal door and wiped water off my face. I'd wait out the rain here, but I hunkered down near the doorway so that it would be clear I had no nefarious notions in mind.

I smelled paint. Oil paint. The wooden frame of the twenty-foot high sliding door had recently been slathered with silver paint. I reached out. It was still tacky and left a smear on my finger. The odor moved in closer, wrapped around me… transported me back through the years.

***

After dropping out of graduate school, I drove down to stay with some fellow academic failures who had moved to the little town of Blanco. Milton was somewhat older than the others. He walked away from an MBA and took over a dilapidated building in the town square his family no longer had any interest in. The place used to be a paint and wallpaper store until it had gone out of business in the 1970s.

When I arrived in the middle of the spring semester, Milton was living on the second-floor with his friends, Lyle and Forest. Back at the university, the three had gigged around performing appalling amplified racket. The ground floor of the building in Blanco was one large, well-lit space which the three had painted silver, after, I assumed, Warhol's Factory. The fresh paint had the metallic, chemical smell of a car radiator when it boils over. Milton and the others practiced there in long, pointless sessions. They weren't just making music, but involved in a greater social experiment embracing performance art, multimedia presentation, postmodern disinformation campaigns, and so on. The place reeked of marijuana and was littered with Dairy Queen cups and burger wrappers. My visit couldn't have lasted more than two days, but in my memory it was weeks. The air was thick with acrimony; the stoned, rambling vituperations piled to the rafters. They were at each other like rats in a sock. I made my exit early one morning without being seen.

Some years later, I looked up Milton. He still lives on the second-floor. Lyle and Forest long ago abandoned him (one for Jesus, and the other to become a diving instructor in, of all places, Norman, Oklahoma). The years had not been kind to Milton—they'd left crags on his face, and sagging bulges everywhere else. He was sponging off his folks and continuing to make music. His studio was a cramped room overlooking the courthouse, choked with computers, cables, speakers, and assorted devices. He showed me his back-list of dozens of CDs he sold through the mail. He claimed to have a following in the Netherlands, and I had no reason to doubt him.

We ate the soup his mother brought over and talked about the years gone by. Milton would sometimes drift off like a weak radio station heard while driving. He claimed to be a narcoleptic, but his brain was just wired badly. The last memory I have of him, he was wearing headphones and watching a computer monitor as he bobbed his head to the drone of a looped recording of a train whistle mournfully stuttering ad infinitum.

On the way out, I stopped to peek through the window on the street level. The huge ground floor space still had the silver paint, but it was tarnished by the years, and furred patches of dust clung around the window casements and up in the crown molding. It wasn't until I was driving through Dripping Springs that it occurred to me I'd forgotten Milton's parting gift—his entire musical oeuvre. "Don't think of it as music," he'd cautioned me. "It's collage. Sound collage."

✲✲✲

There, off Probandt, sheltered from the downpour and surrounded by the odor of paint, I heard a long rumble of thunder far in the distance. The rain tapered off. Soon it was just water dripping off the building. An old man in bib overalls and a grimy t-shirt ambled across the gravel. He lit a cigarette as he entered the building and passed by me. "Looks like you got caught out in it," he said to me with a grin. And he disappeared back there, somewhere, into the shadows.

TWO QUARTS LOW (MAY 28)

My truck has been running rough, so when I stopped this afternoon at the Handy Andy on Flores for coffee and laundry detergent, I picked up a couple of quarts of motor oil. I tossed the groceries on my front seat and popped the hood. I was right. The dip stick came out dry but for a varnish-y drop on the tip. I have recently started drinking again. Not a wise decision by any arithmetic. I was sick with a hangover, and I wiped at a constant scum of sweat on my forehead. When I opened one of the oil quarts, I was afraid I might make a mess. I wasn't exactly shaking, but I sure wasn't feeling steady. I dipped into the cab and rooted around behind the seats. There was a flyer I had pulled off my windshield last month advertising a Klezmer band playing downtown at the Sons of Herman Hall. I fashioned it into a paper funnel. It worked like a charm.

As I was opening the second quart, a shy girl who works at the grocery store sat down on the bench next to the coin-op dispenser of sanitized water. Her name is Laurena. I first met her a couple of years ago before she started her job at Handy Andy. Back then she attending a high school film program. The instructor had brought me in—an industry professional, was how he'd introduced me—to judge the students' work. For some reason Laurena had remembered me and always spoke to me by name when I came in for groceries.

"Is it okay?" she asked. It took me a beat to realize she had spoken to me. In this era of cell phones, it's difficult to recognize when a solicitous voice is directed your way.

"It'll be fine." I turned to give her a smile. "I think I caught it in time."

She began unwrapping an ice cream sandwich. An old man shuffled up, hugging a paper bag of groceries tight to his chest. He spoke with Laurena in Spanish. I wasn't trying to eavesdrop, and beside my Spanish isn't what it once was, but I gathered the old guy was asking after Laurena's grandmother. It didn't sound good. The man touched the brim of his hat and headed off. Laurena ran her tongue around the edges of the ice cream sandwich. That's the way I do it, too. Next, you wait for it to melt a bit and do it again.

The film Laurena had written and directed showed promise. In fact, it received prizes at a few student film festivals. Like so many movies by young filmmakers, it was obviously autobiographical. Filled with trouble and angst and an abundance of tear-filled scenes. The young actress playing the lead role was beautiful. Thick eyebrows, strong cheekbones, full, soft lips. Her face was more solemn than serious. She played a charismatic and witty young woman. All the things Laurena was not. I remembered the words that Laurena's film instructor had whispered to me that afternoon as the class viewed each other's films. "Perfect casting," he'd said of her film. "Don't you think? Clearly, the protagonist is an idealized version of the student herself. Gorgeous, confident, articulate. The actress does a magnificent job showing a great sadness back behind those eyes."

I had to agree.

I knew quite well how the arts can be a wonderful place for those of us not satisfied with who we are. We can insert the best of ourselves into those narratives or visual depictions we create, and edit out all the things we don't like.

I've known of so many teachers who work in theater, dance, art, and cinema departments who have spoken overtly about how they offer a safe place for sensitive kids to figure out how to fit into the world. There's a variety of practices and modalities wherein people can put on and take off this guise or that persona until they find one that works.

Art as therapy.

I absolutely do see the value in that.

But what of those of us who get stuck? Incapable of settling on this or that? Spending decades engaged in false starts?

Well, I'd rather not dwell on the nuanced purposes of art. Certainly not today. My mind was mostly occupied with this morning's visit from my landlady's son. He came to tell me in person that he now owns the property. Furthermore, he wants me to know that once my lease is up, I should expect big changes. He then spent half an hour touring the property with a clipboard-toting contractor.

Before I moved to my duplex in San Antonio, I had flitted from town to town. But this last decade, settled in the same place, I had finally become that most common of citizens. One who is easy to locate. That's all about to change, I gather. It's unlikely I'll be able to afford a rent increase. This also explains my desire to look after the health of my truck. My subconscious is preparing for flight.

I dropped the two oil cans and my makeshift funnel into the trash barrel beside me. Laurena wiped her hand on the denim of her thigh. I watched as she got up and tossed her ice cream wrapper into the trash. She stood beside me in the shade of my opened hood.

"What's Klezmer?" she asked.

"What?"

She pointed to my funnel in the trash.

"Oh. It's a kind of Jewish music."

She blinked, waiting.

"It sounds like what gypsies play in the movies," I added, lowered my hood until it made a satisfying click.

"You like it?"

"I don't know. It was on my windshield."

At the sound of a car honking, Laurena excused herself. "My mom's picking me up," she said, hurrying off to get into the car waiting at the curb.

CALLISTO LOOKS DOWN (JUNE 2)

I have, for the most part, given up on my neighborhood as a place to encounter anything of interest. The current wave of development has priced out all the relevant, exciting creative venues, and replaced them with a slew of galleries run by callow trust funders who are delighted to hang on their walls the sort of soulless abominations that only an MFA can squeeze out, bereft of all intellectual honesty and cultural depth.

Nonetheless, Melinda (one of the holdouts up on the second-floor of Blue Bird) had invited me to a preview party at a new gallery in the space beneath her. The group show featured her hand-painted photomontages along with the work of half a dozen other artists. As I always made it a point to support her, I said I'd go.

It was as I expected. The wine, though it came out of a box, was drinkable. The mini quiches, which I suspect were from Costco, weren't too bad. I even enjoyed much of the art on the wall. It was the patrons, the punters, the vapid idiots pushing in front of me in the wine and chow lines. They were all talking about real estate investments and the private schools where they send their awful kids to. After three quiches and four glasses of wine, I felt I'd done my duty as a good friend. I beat a quick retreat in the direction of home.

Beyond the parking lot, through a stand of trees, you'll find the stone steps that lead to the San Antonio River. I headed down to the unhurried serenity along the flowing water. All around me the songs of the crickets and the frogs drowned out the city sounds, and I felt I could breathe again.

***

On the other side of the river, the paved path lead to my neighborhood of old homes and huge, mature trees. There was a full moon throwing down shadows from the leaves.

When I turned onto my street, everything was quiet, wrapped up in the night. A car drove by, its headlights illuminating my neighbor, Brian. He stood in front of his house with a spindly tripod that supported a little Sony Handycam. He was videotaping the full moon.

I rushed inside my place and grabbed my fifteen-dollar Galileoscope. I had bought the thing online during the International Year of Astronomy. That was years ago! The plastic telescope was an educational toy which promised to give the viewer an experience akin to that of Galileo. You'd be able to see the rings of Saturn, the four Galilean moons of Jupiter, and a wonderful prospect of craters on the moon.

Back when the telescope arrived, I made quick work assembling it. But the weather had me stymied. There were overcast skies for the next three days. I put it away, and forgot all about it.

But tonight was the night!

I fastened my cheap plastic telescope to an eight hundred dollar Italian tripod that has a massive fluid head. Overkill, no doubt. But it was the closest at hand. I trundled the whole thing outside, walked down the sidewalk, and set it up beside Brian.

"Hey, man," Brian said in his soft British accent. As I set up my tripod and tinkered around with my little plastic toy, we stood there, side by side, silently, as men tend to do. Eventually, Brian turned to me and said he was experimenting with his video camera to see if he could get a good shot of the moon. I glanced over. His camera was zoomed in all the way. It had an automatic exposure, and I was sure the image would be blown out into a hazy white blob.

I had just tilted my telescope so that the moon filled the view, when

Brian asked me: "What you got there?"

I couldn't help myself.

"Whoa! Check this out! I mean, this telescope cost me fifteen dollars!"

Brian peered into it to take a look at the moon. He murmured in agreement.

"Impressive," he said. "But the moon's upside down." There was a note of pity in his voice. Sort of along the lines of, you get what you pay for.

I considered explaining the rudiments of optics. That's when I heard Minnie open her door to call the cats in for the night.

"What's up, guys?" She walked over to look at Brian's camera, and then into my telescope. She stepped back and just gazed at the moon in silence.

"It's so big tonight," she finally said in a hushed tone.

Minnie's husband, Trip came to find out what was keeping her. He squinted into my telescope.

"Hey," he said with a chuckle. "You can even see the moon moving. Pretty cool." He tapped at the telescope. "You know, for plastic."

He asked what else might be worth looking at. I spotted Jupiter and shifted the telescope over there. Once I saw the four little points of light near it, the largest Jovian moons, I let Trip take a look.

The telescope, as cheap and clunky as it was, made a huge difference. The stars were never impressive when seen in my neighborhood. One of the problems tonight was the light from the full moon; however, the real culprit was the city's light pollution.

***

I remember when I lived in the desert how I was constantly bowled over by the endless run of stars carpeting the sky.

There was one time when I rode my mountain bike about seven miles back into the Bofecillos Mountains, in search of an archeological site

Rogelio, the local postmaster, told me he had discovered decades ago when he was a boy.

We'd been sitting out in front of the post office. He indicated a mountain in the distance.

"That one, like a loaf of bread. There's an arroyo at the foot of it, and on a little rise is where I found them. I was out hunting with my uncle. We were riding horses. I saw this circle on the ground made of sticks. The circle was four feet across. We started digging, thinking it was treasure."

Rogelio said they uncovered a human skeleton. It had been buried in a large basket with its knees up, like sitting in a squat. The sticks were the support frame of what was left of the basket. They then noticed about six other similar circles. It was an old Indian burial site. They covered the body and left.

"No treasure there," Rogelio said with a wry smile. "Just ghosts."

I didn't go looking for treasure. And, really, I wasn't even trying to find an archeological site. Mostly, it gave me a reason for an adventure. I had a backpack with sandwiches, water, and a small battery-powered lantern. I had lashed to the back of my bike a thin padded ground cloth and my sleeping bag. The topographic map brought me to the arroyo Rogelio mentioned. It'd been a circuitous route down a couple of disused jeep trails and a curving dried water course.

It was early afternoon when I reached that little valley. I encountered nothing unusual. Just a lonely wasteland of rocks and a host of plants cunningly evolved to stab, snag, or otherwise mess you up. During the rainy season, the ocotillos, catclaw, and assorted cacti enticed you with vibrant flowers. That day, however, there were no such picturesque displays, for it had not rained in over three months. I had been on foot for the last half mile, rolling my bicycle beside me, as it was easier to navigate on foot through the gravel and sandy floor of the arroyo. When I realized I was where I wanted to be, I picked up my bike and balanced the crossbar of the frame over my shoulder so I could climb up to a low, flat-top hill; a four or five acre uplift, about twenty feet above the arroyo. It was clear that this was Rogelio's hill. I laid my bike down on an empty patch of ground well removed from thorny, spiny plants. Then I spread out my ground cloth and sleeping bag.

I decided to climb to the top of the mountain, that bread loaf Rogelio had pointed out. The mountain rose up at the far edge of my hill. I estimated that the summit was five hundred feet up.

For the first four hundred feet, the going wasn't too steep. I didn't have trouble zig-zagging my way up. I had to make sure to hit the upper portion just right, because it was nothing but straight cliffs, except for a little break, like the gap of a missing tooth, which continued to the flat summit.

From the top of the mountain, I saw the river valley spread out in front of me. The tiny Mexican town of El Mulato was to my left, with the hulking form of Sierra Rica, a massive long-dormant volcano, in the far distance.

A mild wind came in from Mexico. If I strained my ears, I could hear it passing over the ocotillo and lechuguilla. The other sounds from the desert were missing. Were I down in the arroyo, or even at my little camp on the hilltop, I'd be hearing the buzzing of curious flying insects.

I climbed down off the mountain, back to the bees and the flies. I began to make a systematic survey of the hill.

The sotol plant is like an agave or a century plant. Its base is a series of spear-like claws curving up in a spherical clump. In the center grows a woody stalk, four to six feet tall, which, in season, terminates in flowers. After blooming, the flowers die and this central stalk falls away. It makes for a great walking stick.

I found a long, sturdy sotol stalk. I used it as I walked across the hilltop. Anytime I saw something that might be a stick coming up from the ground in the manner of Rogelio's burial sites I'd poke and dig around with my sotol. I made a mental map and basically placed a grid over the area. After an hour, I felt confident I had covered the entire surface. I discovered nothing man-made.

When the sun dropped down enough to put the whole hilltop into shadow, I sat down on my sleeping bag and ate one of my sandwiches. I thought I'd probably not need any thing to cover me up during the night. The desert, even in the warmer months, can get cool at night. But on those days when it climbs above a hundred, it can take most of the night for the heat of the day to leach out of the ground.

That night, when the sun finally set, the sky was a wonderful abstract arrangement of ghostly stellar light. During the early hours of darkness, I laid on my back, looking up at the stars.

I guess I drifted off. Something woke me up. I don't know what it was. I checked my watch. It was 4:47 in the morning, and still not cool enough to unzip my bedroll and get in. I turned over on my back to stretch. When I looked up, I had to catch my breath. The sky was filled with light.

It was the Milky Way. Directly overhead. Now this wasn't the first time I'd seen this sight, but even when sitting outside of my single-wide trailer down on the river in Vado Rojo, there was still spillover light from the neighboring farms. But that night, in the serious darkness, it was powerful, intimate. It took me a moment to realize I'd forgotten to breathe. I gasped and started breathing again.

Then I heard a scraping noise. Like sandpaper on rough wood. I suddenly knew it was the sound that had woke me. It seemed close. I glanced around. And there, silhouetted against the sky no more than fifty feet from me, was a cow. No. More slender. A deer? The animal was pawing the ground. Digging at something. A mule deer. That must be what it was. It was big. It stopped. I watched it lower its nose to the ground, sniffing around. It lost interest and wandered off, disappearing down into the arroyo.

I made a mental note of the spot by fixing, in my mind, a mountain peak in the distance. I turned back to looking at the sky, before eventually falling asleep.

In the morning, I walked to where the animal had been digging. It was easy to locate. A large area was disturbed. I used my sotol stick to dig deeper. There was a flat rock that I had to dislodge and pull out. Underneath I found three stone triangles which I thought, at first, were fossilized shark's teeth. But, upon closer inspection, it was clear they were small arrowheads, delicately chipped from caramel-colored flint.

I kept one and placed the other two back on the ground and set the flat rock over them. Ever since, I've carried that arrowhead with me. At the moment, it's in the little zippered coin compartment of my wallet. I don't know what it represents. If anything. But I keep it with me.

That's the closest thing to treasure I brought back from my excursion.

***

Minnie pressed her eye to the telescope. She asked me the names of the moons she could see around Jupiter.

"Io, Europa, Ganymede, and Callisto. No idea which is which. But those are the four that Galileo saw."

"So, he gave them those names?" Minnie asked, stepping back.

"That was Kepler's doing," Trip said.

Minnie and Trip lost interest after a few more minutes. Brian was still obsessed, adjusting the settings of his video camera. I headed home around one in the morning.

It was clear I needed a treasure hunt to inspire me. I was itching to explore a new valley or mountain top.

EMBALMING ROOM (JUNE 6)

Rachel received the same email as had I, from a local gallery celebrating its ten-year anniversary. The invitation had gone out to various community artists to submit proposals for work somehow involving the number, word, or idea of "ten." As there was no money involved, and because I was pissed off with the gallery owner (though why, I can no longer recall), my response was simple. I hit the delete button. Rachel, however, had a flash of inspiration. She desired to create a series of photographs of her bare feet, titled "Ten Steps." Each image of a single foot (alternating left right left right) would represent a time in a person's life, from cradle to grave. She planned on using her own feet, so she asked me to do the camera work. A collaboration. That was an easy yes for me. But I wanted to provide more. So I suggested we produce the piece as a short film presented on a digital frame. I'd use the feet pictures and create an animated morphing slideshow.

It was agreed. After a couple of days, she sent me a list of possible locations. We spent an enjoyable week roaming around town, shooting her feet. When we came to the shot listed simply as "beach," we considered possibilities. The shore of Woodlawn Lake? A gravel sandbar in the San Antonio River? But nothing had that iconic appearance of beach sand with a line of foam-edged water coming in.

"How do you feel about a road trip?" she asked.

"Absolutely!"

She mentioned Padre Island. I countered with Galveston. She agreed.

So this morning we pointed my truck east and headed down Interstate 10. The weather did not look promising, but all we needed was a close-up shot of a foot in the sand with some water. Even if it rained, we could make it work.

I was afraid things had become weird between us. I finally sent her an email explaining that because I had a few long-term projects "up in the air" I wasn't in a position to commit to moving to another city at the moment. The closest she came to acknowledging my email during the drive was to tell me: "The offer still stands if or when you change your mind." I nodded, muttering that was nice to know. Mostly, it was nice to know we were still fine.

Somewhere outside of Flatonia, we hit heavy traffic. The clouds raced toward us, low, ragged, and more black than gray. It must have just rained. Water pooled on the edge of the highway. I needed to keep pressing on the brake, as we rolled along, until we were moving more slowly than if we were walking. I spotted the flashing lights of emergency vehicles up ahead. Rachel ate a piece of beef jerky from the last gas station stop, and began telling me what she'd do if she were to wake up and find herself alone on the planet, the sole survivor of a virulent pandemic to which she was the only one inexplicably immune. There was this funeral home, she said, Orlando and Sons. A huge stone house from the 1800s with a deep wraparound porch. She visited once to arrange the funeral of a niece, who died in a waterskiing accident. The casket display room had impressed her. "Don't ever confuse a coffin with a casket," she said as an aside. "It's the unmistakable mark of a rube."

When the rain began drumming on the roof of my truck, she seemed not to notice. She continued, explaining how she'd let herself in the side door so she could walk through the tiled embalming room, careful not to tangle herself in the network of rubber tubing which snaked around the glass vats of formaldehyde and bodily fluids. The vapor locks on the formaldehyde tanks are adjustable to allow some off-gassing, and the whole place would have that sharp scent. But it was the caskets she wanted to visit. What a thrill to run her hands over the polished hardwoods of the more elite models; feel the yielding foam form of the silk-lined interiors.

There was a rattle of tiny pellets of hail on the windshield.

"So, the rest of humanity has to die for this to happen?" I asked, as we passed an ambulance with its back door open. Cops and EMTs were clustered around.

"Well," she said with a shrug, "that's just for starters. I'd do other stuff, I'm sure."

I was well aware of her preoccupation with matters of death, and I had made a plan that was seeming more and more well-crafted. When we reached Houston, the rains were still with us. I pulled into the parking lot of the National Museum of Funeral History. I knew I'd scored a few points with her when she said excitedly that she'd never even heard of the place. We spent over an hour wandering the exhibits of hearses, ornate caskets, and dioramas of mummification procedures and Day of the Dead celebrations.

By the time we got back and the road and made it to Galveston, the clouds had blown away. There was standing water everywhere. It steamed up off the sidewalks and streets. We got our perfect shot of foot, sand, and surf. This left plenty of time to explore about under the pier, poking at shells and kelp. Before returning back home, we stopped for sandwiches at a cafe in the Strand. We decided not to ask why their windows were boarded-up. We were afraid we might come off as out-of-town bumpkins. Were they expecting a hurricane? Maybe just construction? It wasn't until I was home at my computer that I learned we began the day driving right into a major storm—an almost-hurricane of a threatening enough nature to warrant a name (in this instance, Bill). It had shifted and moved inland while we were perusing the replica canopic jars in the Wonders of the Egyptian Afterlife exhibit. I guess we were too busy exchanging whispers of inappropriate commentary to have noticed the growing power of the squall outside and its eventual dissipation.

There are times when I so enjoy being wrapped up in the cocoon of someone else's company that a typhoon is nothing more than a bit of set dressing, an unseen atmospheric backdrop to a close-up photograph.

THE BRIGHT GREEN SCUM (JUNE 15)

Today, as I rode my bike past a pond of still water, I noticed that it was covered edge to edge with a bright green scum. I was struck with an odd desire to take off my shoes, push the scum aside, and dangle my feet in the water. As that thought crossed my mind, I mourned the fact that I wasn't that sort of spontaneous person. Then another thought surfaced. Maybe one can *become* such a person by pouncing on those impulsive desires with proactive intent.

I hit the brakes, raising a low cloud of dust. I sat down on the grass beside the pool to remove my shoes and socks. As I brushed my hand across the green surface and lowered my feet into the water, I realized it wasn't a film of algae, but thousands of tiny, floating plants. Duckweed. My feet vanished from sight as the duckweed drifted back in against my skin. I took a deep breath, closed my eyes. My pulse slowed and the only noise I could hear was the thin, electric harmony of the cicadas.

I remembered back when I was still in my teens. I was out camping with some friends. After a long hike, we emerged from the trees and looked out across to the little lake where we had reserved a campsite. One of us, without any care or contemplation, ran straight toward the water, dropping her clothes along the way. She was naked when she reached the shore, and in she went. The rest of us took our time, shyly changing into swimming suits. By the time we were dipping our toes into the water, she was already out, seated on a rock, and nonchalantly plucking a couple of leeches off her body. I've never forgotten the expression of undiluted joy on her face when she jumped into the water.

Taking a deep breath, I opened my eyes to peer down at the green pond. I pulled my feet from the water and brushed off the duckweed with a sock. No leeches. I put my shoes back on and cycled off, feeling an absurd welling of virtue from my prosaic detour.

TRINKETS AND TREASURES (JUNE 23)

I helped myself to a couple of blueberries off of Samantha's fruit plate. We were seated at one of the outside tables of LeAnn's Taqueria and Bistro. My egg white migas were a flavorless affair, but the coffee was good. Samantha pushed away the little plate that had held her piece of carrot cake. She muttered while she scanned some official paperwork from the Alamo Community College District. "Motherfuckers pay me next to nothing, force me to buy their parking permit, and now I have to fill out this code of goddamn conduct form?"

I was tempted to remind her that I had used my Photoshop skills at the beginning of the semester to create a flawless parking decal, good for all campuses. A service I had provided to her for free. Instead, I pointed out that the document that she had begun to scribble on only had four fields to fill in. "See, Sam?" I added. "You're already done."

"It's the indignity. Besides, I have to hand-deliver this to an administrative office all the way out at the Palo Alto campus."

Samantha is, among other things, an artist's model. She is constantly networking with various painting instructors and college art departments around town, trying to get gigs. Not such an easy task for a woman in her fifties, but she manages to keep busy. To soften her mood, I told Samantha about meeting Maisie, an agoraphobic shut-in on the southside. "She owns an original Matisse. Might have sold it now—she's very poor. Never left Texas, but that doesn't stop her from convincing herself she's French."

"Becoming French sounds like an excellent coping mechanism," Samantha said. She folded the forms and slid them neatly into a manilla envelope. "I need to remember that. It's nice to have those sorts of things in one's back pocket when anxiety comes calling."

At that moment, Eveline Deschamps rounded the corner onto South Alamo Street. She was rummaging through her handbag, so I saw her before she saw us. "Speak of the devil," I muttered. Samantha seemed to be ignoring me. She slipped her ballpoint pen into her pocket. I turned to her. "Don't look now."

Samantha removed her reading glasses and, with a playful smile, whispered: "Are we being watched? Is it your faux French friend, Maisie? Venturing out into the sunlight?"

"No, but close. Over at the bus stop. Your sworn enemy."

"You need to narrow the field," she said, still not looking up.

"Check it out for yourself. She's bound to notice us before her bus arrives."

Just as Samantha lifted her gaze, I knew we were spotted. I heard the unmistakable rasping smoker's voice and that thick French accent.

"Samantha, my darling!"

"Evie!" Samantha said with the authentic enthusiasm that can only come from decades of theater training. Eveline bustled over. Samantha stood, and they both embraced in the graceful choreography of the Gallic double-cheek kiss. Before I could get up, they both sat down and began a quick exchange in French, which ended in laughter. Eveline acknowledged me with a tilt of her head. She squeezed my hand before fishing a cigarette from a shoulder bag.

"Do you remember my friend?" Samantha asked, giving her my name.

"Of course," Eveline said, but it was clear she had not.

"How remarkable," Samantha said. "You being here right as we were talking about, well, French people."

Eveline smiled benignly and gave us a little noncommittal shrug. Samantha and I met her the previous year. Back then Eveline had entered into an agreement with Kelton Dermott, artistic director of the Prometheus, to stage her one-woman show at the theater. Samantha had been commissioned to translate the French text into English, and my job was to create animated subtitles of Samantha's translation, which would be projected onto the back wall of the stage during the performance. Somewhere along the way, the production was canceled. Eveline had insisted that she wouldn't be able to memorize her lines in time for the performance dates. Samantha, however, was convinced Eveline had a mental breakdown. Not that the specific reason made any difference to Samantha. She'd been promised a fixed figure for the translation, and she needed the money. She was barely scraping by on her modeling gigs. Worse, she had spent a week laboring over the translation before Kelton pulled the production—hours of work that had never been compensated. With all that in mind, I found myself incredibly impressed by Samantha's willingness to forgive Eveline. It's not her style.

"I've never eaten here before." Eveline said, glancing about.

"It's awful," I said.

Eveline looked at Samantha, who just shook her head.

"Don't listen to him," Samantha said. "Mine was fine. However, I suppose it's hard to fuck up a carrot cake." She drained the last of her coffee.

As I waved down the waitress and paid, Eveline asked what we were doing with the rest of the day.

"Trinkets and Treasures," Samantha said.

"Pardon?" Eveline asked.

"It's the first Tuesday of the month," I explained. "That's when the State Hospital has a sale at their thrift store. They call it Trinkets and

Treasures."

"Why not join us, Evie?" Samantha suddenly said, her eyes big. "It's refreshingly rasquache, which is South Texan for gauche." I shot Samantha a questioning glance. "It'll be fun," she said, giving me a wink. "Usually, it's more trinkets than treasures, Evie, but you'll not know if you don't go."

It was a tight fit with all of us in my pickup truck. Eveline pouted like a child because I wouldn't let her smoke. We drove all the way down South Presa, past Che's Chicken, past the ruins of the old Hot Wells resort, and, at the huge arched iron gates to the San Antonio State Hospital, there it was. A tiny hand-painted sign with a faded orange arrow pointing the way to *Trinkets and Treasures*. Several similar signs guided us through the sprawling complex of sun-charred grass and buff brick buildings.

"It's so big," Eveline remarked.

"Yeah. Five hundred acres or so," I said, turning at an abandoned security kiosk.

"This doesn't look like any hospital I've ever seen," Eveline said, glancing about.

"What did it used to be called?" Samantha asked. "The Southwestern Lunatic Asylum, right?"

"Been around since the 1890s," I added with a nod.

"Where are the security guards?" Eveline asked.

"Now, now," Samantha said, patting Eveline's knee. "I'm sure they have it all figured out."

The facility was a shadow of its former glory days. Most of the buildings appeared abandoned. Perhaps they were. But patients *were* still cared for at the hospital. In fact, only last month, while working on a film set, I had overheard a young actress telling the makeup artist about the indignities she suffered as a teen at the State Hospital. When I remarked how terrible it all sounded, the woman shook her head. "You don't understand," she told me. "I was fucking nuts, completely out of control. That place is why I'm alive today."

We pulled into a parking slot in front of Logan Hall. As we walked to the entrance, I looked up at the second-floor windows, which were covered by heavy-gage wire mesh. The entire ground floor of the building was given over to the thrift shop, but I always wondered what might be happening up on the level above.

"Daphne!" shouted one of the older women who volunteered at the thrift shop as we entered the lobby. Samantha grinned and hurried over to the curved counter of what had once been the nurses' station. That's where the volunteers will add up your trinkets and treasures on a battered Casio electronic calculator and make change out of a tin box.

Daphne. That would be Daphne Cannard, one of Samantha's aliases. It's all part of her ceaseless pursuit to add color to her world. I'd actually forgotten that she was known to the old ladies at Trinkets and Treasures by one of her assumed names. Eveline didn't notice. Or maybe she considered it another American eccentricity. She wandered over to a dusty display case which held a meticulously carved wooden replica of Logan Hall that a patient crafted back in the 1940s, complete with green-tinted cotton shrubbery. Certainly a treasure, but, in this case, not for sale.

I scanned a few shelves of books, each priced at a dollar. Mostly book club mysteries. Samantha came up behind me, excited. Two of the volunteer ladies were with her, one held a clipboard.

"We can take the tour!" Samantha broke a Rice Krispies Treat into two halves and handed one to me. "Aren't they so sweet," she said of the volunteers. "They gave me their last treat."

Ah, the Tour.

Samantha thought I shared her fascination with the State Hospital. I mostly found it to be an interesting diversion. Some days, I'd pick up a sports coat or a coffee carafe. But that was it. However, Samantha was constantly trying to get on the list for the monthly tour of the facilities. It always seemed we arrived after the tour had departed. But not today. Lucky us. There was still a wrinkle. The tour wasn't for the curious public, but rather for those who were thinking of placing a beloved family member into the charge of SASH. And thus, I was now afraid I'd need to pretend to suffer from some mental affliction. Though I've been involved with theater for a few years now, in all candor, I'm not a very good actor.

A stooped-shouldered black man in a lab coat came to join us. "This is Doctor Dante Phelps," said one of the volunteer women. "He'll be heading the tour." Phelps shook our hands, holding mine a bit longer. He leaned in to get a closer look at me. "Oh, no," Samantha said. "My brother and I brought our sister, Evie. It's just the two of us taking care of her. And she can be quite a handful. I mean, it's not like she's dangerous, or anything." Samantha turned to me, her eyes wide. "I mean, we'd call them verbal outbursts, right?" She smiled. Nodded. "Deep down inside," she said, glancing up at the doctor, "well, she's a gentle soul."

"Only really difficult in the evenings," I decided to add.

"She's such a small thing," Samantha continued. "You'd not expect such strength. It's like those cute little chimps. You put 'em in diapers and a bowler hat and you want to hug and tickle them all day long. Until they revert back to the jungle and tear your face off." She laughed and playfully punched the doctor in the arm. "But I don't have to tell you that, do I, Doctor Dante?"

Eveline turned and looked over at us. "Evie!" Samantha chirped, waving Eveline over. As we watched her approach, Samantha explained to the doctor in a low tone: "It was a rough morning. And not so easy to coax her out of the house. I think she's expecting ice cream." Eveline joined the group, smiling at everyone.

"You do have friends everywhere," Eveline said warmly, in that heavy accent of hers.

"Well," Samantha said with a smile to the doctor. "It looks like she's French today."

"I'm sorry, what was that?" Eveline asked, confused.

"Evie," Samantha said. "You are such a joy." Samantha turned to the two women volunteers. "Isn't she? She's a joy. A treasure. Now, Evie, let's go see what trinkets and treasure we might find." And as Samantha guided Eveline to one of the side rooms with the clothing and kitchen items, she whispered over her shoulder to the doctor: "You let us know when the van's ready to show us around."

I continued to wander about, picking through the humble offerings. As I examined a four-foot HDMI cable on a folding table near the janitor's closet, Samantha grabbed my elbow.

"Where's our darling sister?" I asked.

"Trying on a green pastel skirt suit." She peered up and down the empty corridor. "Follow me," she said. But there was no following. She still held my elbow and pushed me in front of her, steering me through the side door. Outside, on the steps, I heard the door lock behind us. I had thought she was going to share another Rice Krispies Treat with me. I was wrong. "No time to talk," she hissed. "We gotta move." I followed her around to the front parking lot. She took the keys from me and we got in my truck, with her in the driver's seat. She spun the wheel as we reversed. We took an unpaved shortcut to South Presa, gravel flying behind us.

It wasn't until she made a left on Southcross that I asked: "So, where's Eveline?"

"In a padded room, trussed up in an extra-long-sleeved canvas smock. You know, if we're lucky. Ungrateful bitch."

Five minutes later, we were seated in a booth at the back of Taqueria Guadalajara drinking bottles of Bohemia and sharing a basket of tortilla chips. I asked how she felt about not being able to go back to Trinkets and Treasures. Or ever having a chance to take the tour.

"I mean, was it worth it just to get back at Eveline?"

"Sometimes you disappoint me. The fine people at T and T will never again set eyes on Daphne Cannard. True. But they'll be happy to have Vivian as a new customer."

"Let me guess. This Vivian, she's French?"

"Vivian McNaughton," Samantha said, slipping into a slight accent, "is Scottish all the way down to her sturdy, polished brogues! And a redhead! Oh, and I do hope she'll be joined by her gentleman friend, Randolph, who I suspect would look quite dashing in an ill-fitting toupee and a paisley ascot." Samantha lifted her eyebrows and reached over to tug at my collar.

What can I say? Samantha understands my weakness for a bad toupee.

PEDRO MORALES' LOVE NEST (JULY 1)

On an overcast weekday afternoon back in May, Johnny and I discovered Pedro Morales' love nest.

We were riding bikes on the westside, on the edge of downtown, to all appearances just two shiftless slackers killing time. Johnny kept darting into alleys to peer into dumpsters, always searching for treasures. I started grousing that if we didn't hightail it over to Travis Park before two, the guy with the hotdog cart would be packed up and gone. As these were Johnny' favorite hot dogs, he picked up the pace. We doglegged from Guadalupe to El Paso Street. As we passed Café Insurgente, Johnny gave a shout—"Just one more!"—and sped down a narrow drive alongside a crumbling two-story building. When I caught up, his bike was on its side in a gravel parking lot, its rear wheel still spinning fast and free. He had crawled halfway inside a cavernous dumpster, his work boots flailing. As I leaned my bike against a mammoth oak tree, he shouted out, "Jackpot!" The last syllable reverberated like the single note from a kettle drum, hanging in the air and slow to decay.

"You okay?" I asked, walking up behind him.

"Dude, pull me out." I grabbed his belt and hauled him to his feet. He was grinning. He hooked his thumb for me to take a peek. I opened the sliding side hatch and leaned in. Taking up most of the dumpster was a small, elegant sofa in immaculate condition. "One hundred percent leather," he said with hushed excitement. "Tender calf skin, I betcha." I turned around, nodding. It was quite a find. "What do you think?" Johnny asked.

"Nice."

"Nice? I'd lay odds Sherlock Holmes never parked his keister on something so fine."

There was the squeal of a rusty hinge above. We looked up at a iron fire escape as an old, muscled man stepped out. The sun cut through the clouds as if on cue to glisten off his sweaty bare chest, covered with nautical tattoos. He acknowledged us with a raise of his chin. He pivoted gently up there on the landing and brought out a large crystal chandelier, holding it up free of the metal railing.

"Whoa, man!" Johnny shouted. "Careful." He took the stairs two at a time, calling to me over his shoulder, "Looks like a Tiffany!" I wasn't so sure about that. I followed him up the fire escape. When I made it to the top, Johnny spun around and slapped me on the back. "It's getting tossed, too!"

The old man handed over the chandelier. "There's more," he told Johnny, tilting his head toward the door. "Inside."

"This I gotta see," Johnny said, giddy. He passed the chandelier on to me, which I found to be surprisingly light. Johnny followed the man inside.

I took the chandelier down and placed it carefully beside the dumpster. My stomach growled, but there wasn't much I could do. From a dense tangle of weeds, I pulled an old metal folding chair with a ghost of pink paint still on the seat and dragged it into the shade of the oak tree. After a few minutes, Johnny yelled down to me from the fire escape. "What are you doing down there? You have to come up and see this place!"

I expected a dark, dusty warehouse space. So when I got up there, it took me a moment to make sense out of the polished maple paneling, brocade wingback chairs, dark maroon curtains, and oriental rugs tastefully scattered about. It was a two-thousand-square-foot hybrid of a gentleman's club and a Victorian bordello. I was speechless as I approached the gigantic circular bed. Johnny ran his hands over a large ebony chest beside it. "It's filled with paddles, leather masks, and all sorts of goodies." I asked if he planned to rent a moving van to haul it all off. "Don't have to," he said. "They can leave everything here because I'm taking over the lease. The last tenant, he died. Anyway, the dude with the prison tattoos is downstairs, trying to find the property manager."

"You sure about this?"

"It's only five hundred bucks a month. I'd be crazy not to!" Johnny had recently begun working for a limo service, and, as prom season was giving way to wedding season, he was feeling prosperous. "Besides," he said, peering around in reverence. "This is a piece of history. We're standing in Pedro Morales' fabled love nest."

"Pedro who?"

"Good Lord, man!" He rolled his eyes. "Not that I expect a güero from Dallas to know anything about history." He sat down on the chest. "Pedro Morales was a big-time Chicano activist here in San Antonio. The right-hand man of Miguel Cantú. But Pedro had the charm. My father talked about him all the time. When big stars from Hollywood came to town, Pedro would show them a good time. You know, Tom Hayden, Jane Fonda." Johnny winked at me and patted the mattress. "Barbarella, I betcha! Right here, right here! What do you think?"

"I guess you could put up some sort of historic plaque."

"No way. Pedro kept this on the down-low, and I think that's best. They said the old rooster couldn't keep it in his pants. What a life!"

A door on the far side of the room opened and the old man entered, now wearing a shirt. He was followed by a small black man in sunglasses and a Nehru jacket who clutched a clipboard. "What I could do with a place like this!" Johnny said in a knowing whisper. He pantomimed the grasping of something so grand and lascivious that it lay beyond even his comprehension. "Wow!"

***

I'd forgotten all about the weird time capsule of a place over on El Paso Street. But it all came back to me last night. I was sitting at a table toward the back of Taqueria Cósmico off Cevallos Street, specializing in upscale Mexican "street food," trying my best to enjoy the vegan carnitas. I sat across from Benny Jordan, the artistic director of a small poetry non-profit. Benny had just got a grant from the Ford Foundation, and he wanted me to produce a series of videos featuring the work of some of the more accomplished emerging local authors. He envisioned twelve poems, shot and cut in music video style. It sounded fun. Also, the budget he had available meant I could finally pay off a pack of pesky creditors who had me screening my calls and avoiding the mailbox. As Benny waved the waitress down for more lime wedges and chopped onions, I did some quick mental math. Goodbye weddings and quinceañeras.

"So, we can work together?" Benny asked me, while he added creamer to his coffee.

"Absolutely!"

"Great! I'm looking forward to putting things in motion."

Benny's cell phone rang. He glanced down, held up a finger apologetically to me, and answered the phone. As he talked, I pulled a tortilla from the little round box and began making a taco with the faux carnitas, adding onions, cilantro, avocado, and salsa. There was a stubby guy, almost all torso, in a down vest walking from table to table. I'd seen him before. He sold pirated DVDs. Mostly he worked the southside cafes and taco joints. I'd never expect him in a hipster place like this. Yet there he was, totting his three-ring binder with color photocopies of the movies he had in the trunk of his Lincoln Town Car, which, I knew from experience, would be parked out front. That's when I noticed he was working the room with a partner. An energetic man in chinos and a denim jacket who also carried a binder from table to table. When this other fellow turned to approach us, I realized it was Johnny. When Johnny spotted me, he sauntered up, grinning. Before I could say anything, he took a seat at the table.

"What's up?" I asked him. "Selling blackmarket movies?"

"We all do what we must," he said. He leaned his elbows on the table and looked at me. "I will say this. I'm holding on tight to *my* street cred. But I come in here and see *you* eating tofu tacos? I'm hardly the one who needs to explain himself."

Benny, having finished his call, put down his phone. He glanced over at Johnny.

"This is my friend, Johnny," I told Benny. "Johnny, Benny Jordan."

"It's a pleasure to meet you," Benny said, offering his hand.

"Oh, we've met," Johnny said, taking Benny's hand. "It's been awhile. I can't fault you for not remembering. I had to give you a drive home you were so wasted after a Trinidad Sánchez reading. When was that? Fifteen years ago?"

Benny laughed. "Sounds like me. And you, you sell movies?"

"Johnny is a man of multiple talents," I said. "Painter, photographer, entrepreneur. Also, he's the greatest dumpster-diver I've ever met. In fact, that's how he discovered Pedro Morales' love nest."

"No!" Benny was impressed. "That's gotta be good for a footnote in the story of anyone's life. Supposed to be just to the west of downtown, yeah?"

"El Paso Street," I said. "And this is the fellow who is keeping the dream alive. He has rented the space and—"

"Well," Johnny managed a weak laugh. "They kicked me out. It was a good ride while it lasted, but I couldn't keep up the rent."

"Johnny! That place was perfect for you!" I turned to Benny. "It had a big round bed, mirrored ceiling, a wet bar, and a *bidet* in the bathroom." I shot Johnny a look. "Man, what happened?"

"I heard Pedro seduced Dyan Cannon and Barbara Hershey there," Benny said. "That place is history."

"Yeah." Johnny sighed. "It was great at first. I was doing my art there. Feeling inspired and all. But the rent was getting to me. By the second month, I was hurting. And then, well, you know Archie? He heard about my place and he offered to pay to use it to make his—"

"His porno movies," said Benny. "Yes, I know Archie Ivy."

"I found myself at the top of a slippery slope. Archie's loaded, and I'd be an idiot to say no to all that sub-lease money. But I could hardly ever use the place. And after a while, well, I didn't want to."

"So I'm guessing Archie got busted?" Benny said.

Johnny nodded. "And the property manager gave me the boot."

"Kind of like Pedro Morales." Benny stroked his chin and raised his eyes to the ceiling. "The man was doing so much good. But he was brought down by his own appetites. With him it was lechery. Where as with you—"

"Hey!" Johnny said, grabbing his binder. "I don't know where you're headed, but watch it!" He stood up. "All I wanted was a cool place to hang out."

"Calm down," Benny said. "By the way," he tapped the binder, "you got any copies of the movies Archie Ivy made?"

Johnny grinned. "Maybe I do." He sat back down.

"I'm especially interested in anything shot in Pedro Morales' love nest." Benny turned to me. "That's what we're calling it, right?"

Before I had a chance to say anything, Johnny leaned in close to Benny. "On the day of the vice squad raid, I gathered up all of Archie's original tapes and DVDs from his secret stash in the rafters while he was still being fingerprinted." He leaned back and gave a pained laugh. "Only fair. I mean, after what that jerk put me through!"

"I'll buy up everything," Benny said. "I'm serious."

"Well, I'm thinking we can do some business," Johnny said in a conspiratorial tone. He stood back up. "So, if you'll step over to my office. And by that, I mean the trunk of my car." Benny laughed. He looked over at me. I shrugged. I watched them head out the door. It turned out to be more than just a quick trip to the parking lot. They never returned. I was left to pick up the tab.

***

This morning I received a short email from Benny. It seems that the poetry video project is off. Something about a budgetary shortfall. Good lord! The lack of commitment in this town is, at times, breathtaking. How often have I found myself caring more about other people's projects than they do themselves? Of course, this is what comes from not pushing my own personal work. Benny with budget issues? Please! I suspect that Benny Jordan has begun the process of tainting that Ford Foundation money by branching out into the porn industry. I'll have to wait and see if he, too, is brought down by his own appetites. Unfortunately, these things take time to play out.

A LONG LINE OF SALT (JULY 17)

This afternoon I was hanging out at Melinda's studio over at the Blue Bird Arts Complex. We were drinking peppermint tea and talking while she worked on a dozen photographs for a gallery exhibit. They were street portraits she'd taken on a recent visit to Bangladesh. She had mounted the photos on cradle boards. Now she was delicately painting geometric designs on the wooden edges. I had walked over to her studio because I needed company, and Melinda never asks probing questions.

I had slept late, and while drinking my first coffee of the day, I stepped out onto my porch for some fresh air. There was a box beside my door. It was filled with books I'd loaned to Rachel. She'd added a note written with a felt marker to the top of the box saying how she was sorry she'd missed me. She hoped I'd come visit her soon in New Orleans. We must keep in touch.

At the bottom was a postscript in capital letters. "My offer still stands." I felt sick. Not just because I knew I'd miss her more than I'd care to admit. But it was obvious I'd slept through her knocking on my door. So, that was it. Rachel had packed up her clothes and books, her dog and two cats. She'd taken the highway east, to New Orleans. I finished my coffee, got dressed, and made my way across the Alamo Street bridge to Melinda's studio. It wasn't that I desired to talk with someone, but I didn't feel like being alone. I was fine with drinking Melinda's tea and watching her work.

"What's that?" I asked Melinda.

"What's what?"

I picked up a padded mailing envelope about the size of a small throw pillow sitting on her desk. It was heavy. The return address was a town in Kentucky. "Oh." She smiled, her eyes never looking up from her brush. She kept painting in silence. I thought we were going to ignore the subject, but finally she said, "Dirt."

"I see," I said. But I didn't.

"My friend Daisy is visiting her aunt. So, I asked her to send me dirt from…well, wherever she is."

"Kentucky," I said, tapping at the mailing label.

"Right." She switched out to a more slender brush and loaded it with red paint. "There's this book I read that described a banishing spell."

"You have an angry spirit?" I asked, peering about the studio with no little amusement.

"Don't I complain about *her* often enough?" she whispered. She raised her eyes, looking at the wall behind me.

Ah, Felice, the noisy, belligerent, and perpetually drunk ceramicist who rented the studio next to Melinda. Everyone on the entire floor hated her. I would think that they'd sign a petition or something. Force her out.

"Ground glass in her sugar bowl," I mused. "Isn't that how it's done in those Agatha Christie novels?"

"The way it works," she said, ignoring me, "is that if you want someone to leave, you get dirt from far away—"

"Like Kentucky."

"Like Kentucky. You sprinkle it along the threshold of their front door. You know, so they'd have to step over it. Repeat as needed. Shouldn't take more than a few days. So the book says."

I leaned over to inspect the package.

"It was postmarked a week ago." I looked across at Melinda. "And it's still sealed. What's the holdup?"

"It all sounds silly now." She smiled. "See? You're laughing at me."

"No," I said, quickly. "Well, okay. A little. But you *have* to do it."

"Maybe. I'll think about it."

***

The dirt made me think of salt. A long line of salt. That memory was from back when I lived in Vado Rojo, deep in the West Texas desert. The homes face the highway, and the fields behind them gently slope down to the Rio Grande. In better times, they used to farm cotton, squash, and cantaloupes. Every time I go back to visit, there's more poverty, and more crosses in the cemetery. It's quiet there. You can hear the bees darting amid the greasewood. The wind, when it picks up, can be fierce. There's a dirt road down to the oldest part of town. That's where the river crossing used to be, before the Border Patrol shut it down. An old man would row you across in his little chalupa. A dollar for a round trip. Mostly it was used by families who had lived on both sides of the border for as far back as they could remember.

In the dusty plaza, is an abandoned adobe church. For a while, a group of people lived there. They called themselves the Iris Collective. Five of them. Four adults and a little girl. They used silly names like Clint Westwood and Lorelei Wonderbrook, but their words took on a serious tone when speaking about their spiritual practices. Practices which no one in town was able to understand. They invited me to tea once. They lived simply, but for some reason had a set of fine china teacups. The little girl, however, drank from a tin cup, because she might break the china. I remembered, during a lull in the conversation, asking them about the line of salt that had been poured in the dirt in front of their door. They fell silent. Then the little girl spoke up and said it was the people from the town. They did it at night. One of the adults interrupted, explaining that no one knew why. The girl's eyes fluttered to me for a moment. I suspect she knew why. But they changed the subject.

191

At some point, I realized the little girl wasn't related to any of the others, and none of the adults would do anything without first asking her if she approved. I don't mean to suggest the girl had been kidnapped. Nothing like that. But none of the adults served the role of a parental figure. In short, the power dynamics were all off between the adults and the one child. With that said, it might seem strange I found an innocent sweetness about it all. Of course, there was the additional element of the unwholesome aroma of something which would end badly; however, there was not enough time for me to see their story play out. Someone from the sheriff's office visited them, and the next day they were gone.

***

I was thinking of telling the story to Melinda, but her boyfriend dropped by to take her to a late lunch. When they invited me to come along, I muttered something about having a busy day. I headed back home, with the memory of those Iris folks still in my head. My favorite stories are the ones without endings. This way I can, during an idle moment, let possible scenarios play out in my head, the outcome dependent upon my moods. Give me a beginning, just a taste, a whiff, and in my mind I can spin together something as audacious and irrevocable as in any Greek tragedy.

Then there are the stories which have not yet begun. They lodge inside me, inert and heavy. All day I kept seeing, in my mind's eye, that parcel of Kentucky dirt sitting on Melinda's desk. I think I have a key to her studio somewhere. I want to let myself in and open up the dirt and put it to work. What I *really* want to do is get a truckload of magical imported dirt and just spread it around the entire city, forcing out everyone. Or, perhaps, just me.

PUDDLES IN THE SUMMER (JULY 28)

My plan was to disconnect from the world and spend the afternoon in lazy solitude. I walked all the way out to a park near Mission Concepción. When I came to a little footbridge, I climbed down into the shade underneath in the dry concrete spillway. I sat down with my back to a low brick wall, musing on the vague, faded graffiti.

My cell phone began ringing. I thought I had turned it off. Against my better judgement, I answered. An artist friend was in a panic. He needed to meet a funding deadline and had two hours to upload digital work samples. The problem was, his media files were too big. As I walked him through the procedure to compress the files to more manageable sizes, I watched as two boys made their way down from the bridge above. They were teenagers with skateboards under their arms. They didn't notice me at first, but when they did, they just nodded. I kept up my phone conversation as the kids set up a small video camera on an even smaller tripod. When the artist finally managed to upload his work, I hung up. The boys began to videotape themselves careening down the paved slope to where a thin trail of water flowed through the middle of the spillway.

The first couple of times I found myself watching in horror as they wiped out when the wheels of the skateboards hit the water. Then I realized they were intentionally trying to skid out of control in the water with the plan to regain control and make it up the opposite side. Each run took them closer to serious injury. But by maybe the sixth time, with the both of them taking the slope together, they performed a perfect tandem skid, which threw up water, soaking them, but they each recovered and made it halfway up the other side, cheering and laughing, and completely unconcerned about my presence.

"That's it," one of them said, with confidence. "That's the one we use!"

They packed up their camera and climbed back up to the street. I was surprised how quickly the water they had splashed out of the stream dried in the sun. Soon, there was no indication they had ever been there at all.

JUST ENOUGH TIME FOR GIN
AND TONICS (JULY 31)

If I leaned far enough back on the railing of my neighbors' front porch, I could catch a glimpse of the Tower of the Americas and a couple of the tall buildings of the San Antonio skyline. I had been invited to last night's impromptu get-together. A small gathering of just Kathy and Cal, who owned the house, and Trip and Minnie from across the street. You might think I'd have something in common with these people, as we were all close in age; however, both these couples had children, they owned their homes, they had professions… The list could go on. So as the conversation drifted, touching on topics of lending rates, school-board elections, retirement plans, I quietly pretended to listen, enjoying the gin and tonics, which were already mixed in a pitcher, and the vanilla ice-cream, which Kathy made earlier in the afternoon in her grandmother's old crank-handled machine. Eventually, the conversation turned to matters of more interest to me.

"We're so glad she bought that second house," Kathy said, placing a hand on her husband's knee. "You know, the one on the corner, across the street from where she lives." She was speaking of the famous woman who lived at the end of our block, the sole undisputed celebrity on the street, undisputed as well by the MacArthur Foundation, who conferred upon her one of their "genius grants" in recognition of her literary successes.

Trip speculated it was for investment purposes, but his wife Minnie shook her head. "Well, maybe," she said. "But she's putting it to use. The girl who moved into the house last week is writing her biography."

Meaning a biography of the celebrity genius.

Cal snorted. "Hell if I'd want my biographer living across the street from me." He drained his glass.

"You can cross that bridge when you get to it, dear," Kathy replied drily.

"At least that weirdo's gone for good," Trip said. He fiddled with his long gray ponytail.

"You never met him," Minnie admonished. "You can't call him that."

"He had been locked up in that house for twenty years, at least," Kathy said. "Margaret remembers the family. She told me the guy's mom was a sweet woman. And the son was, well, okay. Kind of squirrely. And that would be Margaret's choice of words. Once his mom died, he never left the house again."

"Yeah," Trip said, running his finger across the bottom of his bowl. He licked off the last of the ice cream. "Until the guys in the white suits came to drag him away."

"I heard it was the constable's office," Cal added. "Defaulting on property taxes."

"Whatever," Trip said. "But I'm sure mental health workers were involved."

"A mystery it will remain," Minnie said.

"His name was Blake," I told them. "I met him last year."

They all stared at me.

Finally Trip asked, "What, did you invite yourself over for tea?"

"No. It was coffee." I let my eyes drop to the empty glass in my hand. Cal got up and filled it. "And *he* invited *me*."

I told them about the day I encountered the notecard in my mailbox. It took me a moment to recognize it for what it was. A personal communication. Handwritten address, first class stamp. For years mailboxes have harbored little more than junk mail and bills. What caught my interest was that the return address was for a house on my block. The note was floridly written with an unnecessary amount of semicolons. Blake was the writer's name, his first name. He mentioned "an excellent academic paper of yours I have recently read," and he suggested a day and time I might come for a visit to talk about my studies. "I'd drop by and introduce myself in person, but I am somewhat housebound, and as such unable to make it even the short distance to your home."

Minnie cleared her throat. I looked up.

"Academic paper?" she asked.

I explained that a decade back, while still in grad school, I had a piece published in a multidisciplinary journal, *On Time*, which was, as the journal's title indicated, all about the concept of time. I'd done an essay about time in modernist literature. The obvious stuff, Proust and Woolf. Very dry and as pompous as those things tend to be. Yet it struck a chord with this fellow, Blake. He had tracked me down. And, thrilled that I was in the neighborhood, he wanted to have a chat over coffee about his favorite topic. Time.

***

I'd never before given much thought to the house on the corner. The lawn was kept neat, with little flower beds of marigolds circling two stunted magnolia trees. Climbing ivy covered the sides of the house. When I knocked, Blake answered the door. I shook his hand, which was cool and dry. When I stepped in, he closed the door behind me. Blake was about my age, mid-forties. He had the brittle appearance of an aging punk rocker who refused to let go of his anti-establishment rebelliousness: spiky tousled hair thickened by black dye, straight-legged black jeans, black t-shirt under an unbuttoned and untucked white dress shirt worn like a jacket. I'm pretty sure he had on a bit of eyeliner, which made his pale, bloodless skin even more cadaverous.

The living room had been appointed like a Victorian parlor. Persian rug, William Morris inspired wallpaper, wingback chairs, in fact, the only discernible artifact of modernity was the window unit blasting out cold air, which I found welcoming on a summer day in Texas. Blake motioned me to a maroon chair. Once I was sitting, he walked through a dining room and then through a swinging door into the kitchen. Seconds later, he returned carrying a tray with two mugs of coffee and two plates of scones, already buttered.

He leaned back in his chair, placing his slippered feet atop the coffee table. He blew across the surface of his coffee. We chatted about books. Literature at first. Then things moved toward science. I was able to hold my own on digressions concerning the work of Marconi, Einstein, and Heisenberg. Blake became excited when he brought up the names of two Russian physicists who wrote a paper about how electromagnetic oscillations can impact the movement of time.

"If it was winter," Blake continued, after taking a moment to catch his breath, "you'd be able to see under all those vines outside. This house is wrapped in 16-gauge copper wire. Seven hundred and forty-three loops of wire. Sure, the wire has to meander around the doors and the windows, but it's all out there. The ivy loves it. Damned if I know why. There is a constant low voltage, fed by a slow-spinning electromagnet inside an old water heater on the back porch. A 4.3 cycle AC generator. This is all, of course, privileged information." I gave him an indulgent smile and then pantomimed zipping my lips. "What we have here," Blake lifted up his hand, indicating his home, "is a time machine. Not like H. G. Wells. I'm not able to travel back and forth. But the special wiring here shields me from time. Time is a substance. A thing. A force which can be hampered by a specific electromagnetic field. In this case, the wires girding this house." Blake looked at an old 1980s style digital watch on his wrist, it had a red LED readout. He laughed. "I'm a prisoner of my own experiments—can't leave until it's run its course. Time, it's a bitch."

I'd finished my last bite of scone and was patting at my lips with a paper napkin. I was tempted to check my own watch, but all I had to mark time was my cell phone. It was in my pocket. "I see," I said. "That's extraordinary."

"It might surprise you to learn, my friend," Blake said with a smug grin, "that I'm 46 years old. That's right!"

Actually, I had no trouble believing *that*.

"I'm going to find my passport, so you will know I'm being truthful. The world will gasp in astonishment when my experiment ends in 75 more years. I will then emerge, looking just as I do now. A youthful 25 years old!" Blake put down his mug, brushed the crumbs from his shirt, and leaped up. He hurried off into the back of the house, where I presume he kept his passport.

I was trying to figure out the best plan of escape when I heard a loud knock at the front door. I waited, thinking Blake had heard it over the air conditioning. But, no. The knocking repeated. I went to open the door. The delivery man seemed startled to see me. I explained that Blake was busy and took from him the two bags of groceries. I placed them on the floor just inside the door.

"That would be for me," the man said quietly, indicating an envelope on a low table beside me. His payment. I handed it over.

As I stood there watching the delivery man return to his van and drive off, my gaze drifted down. I noticed a wire running along the threshold of the front door. Until then I'd never heard of 16-gage copper wire, let alone knowingly seen any. It was skinnier than I'd have guessed, and the bit I saw had collected a dull green patina with age. I leaned down, running my finger underneath it. I felt a tingly vibration. I crossed over onto the porch, out into the world where time's arrow was unshielded and thus allowed to continue its slow ravages. As softly as possible, I shut the door behind me and walked home. I never received another letter from Blake.

***

Trip looked down into his glass when I finished my story and said that "maybe if you'd waited around you'd have seen that crazy bastard return wearing a silver jumpsuit and waving a plastic laser gun." The others laughed. Cal suggested we sneak over to the house and "give those wires a feel," but then someone brought up the subject of homeowners' insurance, and I soon said my goodnights.

Last night's cozy, neighborly gathering would have probably dissipated quickly enough from my memory were it not for a strange coincidence that happened this morning. My neighbor, two doors down, Brian, told me that the celebrity author's biographer had fallen into a catatonic state from which she could not be roused. He had been up early enough to have witnessed the ambulance crew who came to spirit her off to the hospital. He attempted to place the blame on black mold or perhaps an allergic reaction to a spider bite. However, I suspect the real culprit was a 4.3 cycle AC generator hidden in plain sight on the back porch.

ONCE AROUND THE CAROUSAL BOWER (AUG. 3)

There are trails I discover in the city. Unpaved, unplanned, and they meander across boundary lines, unconcerned with property, whether it be public or private. If I were to encounter these in the country, they'd likely be the result of animals on their daily rounds. In the city, they are the product of human movement. Sometimes it appears that a well-trodden path is a shortcut used by mail carriers or meter readers. However, the ones that take you into the unexpected places are commonly used by shy, wary indigents, who desire a quiet nest within a dense stand of shrubbery.

These trails are often where you think they *should* be. Walk along the fence line of an abandoned brewery. See that portion of the wire fence? Where that little flap down at the base of the iron pole can be pushed aside? Drop down, roll through. Don't overthink, just do it. Hundreds have done it before. The next thing you know, you're on the other side, on your feet, and slipping between grapevines and a rhododendron bush, and it happened so smoothly, so abruptly, that the security guard, who might have been trailing you, is baffled, uncertain as to what became of you.

Urban exploration, they call it. The serious folks suit up like ninjas. They usually go out at night with climbing gear, night vision goggles, all manner of exotic toys. Me? I just explore. A bit of trespass, I guess. I've never been much for rules.

I've only ever been confronted once by someone in uniform during such explorations. I was nine years old. It was a Saturday afternoon, and I was wandering around my elementary school, which was just a few blocks from home. I noticed that a metal grating under the steps to the gym was loose, hanging by a single rusting hinge. Of course, I squirmed through. I was in there for an hour, winding my way around a series of low tunnels where the electrical and plumbing lines ran. When I got bored, I crawled out. A policeman stood there, waiting. I'm not sure how he knew I was under the school. A neighbor had likely seen me and tipped him off. He lectured me for some time about the dangers under there. He painted a grim (and to me, somewhat amusing) scenario which had him standing on my front porch telling my parents I had been killed. Kill by what, he didn't say. He kept me in the back of his patrol car for about twenty minutes. When he thought I had been sufficiently scared and humiliated, he let me go. A sort of catch-and-release character-building exercise. Ever since then, I've learned to keep a vigilant eye out for anyone nearby while I explore.

Living around downtown San Antonio gave me many opportunities to wander through decayed structures and decommissioned factories. I've made movies and run fashion shoots in places which have now been destroyed, gentrified, or are currently under the soulless speculative gaze of property developers. I find I have, unintentionally, documented so many quiet, unique corners of this city that no longer exist. The Big Tex Grain Company, Hays Street Bridge, Hot Wells Resort, the Friedrich Building. All instantly identifiable landmarks of this city's past which have been destroyed, Disneyfied, or are currently in the crosshairs of the surveyor's theodolite.

So, today, I made a pilgrimage to the grounds of the old Lone Star Brewery across the river from Roosevelt Park, on the edge of my neighborhood. The huge complex has been abandoned and surrounded by a wire fence for at least the decade I've lived in town. A couple of plans to develop the area over the years faltered, fizzled. The current group of owners sound like the ones who will finally push it through. The plan will be another "mixed use" development. This has become code for a semi-gated community of condos, bars, boutiques, and restaurants specializing in cuisine that those residents displaced by the process of urban renewal would likely not even recognize as food.

Even my tepid form of protest seems laughable. *Trespassing.* See? You're already smiling. Call it what you will. The fact is, it couldn't be easier. As easy as dropping and rolling. Most wire fences function as psychological barriers. It's expensive to make them truly secure. Sure, I saw the signs about video surveillance. But it was obvious that the cameras attached to a couple of trees and on a light pole were at least ten years old and not even plugged in. I did take the warnings of *Security Guards on Premises* a bit more seriously, because I've noticed the portly man in khakis rolling about in his motorized golf cart—the kind you can hear rattling and sputtering from fifty yards off. It'd be different if there were guard dogs. I knew there weren't.

So, once inside, I wandered the grounds, unconcerned and unmolested, trying to envision what this old brewery *should* become. Maybe a community center for the surrounding neighborhoods. Shops with rents affordable enough for the lower-middle-class residents across the river or on the other side of Probandt. Possibly even studios for all the artists pushed out of the Blue Bird Arts Complex across the Union Pacific tracks. The pond beside the drained swimming pool was empty. I heard that years ago, when the brewery was in service, that they'd open up the place on weekends to the families from the neighborhood. The kids swam in the pool. There'd be barbecues. People picnicked around the pond. I'd been told the pond was once fed by a natural spring, but now it was capped.

I walked across the cracked parking lot to the main factory building, which I guess once held the fermenting vats. Through a wall covered with shattered windows, I saw half a dozen dull silvered tanks the size of dump trucks. I climbed, as quietly as possible, a metal staircase up the side of the building to the tar and pebble roof. From up there I had a view of the entire complex and beyond, from the scrap metal yard all the way over to the old slaughterhouse, recently shut down, and no doubt soon to be condominiums as well. From up on the roof, I was also able to keep an eye on the security guard over by the west entrance gate. He was napping in the padded seat of his golf cart. I removed my DSLR from my messenger bag and took a few obligatory shots. The sun was overhead, so the light was flat, uninspiring. I climbed down.

As I headed back out the way I'd come in, I tried to figure out why I felt so dejected. Then it dawned on me. I wasn't *drawn* in here. I had pushed my way in. An adventure is supposed to be natural, free of this deliberate premeditation. I had shoved my way onto the Lone Star grounds like it was a job. I don't like jobs. The pull of the trail should be gentle. You need to let it guide you. Let it entice you through the clutter of vegetation, which seems friendly and obliging, with no bramble tearing at you, no nettle tall enough to sting. Suddenly you're no longer in the city. The sounds of sirens and construction sites are muffled.

The trail pulls, it does. If you're lucky. But it leads to no real terminus. True, there might be hasty camps or carousal bowers, but the trail mostly leads to another trail. And that then to others. And on and on. An endless network, constantly being renewed. I felt it was well past the time for me to succumb to that pull. To wander down new trails, with their promise of new sights, new experiences. But, instead, I headed home.

THE ELMENDORF BEAST (AUG. 5)

This afternoon I took Sammy for a walk. He's a big, friendly black Labrador, and I refuse to call him by his given name of Sambo. His owner, Howard, lives down the block. The man's an octogenarian from a generation preceding political correctness. He's in the hospital for a venous thrombectomy to deal with a clot in his leg and no one else wants to look after his dog. He's not very popular. Well, Sammy is, but not his owner. Actually, it was nice to have an excuse to get out of the house. My landlady's son…well, I guess he's now my landlord. Anyway, he changed his mind. He has decided to sell the house. This I learned today right before my dog walk. He was stomping around the front and back yards making notes and snapping pictures. As I locked the door behind me, he excitedly told me he'd already received three offers.

"And I haven't even put the place on the market! Oh, and don't worry. When the transfer goes through, you'll have thirty days' notice. Of course, my realtor might tell me to do a few repairs first." He trailed off, his eyes scanning from the foundation all the way up to the rusty tin roof.

I said something along the lines of, "Thanks for the heads-up," and hurried down the street to Sammy's place. I used the key under the doormat to let myself in. Sammy, who loves company, performed a short, excited dance, ending in a single low-pitched *woof.* I clipped on his leash, and we headed out. Just down the block, there's a short dead-end street that terminates at a footpath above the river. We stopped there. I politely looked anywhere but at Sammy, who was peeing on a clump of trompillo. I turned to watch as an old Ford Fiesta with peeling paint pulled to the curb near an abandoned house. When Sammy was done, we continued on our way, walking alongside the car. A man of about thirty stepped out. We nodded. He wore work boots, white painter's pants, and hadn't shaved in several days. He took out a fine mesh fish net and closed the door of the Ford. He moved in a furtive manner, keeping his back away from me. Then he glanced at me and laughed.

"I just ripped my pants. It's kind of embarrassing." He wanted to establish that he, clearly a poor man in a somewhat upwardly mobile neighborhood, was not to be viewed with suspicion. But, hell, I didn't look much better than him. He showed me the tear, which was impressive. A pair of tartan boxers peeked out. Sammy closed in, his tail wagging, and the guy with the net leaned down to pat his head. The man introduced himself as Claudio and he told me he owned a metal shop over on Presa. He popped the trunk, removing two cans of Lone Star from a cooler. I took one. It was a huge 24-ounce can. I felt like a five-year-old holding his daddy's beer.

Sammy and I followed Claudio down to the river. He knew his way around. He took us to a secluded pool that's fed by a stream gurgling from a culvert and then it seeps into the river through a marshy patch. The pool is shaded by a massive cypress tree. It's one of my favorite places along the river, and most of the people in my neighborhood aren't even aware of it. In fact, it was that very place Johnny and I had come when we went in search of the sacred underground springs. I looked at the metal gate that kept people out of the culvert and saw that the padlock had not been replaced. It was still there, dangling useless. You could barely see the gap in the shackle where we'd used my bolt cutters.

I sat in the shade on a large, flat rock. Sammy settled down beside me. We watched Claudio. He removed his shoes and socks. Rolled up his pant legs. When he waded out, he held his net aloft like a dowser awaiting psychic inspiration. He peered down at the mossy rocks through the clear water. He nodded to his reflection and made a firm, calculated sweep with his net. Then, with a deft series of movements, he pulled a Snapple bottle from one of his roomy pockets, filled it with pond water, and, with his bare hand, transferred half a dozen minnows from the net into the bottle. In under ten minutes he loaded two bottles with tiny fish. He took a seat beside me and cracked open his beer.

"I've got some catching up to do, I see," he said, glancing at the can in my hand. He placed the bottles of fish, now capped, beside Sammy. "This is a good place to find minnows. I feed them to my bass in my aquarium at home." I nodded as he spoke. It all sounded natural enough. He was just doing his thing. It wasn't until later that I wondered if I'd heard him correctly. Do people keep bass as pets? "This pond is fed by a creek," he said. "According to my grandmother, it used to meander for miles. Now it has to go underground." He pointed to the circular cement opening from where the water poured.

"Yeah," I said. "I heard." I decided not to tell him about my adventures with the bolt cutters.

"The neighborhood around here has changed a lot since I was little," Claudio said wistfully as he tossed back a good guzzle of beer. "But *this* place hasn't changed at all. It's quiet. Forgotten."

"I guess it helps that the house up there is abandoned." I pointed to the overgrown estate above us. It's a decrepit bungalow on about half an acre. The place is surrounded by a riot of wild plants, and, unless you look hard, you'd think it was an empty wooded lot.

Claudio fired up a cigarette and shook his head. "Naw. There's a guy lives up there. Fitzroy. Darby Fitzroy." Claudio's story unfolded over the course of several cigarettes and another trip to the beer cooler in his trunk. Sammy slipped into a resigned nap, not interrupting once.

It seemed that ten years ago, the house above *was* vacant. Had been for years. And then a young man named Darby inherited the place and began to fix it up. Newly graduated with some sort of bioengineering degree, he got hired on as a lab assistant at the South Texas Bio-Research

Center in their Advanced Technologies department.

"Super nice guy," Claudio said. "Very down-to-earth. You know, for this neighborhood."

Even back then, Claudio fished for minnows in the same pond. He hadn't realized anyone had moved into the house above until one day when he heard a voice calling down to him about how there would be a party later that evening and that he was invited. Claudio looked up to see Darby leaning over a rickety wooden fence grinning down at him.

"He was crazy up there," Claudio said. "The rotting wood on the fence was groaning and creaking. Clods of dirt fell loose and splashed down. It scared my fish. But I went to his party. I was dating this girl. Amanda. No, Sylvia. Yeah. Sylvia. I thought she'd be impressed. And, let me tell you. She was." I looked up. I could see the faint outlines of the fence through the vines. "Darby threw a hell of a party. The place up there used to be a sight. All those string lights hanging around that great deck overlooking the river. It's all rotted and choked with bamboo now. But he had a brisket in a smoker, sausages on the grill. Iced beer and bourbon. Sylvia thought I had quite the hook up! There were scientists from the research center. And some of those airy fairy wackos from the Bexar County Philosophy of Mind Institute. God, can they talk." Claudio followed my gaze up to the fence above. He smiled. "So, we became friends." Claudio turned to me. He was about to say something, but he paused. I waited. "You ever heard of the Elmendorf Beast?" he finally said.

"The what?" I laughed. "No."

"It was all over the news about ten years back."

"Oh, wait. That was like some chupacabra sighting. Didn't it turn out to be a coyote with mange?"

"That's what the news said."

"Some farmer shot it."

"His name was Argos."

"You mean the farmer?" I asked. That didn't sound right.

"No. The beast."

Claudio told me that one of Darby's jobs at the research center was to dispose of the test animals when they were no longer needed. It wasn't his job to euthanize them. But he did have to remove the carcasses from the decompression chambers where they were dispatched and haul them to the incinerator. One day he opened the metal pressurized door, not to a dead animal, but to a frisky, hairless dog.

"It was after hours," Claudio said. "So he was able to sneak the animal home. It became his pet. A secret pet."

The dog had an identification number tattooed on its ear. Darby grew curious. He wanted to be sure the dog wasn't infected with an experimental bug or something. Over the next few days, he made discreet inquiries. He was surprised how candid some of the researchers were. He learned that they were working on rather unconventional experiments.

"Darby told me that Argos—that was the name he gave the dog— wasn't, strictly speaking, a dog at all. Are you familiar with tetragametic chimerism?"

I shook my head.

"Me neither. Had to look it up. The truth was, Darby's new dog was a hybrid of Labrador—like that black dog you got there—and a Russian boar. No shit." Claudio told me that he saw Argos only once, and that was enough. It had seemed docile to Darby at first because it was still sedated. Eventually, it became aggressive. "The Russian boar doesn't fuck around," Claudio said. "Even when it's been half diluted with Labrador." When Argos escaped, an inevitability Claudio had been certain of, the creature made its way south, following the San Antonio River. "Stories started coming in. Argos left a trail of destruction." Claudio laughed. "I know. It's not funny. Pets and chickens disappearing or being eaten. And when the photographs started appearing on the TV and in the papers, Darby knew he had to come clean. Tell his bosses that he'd taken home an experiment for a pet."

"But the news said the animal was tested. I am remembering it right? Coyote DNA?"

"Who do you think did the testing?" Claudio asked. He raised his brows. "It was all covered up. Darby was fired." Claudio glanced at his watch. He muttered something and began picking up his bottles of fish. He took a deep breath, looking up. "We've drifted apart," Claudio said of Darby. "We still talk every so often. But, well, he drinks." Claudio shook his beer. He drank the last swallow. "Not like this. But hardcore. I don't know what he does for money these days. Somehow he gets by. I think they paid him off. Hush money. Probably easier than killing him." Claudio shook my hand. He patted Sammy on the head. And he climbed back up the footpath to his car.

In the calm of the shaded pond, I tried to picture this spot without me. This neighborhood, without me. It was coming. My inevitable departure. Maybe I should be thankful to my landlord for putting into motion forces to push me out of my comfortable bubble. At least I wouldn't become the neighborhood recluse, like Darby. Or the hated crabby old bigot with the bad veins and the sweet dog.

Sammy stood with a thin groan and pointed his nose up toward the street. It was his custom to be fed after his afternoon constitutional, and clearly lunch was on his mind. So we stepped into the sunlight and left the minnows behind.

THE WAGON MASTER (AUG. 8)

I have made a decision to no longer drink during the daytime. That would explain why I was feeling so out of sync with Samantha. She invited me out to lunch today at Erma's Cafe because, of course, they serve beer. We'd finished eating, and she was on her third bottle of Bohemia. She had just ended a lengthy, satisfying rant about the vicissitudes of life in the trenches of community theater. For the last three weeks, she been playing Cordelia in a production of King Lear, "where my father, the king, was played by a twenty-three-year-old undernourished lad with swollen adenoids."

As Samantha rummaged in her change purse to see if she could afford another beer, an oldish woman with orange hair and wearing a wide-brimmed straw hat pushed back on her head flung open the door to the cafe. She came straight up to us with intense deliberation.

"Samantha!" she shrieked, drawing out the second syllable in a high trill, like a smoke detector going off.

"Well, hello, Lois," Samantha said, her expression neutral and untroubled, as though people shout at her all the time.

"I thought that was your Pinto out front," Lois said to Samantha as she sat down beside me. "You're famous. Oh, my goodness, you're all over the newspaper these days!"

Lois was referencing the recent human interest piece in the *San Antonio Express News* about Samantha's art modeling career. Apparently, it is worthy of public attention that a woman of a certain age would disrobe for money. I didn't understand the fuss. But the article had been written well enough and had been accompanied by a flattering photograph of Samantha in which a vase of flowers had been strategically positioned to satisfy the decorum of the front page of the Lifestyle section.

"Would that my theater work might command such attention," Samantha muttered, shooting me a glance.

"You must have people stopping you in the street constantly," Lois added. "You've the very soul of the classic bohemian! Lounging in silk pajamas. Or, my goodness, nothing at all! Posing alongside marigolds, lutes, and plates of fruit. I seethe with envy!"

"Lois attends one of the art classes I model for," Samantha told me.

"Wait a minute," Lois said, leaning in closer to me. "I believe Samantha's spoken of you before. Yes! You're her thrifting partner!" Lois waved off the waitress, who came to check on our table. "You two will enjoy this," Lois said, removing her hat and wiggling into a more comfortable position in her chair. Samantha sighed and returned to counting up her change. Lois pivoted, grabbed my arm, and locked her eyes on mine.

"I was at that flea market at the State Hospital that Samantha told me about. Me and my husband. You'd like him. He's a Capricorn. Everyone likes Capricorns." I snuck a glance at Samantha. She rolled her eyes. "I called Mark's attention—that's my husband, Mark—to a piece of original art. He held it in his hands for maybe half a second. Then he shook his head. He handed it back, and walked away. No accounting for taste, I suppose. I wondered if a patient painted it. Personally, I enjoyed the naiveté of the little watercolor on pasteboard. The image was of a crudely fashioned cowboy smoking a pipe. He was seated at a table playing poker, or whatever cowboys play. The piece was titled *The Wagon Master*. It was priced at a dollar twenty-five."

Lois paused long enough to stuff a tortilla chip in her mouth from the wicker basket on the table.

"When we returned home, I hung it up in the breakfast nook where we ate our meals. It wasn't long before I noticed he, meaning Mark, had relocated it to the opposite wall. Ah, of course, better to catch the morning light. Well, that was my thought. But he confessed that he moved the painting so he didn't have to look at it. Mark explained that the cowboy had the appearance of a serpent. I laughed. A serpent smoking a pipe? Playing cards? Really. Besides, I told Mark, he's not a cowboy, he's a wagon master. But now Mark had ruined it for me. No matter how the light hit it, I couldn't help but see a snake staring down at me. The eyes, mainly. The eyes were like slits. Every meal was fraught with a dull sense of dread. My morning coffee, which used to be the most comforting part of my day, was spent thinking: Is this what the artist saw? Each time he looked at a person? A snake glaring back at him? A few days later, Mark walked up to me. Your coffee's getting cold, he said. And he leaned down to kiss me on the neck. How sweet! But when I lifted my head, what do you think I saw?"

When Samantha realized her friend was awaiting a response, she shook her head.

"His face was, oh it was ghastly!" Lois' voice had a quaver. She took a deep breath before she continued. "I saw a pair of slitted pupils. And a forked tongue! But just for a second. Just a flash. When Mark left for work, I burned the painting. And as I'm an artist myself, that was quite out of character. We never mentioned it again."

Lois grabbed Samantha's arm and pulled it toward her. She dropped her face inches from Samantha's wristwatch. "Is that the time? Good Lord! I'd better move." She patted my arm, kissed Samantha on the cheek, and left with the same breathless energy as she entered.

"Well," Samantha said. "That was an unexpected non sequitur." She pushed her mound of inadequate change back into her coin purse and snapped it shut. She squared her shoulders and looked across the table at me. "Soooo," she began. "The reason I asked you to lunch is because of the Eight By Eight showcase over at the Prometheus. You know, they've put out the call for new work. They're requesting submissions for eight-minute performances to be presented on an eight-foot by eight-foot stage. The show starts at eight o'clock. Admission eight dollars. Et cetera."

"I hadn't heard."

"Right," she said, looking down at the table. "Because you jumped ship."

Samantha was talking about my official resignation from the Prometheus Performance Company. I guess she never thought I'd go ahead with it.

"Hey, I did lots for the Prometheus before I was a company member. And I will do stuff, still. I just had to walk away from the internal bickering."

"In that case, can you write me an eight-minute monologue about an eight-year-old girl delivering a TED Talk about silverfish?"

"Silverfish?" I asked. "As in the bug?"

"The bug. Correct."

"Absolutely," I said.

She stuck out her hand. We shook.

"Now," I said. "Can I buy you beer?"

"Oh, god, yes."

I decided to order an additional one. For me. I'm not particularly good at making promises to myself.

RIGHT BANK INTERLUDE (AUG. 17)

An actor who wanted me to take some headshots had canceled at the last minute, so I found myself with a free day. Nothing unusual there—neither with a flaky actor, nor a free day. My life was full of both. So, I grabbed my bike and meandered my way to the south, to a stretch of river between Mission San José and Mission San Juan. I got off and rolled my bike along a grassy path along the east bank of the river. I angled my way down to the floodplain and walked to the water.

I say the east bank, but sometimes I like to get fancy and do that left bank, right bank thing. I was, at that moment, on the *left* bank of the San Antonio River. Here's how it works. Imagine you're standing in the water, facing downriver. Your left hand is nearest to the left bank, and so on.

The river was roaring through a shallow channel, so I didn't hear the voice at first. I looked up to see an unkempt man, somewhat older than myself, standing on the opposite bank. He stood next to a mountain bike like mine, wearing a cycling jersey, cut-off jeans, sunglasses, and a baseball cap. His long black hair was pulled back in a ponytail. It was Anthony. I'd met him several times before on the bike trail. He painted houses, yet seemed to be constantly out of work. From his gestures I gathered he wanted me to meet him upriver at the first crossing I could find. That would be VFW Boulevard. I waved and headed off. The one thing we had in common, other than our lack of employment, was that even though we both appeared to be sadly out of shape, we could move fast on two wheels. I took it as a challenge, and made it back along the dirt path, up and across the bridge, and met him on his side.

He invited me to his home for lunch. I had no idea where he lived, but apparently we were just a few blocks from his peeling tar-paper house on Pyron, within sightline of Mission San José. When we reached his place, the dogs lounging under the pecan tree didn't bother to get up. They just followed us with their eyes, the whites of which were the same color as their yellowed teeth. A child's wading pool had been overturned across the hood of a derelict Monte Carlo—to dry out, I presumed, but that must have been a year or more back, as it now was dried and cracked from the onslaught of the sun. We went inside, where it was dark and cool. If Anthony had any kids, they were in school. He introduced me to his wife. She was on the phone speaking Spanish to her mother. She ignored him, but offered a smile to me. I watched as she retreated to the back of the house. I sat at a kitchen table and let Anthony make me a sandwich. I saw he'd gotten too much sun. When he removed his sunglasses, they left an outline with his cheeks and forehead in red.

The kitchen was clean, but not quite homey. Several cast-iron skillets hung from hooks above the sink. An open package of paper napkins shared the tabletop with a pair of plastic disposable salt and pepper shakers. Taped to the refrigerator door was the one indication of children. A faded paper plate with a turkey traced around a little hand in tempera paint. Anthony pulled out a can of beer for himself. He raised an eyebrow, but I shook my head. He gave me a glass of tap water. I removed my cycling gloves and washed my hands in the sink with dishwashing soap. Anthony made us each a Spam sandwich with white bread and mustard. He placed a pickled jalapeño on his plate but didn't offer me one. As we ate, I recalled the last time I'd had a Spam sandwich.

***

It was about ten years ago. Ten years between Spam sandwiches is about par for the course, unless you live in Hawaii, where I understand they eat that stuff all the time. It was back when I lived in the desert along the bank of the Rio Grande. In fact, that's where I started the left bank, right bank stuff. I never got the locals to play my game ("you see, Texas is the left bank, Mexico is the right bank"). No surprise there.

I'd crossed to the Mexican town of Ojinaga with my neighbor, Father Theo. Father Theodore Blanchard served the Episcopal Dioceses of the Rio Grande. His parish was huge. For some reason he'd gotten pulled into charity work which had him providing milk goats he raised—a large, hardy Spanish breed—to impoverished families in Mexican towns across the river from Vado Rojo. The legality of all this seemed questionable to me. Regardless, I found myself there in Ojinaga, sitting in a bar off the plaza with Father Theo and my friend Diego, who was there because he knew most everyone on both sides of the river, and he was also much more diplomatic than Father Theo. Why I was there, I can't recall. Muscle, I guess. It had been my job to hold on to the goat in the back of Father Theo's van as we made it to the international bridge and drove across. Besides, when I'd been asked to help, how could I have said no? Smuggling goats into Mexico had adventure written all over it.

Father Theo and I were nursing Dos Equis, and Diego had a Coke. I kept looking at the open door onto the dusty street, even though it wasn't all that clear to me who we were meeting. The midday sun hammered down out there and it must have been a hundred and fifteen. But the beer was cold and the company was pleasant. Diego and Father Theo were talking about the literary merits of Ovid, and my eyes wandered to the bar. I realized that under the counter, on the patron side, the bar was tiled, and on the floor was a porcelain trough. How exotic! The bar was also a urinal. It made perfect sense, especially for the working-class bars that discouraged a female clientele. No awkward stumbling off to the men's room. No fear someone would steal your smokes whilst you left to take a pee. You could park yourself there in the perfect stance and stay all night, a jaunty finger poised on your zipper.

Diego and Father Theo stood up, and I glanced around to see the man approach. I also stood. I learned that he was the local secretary of agriculture and livestock. We needed his official approval to bring a goat into his country.

Apparently things were not going according to plan. It hadn't been foreseen that we'd have trouble crossing into Mexico. And I'm quite certain we'd have sailed through had it not been for a humorless Mexican border guard who didn't like the look of Father Theo. I could see his point. Father Theo had once been described by a *National Geographic* writer as having the appearance of a "mad poet." He was every inch the exiled man of religion, unfit for the canapé and doily crowd in the big city: wild silver hair, an off-kilter laugh straight from the exorcism chamber, and, peeking out from under the hem of his cassock, a pair of flip-flops. Father Theo had misjudged his audience when he attempted an off-color joke to the border official on the Mexican side of the bridge. The stony-faced man decided to pull open the side sliding door of the van, revealing me and that goat crouched suspiciously in the back. And now there we were, trying to sweet-talk a bureaucrat so we could continue our mission of mercy.

Señor Secretario sat down. His unsmiling demeanor conveyed seriousness. We each shook his hand before we all sat down. Father Theo squirmed. He leaned forward, calmly giving his name, complete with his official title. Then he exploded, firing out a barrage of questions, the nature of which was mostly lost on me because he was speaking Spanish. I am pretty sure that he ended on a simple: "Why are we being detained?"

Before Señor Secretario could say anything, Diego took a deep breath and exhaled. He then asked the official a simple question I couldn't make out. The man nodded, still all business. Diego called to the barman and placed an order for something, pointing all around. Diego has a calm, quiet presence. He's a bear of a man, and he towers over everyone. Sure, he can be amiable, but in a polite, deferential manner; and so, when he makes a declarative statement, people pause and give his words serious consideration. He usually wears a Pancho Villa mustache, but when he shaves, he says he looks like a Ute.

A beer arrived for our guest, and he and Diego had a chat about a man they both knew well—either Diego's uncle or Señor Secretario's uncle. My Spanish was (and still it) practically useless. Father Theo sat glum. And me? I grinned like an imbecile—I was still thrilled by the fact that the bar was a urinal. Brilliant!

The barman finally arrived with four ceramic plates, each with a Spam sandwich. In the middle of the table, he placed a large bowl of peanuts, liberally coated with chili powder. Señor Secretario brightened up. He squeezed a lime wedge all over the peanuts and began tucking into his sandwich. He loosened up, and he explained what he could do for us. He would turn a blind eye this once, but not again. In the future, we would need vaccination papers from American officials as well as having the animals examined by a Mexican sanctioned veterinarian. Father Theo slammed his fist on the table. Thankfully, we were the only people in the bar. The bartender sighed and turned up the volume on his TV. "This is charity," Father Theo said between his teeth. "Caridad! Una organización benéfica!" He had a flat midwestern accent that didn't lend itself well to the poetry of Spanish.

Señor Secretario glanced at me, then at Diego. Diego put a hand on Father Theo's shoulder and whispered in his ear. Father Theo sighed and walked to the bar. Diego asked if there were other options. The man just shook his head. But when Father Theo placed another beer in front of him, Señor Secretario held up his hand. We all waited. He took a drink. Then he pulled a piece of paper from his jacket's breast pocket. He unfolded it on the table. All of us leaned forward to peer at a map of the river valley. The official pointed at a spot on the river. An inaccessible region in the canyons. I gathered this was a good place to cross. He seemed to be letting us know that if his agency remained ignorant of our activities, he didn't care what we did.

"The devil you say!" Father Theo spat out. He repeated his oath in Spanish.

The bureaucrat stared beseechingly at Diego. But I noticed Diego wasn't looking acquiescent. Señor Secretario raised a questioning eyebrow. Diego took hold of the map. He rotated it around. He placed his finger on the river where Vado Rojo sits. He said without preamble that we would be crossing the goats there, practically out of Father Theo's pens and into Mexico. The official was about to make a comment, but Diego launched into a controlled, well-thought-out position I had heard him make many times to me in English about how the border is an arbitrary boundary which divides a culture that should be one. He went into the ordeals of the people on both sides of the river, the common struggles they have to put up with that divide families and friends. Hopes and dreams are crushed because of illogical national boundaries. Diego said this in Spanish, but I caught a few words and recognized the rant he so often subjected me to over afternoon cappuccinos in his kitchen.

Señor Secretario—and I think I saw a glisten in his eye—took to his feet. He roared with a laugh. Said something about the family of man. And he pounded me on the back, as if I were the missing part of this grand, confused rubric. And he headed off to work.

"I love doing business in Mexico," Father Theo gushed with a genuine smile. We walked out of the bar and, with no difficulty at all, delivered the goat to a gracious family in the shadow of Sierra La Santa Cruz. "I hope they don't eat it," Father Theo said as we drove back home. "It's a milking goat. Not an eating goat." That summer we transported a few more goats using the river crossing at Vado Rojo. At some point the philanthropic man up in Muenster, Texas, who was paying for the goats, dropped out of touch with Father Theo. Without his money, the charitable smuggling operation stopped.

***

Sometimes it saddens me that I've spent more time on the left bank of the Rio Grande than I have on the right bank. I hope one day to remedy that.

But here along the San Antonio River, I'm all over both banks.

I finished my Spam sandwich and glass of tap water. I wiped the mustard from my lips with a paper napkin. Anthony slapped me on my back as I left. He was holding a new beer. I could hear his wife, still on the phone, laughing somewhere back in the house. As I rode down Anthony's driveway to the street, the dogs didn't even look up. They were flat on their backs like noontime lions under Serengeti trees in a nature film.

HIBISCUS TEA (AUG. 27)

Allison, the girl who lives in the garage apartment behind my next-door neighbor's house, paid me a visit earlier today. She brought along her own toolbox. She spread her equipment out on my hardwood floor, sitting there cross-legged. I sat on my sofa while she rewired my table lamp. She was barefoot, wearing torn jeans and a sleeveless t-shirt. Her hair was pulled back with one of those thick blue rubber bands the supermarkets put around clumps of broccoli. She looked over at me, frowning. She tilted back her head toward the dim ceiling light. With a grunt of displeasure, she got up and opened the drapes all the way and sat back down.

"You're in one of your hermit phases, I see," she said to me. "It's like a cave in here."

She stripped the insulation off a length of wire with a special tool in a single, deft movement. It was almost performative, but I knew better. Allison did not concern herself with how others saw her. In fact, she seemed barely present in her own life. As unengaged as a gourmet chef politely eating your three-bean salad. Dispassionate, methodical.

"So, you really fucked this up," she said without looking at me.

"I tripped over the cord."

I don't think she bought my excuse. It was almost true. I had been chasing a cockroach along the wainscoting, stomping and missing and stomping and missing, and when it darted behind the desk, I made one last failed lunge, knocking over the lamp. I'm going stir crazy. Except for a bike ride to the Dollar General Store for boxes of macaroni and cheese, I've not even left the house for days. So now I'm at war with the roaches and destroying my house. I can't believe I broke the lamp.

Allison had made it for me as a gift. It's hideous, but in a good way. She's an artist who works in that slippery world of mixed media. Sometimes in two dimensions, sometimes three. But never call anything of hers a painting or a sculpture. Three weeks after I moved into my East Guenther Street duplex, I attended Allison's first opening—first for me, that is. The show was held in a gallery co-op over on Lone Star. Of the dozen or so artists displaying their work, her stuff was by far the best. My favorite piece was a bas-relief of Adina De Zavala done in polyester putty and six dozen nail clippers. I made myself a promise. I would keep an eye out for any outrageously odd items that she might find inspiring. And so, a couple months later, while working a temp gig cleaning out a warehouse near Our Lady of the Lake University, I came across a room with thirty mannequin heads. Male and female. Just the heads. They were all the resin-coated plaster style of the 1950s. The owner of the building shrugged when I asked if I could have them. When I dumped them on Allison, she was so excited that she actually smiled. Two days later, she knocked at my door with an unwieldy table lamp that made me think of a totem pole from an old Jack Benny skit. A wooden platter base, with four mid-century heads stacked boy, girl, boy, girl. The girl on top wore a lampshade that came down to the bridge of her nose. "Isn't it disturbing?" Allison wanted to know. I agreed, and I accepted her gift.

And here she was, trouble-shooting. Dispassionately, methodically. I got up and went into the kitchen. I removed a pitcher of hibiscus tea from the refrigerator. It was strong and super-sweet. I like to combine it half-and-half with carbonated water. Taking two large tumblers down from the cupboard, I mixed up the fizzing concoctions. Allison didn't glance up when I placed the glass on the floor beside her. When she finally reached out for the tea and took a sip, she paused. She peered closer. Frowned. Sniffed. She took a deep swig, about half the glass, and returned to work.

***

Gina introduced me to hibiscus tea. It was over fifteen years ago, back when I still lived in Dallas. We had been chosen (and I'm still not exactly sure why) to represent our respective graduate departments at a symposium on bicultural studies in Matamoros. Four days. All expenses paid, with a per diem stipend.

Gina was fluent in Spanish and had been published in several journals. Why they sent me with her made no sense. To compound confusion, the family who hosted our lodging either assumed that we were a couple, or that we should become one. We were given the guest house, which was one huge room with a double bed, sofa, dining table, kitchenette, and bathroom. I played the gentleman. Took the sofa. Maybe I went overboard with the professional relationship stuff, but Gina and I had never spent much time together before. We were pursuing different interests. She was concerned with early twentieth century Mexican land reform, and I was ostensibly playing around with a critical analysis of the nineteenth century fiction concerning the Mexico-U.S. border.

I was old. Well, older. A "returning student," that's the euphemism. Gina was brainy, and I liked that about her. But she was a kid. Giddy and serious. There's something that exhausts me about young intellectuals. Whatever passionate topic of study they've just picked up, I had put down years ago. The only thing that stuck in my mind about that symposium was that Gina made me, every afternoon before siesta (which we decided to observe), a cup of chilled hibiscus tea which, in Mexico, is called jamaica tea. I liked it.

The following semester, Gina transferred to a doctoral program in Nevada. She mailed me a long letter expressing her feelings for me. I'm not sure if I was saddened or relieved that I'd never had those feelings for her. The letter ran three pages, the prose as protracted and sententious as her essays about the agrarian reforms of the Madero regime. That's the

224

only time I've received a letter from a woman professing great affection for me. She ended on an upbeat note hinting at her irrepressible resilience by way of a Ricardo Flores Magón quote (which I knew wasn't Flores Magón, but William Godwin); however, most of her letter went into detail about my cold aloofness. In short, she found me dispassionate and methodical.

***

Allison snapped the lamp on and off and on again. Satisfied with her success, she switched it off and placed it on the table next to where I was sitting on the sofa. She swept up the shards of plastic insulation with her hands and dumped them into the potted plant on the floor next to her. She tossed back the last of the hibiscus tea and rose to her feet without using her hands, simply by shifting forward and scissoring her legs together. I thanked her, and she left.

I turned the lamp on and closed the curtains. In that warm circle of light from the wonderfully hideous lamp, I sprawled out on my sofa and opened a book. After reading the same page three times, I closed it. I had no idea what to do, but it wasn't reading.

CASHING IN THE LOCO CHECK (SEPT. 7)

The mailbox used to be a magical thing. Like Schrödinger's hypothetical box, you didn't know, until you opened it, whether to rejoice or shake your head in dejection. There was a time when a trip to the mailbox could make or break your day. But that's no longer true. Mostly it's bulk mail, of no interest to anyone, which postal employees must meticulously process using their arcane and official protocol. It is sorted, transported, and brought to your door by a trained professional. Just so you can dump it into the trash. This morning, after returning from a quick jaunt to Lila's Tacos To Go over on Nogalitos Street, I paused on the porch to pull the fresh batch of crap out of my mailbox. As is often the case, I wondered why I didn't keep the recycling bin parked beside the front door. Inside, I flipped through a bank statement, a phone bill, and a glossy oblong postcard offering "pristine and sanitary steam cleaning of all your carpets." But, wait. What was this? A square cream-colored envelope, the sort Hallmark provides when you buy a get-well-soon card. There was no stamp. No return address. Just my name scribbled with a dull pencil.

I wondered if it had been put there last night, or during my morning taco run. I sat down at my desk, unwrapped my bean and cheese tacos, and poured salsa verde on them. I put sugar and cream in my styrofoam cup of coffee. Then I opened the square envelope. It was from Wesley. I guess you could call him a friend, but I think of him more as Johnny's friend. The letter was written in pencil on a single sheet of typing paper, which had been folded into a square to fit inside the envelope.

***

I hope you're still living in the old apartment, and I hope you don't mind me contacting you. I feel I might have offended you in the past.

I've joked before about the "Loco Check" I get, but I don't know if you were ever aware of my diagnosis. I'm bipolar. And sometimes I have good days. But not all the time.

I'm now living in a building for the disabled across from San Pedro Park.

I feel I should make it clear to you how much it meant to me when you helped me move after my mother died. I was a real mess.

Johnny told me that you're working for Homeland Security now. At first I thought he was joking. But maybe he believes it.

Of course, he's trying to get his own Loco money. I've told him all my symptoms, and he's been practicing. You know, being off his nut.

My new wife hates him. Last week we were showing him places to get free food, and he said some awful things to her. I had to choose. And I'm always going to choose her. So I cut him out of my life.

I said I have a wife! She's from the Philippines. We send money back to her family whenever we can. They're so grateful they're naming their little island after me. Maybe it's a joke. The humor could be different in the Philippines.

I'm getting good at rapping. My wife wants to promote me and get an album made. She's very patient and supportive.

If we can make enough money, we're going to move to her family's island. She told me that all her sisters and female cousins want to help us have babies. Again, I'm not sure if this is a joke or real. But who knows? Maybe in thirty years you can go and visit and see my face everywhere you turn!

Your friend, Wesley Foster.

***

I'd not known Wesley to have any interest in music. Certainly not rap. To me, he was an artist. An artist of crude, but vibrantly colorful paintings. He worked in large scale, often painting upon whatever scraps of wood he scavenged from neighborhood refuse piles. For paint, it was also what he could scrounge. Half-empty cans of house paint from friends and family, cheap acrylics from the dollar store, and, I suspect, the time-honored five-finger-discount from local arts supply shops. Wesley started making art about five years ago, about the time I met him. He had grown up around Johnny's family, who were all artists, and quite accomplished. And, suddenly, at the age of forty, he decided to try his hand at it as well. I mean, really threw himself into it.

Johnny was his biggest champion in the beginning. He was the one who cajoled me into making a short documentary about Wesley. It turned out well. I shot at Wesley's tiny apartment in the Apache Courts, a subsidized housing development on the westside. His place was crammed with over a hundred paintings, some finished, some not. They were, by turns, beautiful, hideous, sentimental, unsettling. Strong work, but idiosyncratic. Naïve. Devoid of formal training. During the interview I did for the film, Wesley told me he discovered, while reading a book on art history at the downtown public library, that there was a thing called Outsider Art. It changed everything. He no longer felt a need to apologize. "I'm not an amateur," he said, while the camera was rolling. "I'm an outsider." After I edited the little film, I helped him to post it online. I'd like to think the video helped him get that solo gallery show the next year. His work was placed in the context of art by the differently abled. I believe that's the current terminology. In his case, mental illness.

One of the larger paintings became rather well-known because, during a particularly manic period, Wesley had pulled the bottles from his medicine cabinet and dumped all his pills onto the still wet oil paint on the panel of particle board he was using for his canvas. The pills of assorted colors and sizes were embedded in the paint. When the piece sold, a lawyer had to be brought in because a prissy city councilman accused the gallery of selling controlled substances.

I got a sense that I witnessed the full arc of Wesley's art career, culminating at that gallery show. Whenever I'd see him over the years following that show, we never talked about art. I wasn't sure if he was still painting. Maybe that solo show had provided him a therapeutic and final catharsis. Maybe his doctors finally got his meds adjusted so that he no longer needed to paint. Maybe he was now soothing his inner demons weekly through rapping at a local open mic night.

And the whole Filipina wife bit had me curious. Was she real? I checked to find if Wesley had a Facebook page. He did. And there she was. A rotund, smiling woman of about forty who certainly looked like she might have roots in Southeast Asia. There was even a video of them joking in the kitchen. Wesley was cooking scrambled eggs. She was telling him to turn down the heat and stir more often. She spoke with a thick accent, but in fluent English. They seemed happy. I considered adding Wesley to my Facebook friends' list, but after seeing all his posts flogging a herbal weight loss product, I changed my mind.

However, I took his letter with me to the kitchen. I put it on my refrigerator door with a magnet so that the reverse side faced out. This is where he had placed his postscript.

PS: I'm swimming toward all my dreams. I hope you wish me luck!

I took a moment to reflect upon the photo pasted there at the bottom with masking tape. It appeared to have been cut from a National Geographic. It was a picture of a placid sea turtle swimming through a school of colorful fish. The whole scene was lit by the dappled sunlight coming down from the surface.

NICER IN FIRST CLASS (SEPT. 13)

Rolf Medina was the enfant terrible of the San Antonio film scene even before I moved to town. He had produced a series of perverse and transgressive music videos as well as a no-budget feature-length homoerotic western. Everyone seems to have heard of *Chaps-Chafed and Hellbound*, but I've yet to meet anyone who's seen it. Eventually, he headed off to LA, where he's achieved success as a freelance editor working on Hollywood pictures. He's still young—well, early thirties is young to me—but his occasional personal projects have become more mature. This last week he's been visiting family here in town, and, prompted by boredom, he decided to use his vacation to make a quick short film about a masked wrestler who has retired from the ring to become a realtor, though still retaining his wrestling persona (and mask) while working in his new profession. Because Rolf wanted to play the lead role, he called me up to do the camera work.

Rolf is weird and charismatic, and I can't imagine a scenario where I'd say no to him. We had spent the afternoon shooting a scene in Hemisfair Park where Rolf's character, who is never seen unmasked, breaks his lucha-loving mother's heart by explaining that he's giving up the wrestling life.

It was just me (doing double duty on camera and audio), Rolf, and Kat, cast as the masked wrestler's mother. We managed to keep a low profile. I thought we might attract more attention when Kat, hamming it up pure telenovela in her pink pantsuit and dark red lipstick, embraced a masked Rolf and howled in intense lamentation.

"Mijo, nooooooo!"

We failed to get even a second glance from the wandering tourists and students from UNAM. I guess my trepidation about being hassled by the park police proved unwarranted.

Once done for the day, we took the elevator to the bar at the top of the Tower of the Americas for a round of celebratory drinks.

Kat was giddy the entire day. I don't think she'd had many acting gigs in the last few months. In fact, that's why, when Rolf asked if I knew of an attractive middle-aged Latina actress whom he could hire relatively cheap, I thought of her. I'm not always certain what people mean when they use the phrase "middle-aged," but Kat, though barely older than Rolf, has a considerable range as a performer, and I did not doubt she could pull off older well enough. Besides, she's always struck me as dependable. And now that she has finally dumped—so she says—her feckless and perennial fiancé, she was free to come out and play. When the waiter arrived with our drinks, he made no comment on Rolf's mask. However, he did praise Kat's necklace as he placed her drink on the table.

"Is this a cross section of a seashell?" he asked.

"Yes," she said, flashing the waiter a smile. "It's a fossil. From an ammonite."

He nodded, moving off to check on another table.

"Hey," Rolf said, pointing at me with his beer bottle. "Tell Kat your fossil story. It's hilarious. Trilobite, right?"

I demurred, as I don't always like telling stories that put me in a bad light. Rolf did not persist. Nor was Kat curious. Mostly, she wanted Rolf to tell stories of the movie industry. Which was perfect. It gave Rolf a chance to talk about his favorite subject. Which was Rolf. So I tuned them out and took in the spectacular view of downtown through the windows surrounding us, 360 degrees.

***

My fossil story, which Rolf was talking about, happened six summers ago. Rolf had invited me on a classic American road trip out west. We weren't what you'd call close friends, so I suspect he had already asked a few other people. But I was the only who had an empty calendar. We did it all. Carlsbad Caverns, Grand Canyon, Vegas, Death Valley. And, of course, Los Angeles. But before we even managed to take the tour of the La Brea Tar Pits, Rolf had hooked up with an old flame. In fact, that's why he decided to stay in California. I was no longer part of his adventure, but he kindly paid for my return flight.

It was the first time I had flown since 9/11 and the increased airport security. After a series of tedious indignities, I discovered, at the boarding kiosk, that my plane had been overbooked. Before I could voice my disapproval, I was informed that it was my lucky day. The airline would be happy to upgrade me, free of charge, to the first-class section.

There was something wonderfully nostalgic about the Hollywood Burbank Airport. The deco charm was still fresh there around the concourse and boarding areas. As for the final boarding, passengers could cross the tarmac like in a Humphrey Bogart movie. I moved with a knot of travelers up the gleaming metal staircase which had been rolled alongside my plane.

They had apparently already seated the first-class passengers, because when I entered through the flank of the DC10, the stewardess, upon glancing at my boarding pass, expanded her smile and cut me from the herd. She escorted me through a curtain onto the front portion of the plane. I was seated beside a tanned and bearded man in his sixties. He glanced up at me with a pleasant nod. Using his boarding pass as a bookmark, he placed his *Peter Hathaway Capstick Reader* into the little pouch on the back of the seat in front of him. He introduced himself as Gerald Westdale, but I should call him Gerry. When we shook hands, his assertive grip conveyed the fact I wasn't sitting next to any commonplace old man.

"So, what line are you in?" Gerry asked, stroking his beard. I made some vague mention of making independent films back home in San Antonio. "Oh, I've heard all about you Texas movie boys!" he responded with a grin. "My nephew works over at Lionsgate. He says no one fucks with the Texans. Uncle Gerry, the boy will tell me, you don't cross the likes of Tommy Lee Jones, Bill Wittliff, or Robert Rodriguez, 'cause they'll fuck you back harder'n a heifer." I tried my best to convey a noncommittal expression. "Boy don't know much about the cattle business," he added. "But he's passionate."

I asked what Gerry did for a living.

"Ought to be retired," he said. "Least that's what the ex-wife keeps telling me. But I can't sit around playing canasta or teaching myself the ukulele. Nope. I broker large equipment for small outfits. The oil business, you know. Used to be wide open territory here and abroad, especially in my daddy's day. These days I'm working for smaller concerns drilling Texas, New Mexico, and some in the Gulf."

Once we were in flight, with the "fasten seat belts" sign off, Gerry made sure we were both well taken care of with champagne. "The only time I drink champagne," he told me with a declarative simplicity as the stewardess filled our crystal flutes, "is when I'm airborne." The two of us clinked our glasses and took a sip. Gerry looked out his window and then turned back to me. "What else would you drink above the clouds? A beer or bourbon? Naw. It's got to be French, fizzy, and, if possible, drier than a dust devil."

Throughout the flight, I don't think there was ever a moment when we didn't have a drink in hand, and it was refreshed constantly, as if by magic. He did most of the talking, which was okay. As a raconteur, he delivered the goods. We both ordered the poached salmon. And when our lunch arrived, we fell silent as we ate. I discovered one of the reasons to fly first-class is that the aisles are wider, so the flight attendants can always come to your aid with more liquid refreshments, even during the time meals are being distributed.

"I have a little hobby," Gerry said. Then he smiled, his cheeks now flushed from the wine. "Not so little, really. It has become a damn expensive hobby. It's what I've heard, at times, referred to as adventurous gastronomy."

"Oh, yeah," I said. "Like eating those poisonous puffer fish. Or drinking coffee from civet cat scat." I started to giggle because of the way those last three words so gracelessly tripped off my tongue, and, well, because of the wine.

"That amateur rubbish is for kids and tourists," Gerry replied dismissively. "Condor egg omelets, or maybe skirt steak from a giant panda. That's what I'm talking about. Rarities. Don't let anyone steer you otherwise. Endangered meat is the sweetest." He twisted around in his seat and looked straight at me. "There's a pygmy sea tortoise that comes ashore on Tiburón Island, that's in the Sea of Cortez, and the inhabitants of the island, the Seri tribe, make this incredible stew from the little tortoises." He gazed off into space. "Yes, I played the game. All above board. The local government agreed to provide me, as a gringo, with a license to harvest one, and eat it. Let me tell you, it put a dent in the wallet. But if heaven serves lunch…" And then he sighed. "It's unlikely I will ever have it again, what with the new laws in Mexico concerning threatened species."

Gerry watched the clouds go by out his window for a while.

"My next such meal," he said, shifting in his seat, "was a pure guerrilla operation. Completely under the radar of those government agencies. I headed out to Grande Comore, an island in the Indian Ocean. Just me and an adventurous chef, trained at Le Cordon Bleu. We put out the word, and we waited."

"Is this going where I think it is?" I asked. "The Comoros, isn't that coelacanth territory?"

"And that salmon you and I just ate, as dry and soulless as airplane food tends to be, would get four stars from Zagat if compared to the goddamn coelacanth, if you'll pardon the French. Speaking of the French, that's where my chef was from. He tried everything in his repertoire. I mean, the fish was damn big, so we had plenty to work with. We tried it fried, baked, poached, sautéed with shallots and basil. And fresh herbs aren't so easy to come by on Grand Comore, just so you'll know. Um, where was I?"

"Not so savory," I said, smiling up at the stewardess as she refilled my glass.

"The only thing that came close to acceptable was with it boiled and ground up. Like gefilte fish."

"So you don't still crave the coelacanth like you do the Mexican turtle soup?"

"Oh, sweet lord! We spent 12 weeks in the slums of Tsudjini, waiting for a fisherman to find one of those fossil fish. The anticipation was extraordinary. And the reality… Abysmal."

"Hey," I said, with a giddy slur. "I have a fossil fish story. It's not a living fossil. And, well, it isn't really a fish." Gerry nodded with an indulgent and encouraging smile. "About fifteen years ago," I said, "the second time I dropped out of college, I went out to spend a month on my uncle's ranch in West Texas." I tore open a packet of peanuts and let them slide into my mouth. While chewing, I continued. "I was out gathering cactus fruit along a low mesa top half a mile from the ranch house. And I realized I'd found a fossil. At first I thought it was a fish, but as I kept digging, it was turning into a very big fish. Maybe it was a dinosaur? I was getting excited. My uncle had left for a few days to attend a wedding back in Austin, so it was just me and a shovel. When I finally uncovered the fossil, I saw that it was a trilobite. A monster of a trilobite."

"Oh?" Gerry leaned forward. "How big?"

"Volkswagen," I said.

"That's incredible! You're saying it was ten feet from the nose to the tip of the pygidium?"

"The what?"

"Its behind."

"Ah," I said. "Well, yeah. More or less. I measured it at eight feet by three feet."

"It'd be the fucking Loch Ness monster of the Ordovician!" Gerry leaned forward and pulled a bag from under his seat. "This is big stuff. The largest trilobite known, and I can't recall its name, well, it wasn't even close to three feet long." As Gerry dug through his bag, I tried to recall the summer out at the ranch. It was more like twenty years ago. One of the things I didn't share with Gerry was that this uncle of mine often drove his rickety Subaru down to Langtry to buy peyote from a Mexican rancher. The stuff tasted awful, but it was very interesting. We did quite a bit of it over that summer.

Gerry unfolded a geological map of Texas, and then he refolded it so it was only showing the trans-Pecos area of the state. I was about to place my finger on the region, just alongside the thin line of the Santiago Mountains, when I noticed the whole area of the Big Bend region on Gerry's map was colored orange. Now I didn't have to look at the map key to understand that orange represented depositional material. In this case, ancient lava flows and ash fall. The whole region had suffered cataclysmic volcanism, and this happened long after the reign of the dinosaurs, and certainly the trilobite. Any such fossils would be well buried beneath that volcanic material. In fact, that's why my uncle had to drive so far to purchase his peyote. The stuff prefers limestone rich soil.

Having studied a bit of Texas geology, I was well aware of all this. But somehow I never allowed those two things to surface in my mind at the same time: scientific fact, and my dim memories of a druggy summer lost years ago. Strictly speaking, they were not compatible. And then there was the whole thing about this gigantic trilobite. I understood how big a trilobite is supposed to be. True, back then I only knew their basic shape. But, over the years, with reading and nature films and such, I have added pieces here and there, filling in my knowledge of natural history. But this particular memory was somehow never reanalyzed in the light of reason. Let me state, for the record, I had indeed dug up, well, *something*. However, at that moment, sitting in first class, nothing from my past seemed reliable.

Gerry was waiting. With his background in geology, he'd think me foolish were I to point to my uncle's ranch. There's not supposed to be fossils of that age there. So I let my finger drift over to an empty region to the east, near the little town of Sanderson, where I knew there were plenty of exposed limestone beds of the ancient Permian seas which would be logical trilobite territory. Gerry made a mark with a stubby pencil and mentioned something about alerting his wildcatter friends to keep a lookout for weird fossils whenever scouting for oil in that region.

As Gerry dropped off into a doze over the Painted Desert, I began trying to untangle fact and fantasy, those spurious knotted tendrils of memories, reliable and otherwise. After half an hour, I accepted a plump pillow from a flight attendant and decided to give up, and so I allowed the uncertain past to fall away as quickly as the Hollywood Burbank Airport receded behind us in a billowing contrail.

***

I was brought out of my reverie by Kat's laughter, which has a peculiar catch to it, like there's a baby hiccuping down in there somewhere. As I looked around our table at the bottles of beer in front of me and Rolf and the margarita on the rocks for Kat, and out the window at the clouds and the lights of the city starting to wink on below, I wondered why we weren't drinking champagne up here. I'm sure they had a few bottles around. But because this was all going on Rolf's tab, I didn't want to be too presumptuous. Besides, he had removed his mask (I guess not enough people were gawking), and he and Kat had shifted into that stage of overt flirtation where the presence of a third person, myself, was just sad. I managed to make my exit unnoticed.

The elevator of the Tower of the Americas has one glass wall, so you can see the sights. I was happy to have the whole car to myself. I slipped my camera from my shoulder bag and shot a few still frames of the pink evening sky over the city through the windowed wall as I traveled all the way back down to the ground.

CARNAGE GUISADA (SEPT. 19)

It was a meeting to discuss a music video. I'd shoot it. David, who I've worked with on many occasions, would produce it. David was friends with the band, a rock en español outfit named Resistencia. When he asked my help the other week, he'd used the word "favor," so I doubted there would be much money (if any) for me. We were meeting at a restaurant, so I hoped to at least get a free meal. If you're not looking for La Esquinita, you'll never see it. The humble little cafe is tucked around the side of a massive pecan packing plant on South Flores Street, just past the railroad tracks. Across the street at a tire shop, three dogs sprawled out in a tight cluster in the small shadow thrown by the railroad crossing sign. Summer might be coming to an end, but the heat hasn't let up for weeks. Every day, the tar on the streets turns liquid before noon.

I met David in the gravel parking lot. We were the first to arrive. Inside, we took our seats at a table in the center of the restaurant. David grumbled good-naturedly about musicians. "Never on time." But just as he said that, the door opened and in walked Resistencia, all six members together. We helped the waitress drag over another table.

Being in our forties, David and I were the oldest in the group, but not by far. In fact, David had gone to college with Chuco, the accordionist. All the members of Resistencia had been in quite a few bands already. They'd paid their dues, working with the local and regional legends. I forget, too often, how long a shadow the city of San Antonio throws in the world of music. David introduced me to each of them. Even though it was lunchtime, we all ordered coffee. Except David. Always a Big Red for him. I apologized to the group that, even though I had heard of them, I wasn't familiar with their music.

"Rock and roll, sure," said Chuco. "But also soul and funk."

"And cumbia," Hector added. "Lots of cumbia."

Hector was the lead singer. He played guitar and was the chief lyricist. Clearly the public face of Resistencia.

"I loved that video you did for Chingolandia," Hector said to me. "Beautiful and weird. And kudos for surviving a project with Pandora. She can be…well, she does take herself seriously, doesn't she?"

"Yeah," I said. "Somehow, we've managed to remain civil."

He laughed.

Hector and I fell into that dance of association, which no doubt exists everywhere, but seems especially pronounced in San Antonio. It's like two dogs, free of the leash, meeting on the street, sniffing one another with emphatic diligence. It resembles a game of twenty questions. Almost always this begins with "where did you go to school?" Then, "where do you go to church?" In under five minutes—usually much less—the two strangers will have hit upon a mutual friend of whom they both approve. Instant carnalismo.

Because I did not grow up in this town, this one-sniffing-the-other tactic could have proven challenging. However, as both Hector and I are involved in the local community arts scene, it moved quickly. Soon we were even diving into deeper waters, candidly offering our assessments of the *character* of those folks of whom we commonly knew. I'd like to think that my name could become one of the touchstones over which two other people meeting for the first time might bond. I don't think I'd even care whether I was seen in a favorable light. As Hector and I worked our way through the local artists and politicos we knew (often, but not always, in agreement as to whether he or she was a saint or a sinner), the rest of the table looked on with mild amusement, as though watching some low-stakes and low-energy game like shuffleboard.

"Simone? I don't trust a word she says," I said when Hector mentioned a woman who worked in public relations.

"Ah," Hector said, raising a finger. "I think you'll find she only stretches the truth when it concerns herself. Besides, she's *always* been a friend to Resistencia."

The band nodded in agreement. At that moment, David caught the eye of a woman walking by. It was the owner of the restaurant, Lupe Sue. David introduced her to me and the band. She sat down, and a waitress appeared to place a cup of coffee in front of her.

"Lupe Sue does water aerobics with my mom," David said.

"Every Wednesday and Saturday at the Natatorium," she said. "Eight years and running."

"You mean swimming," I quipped.

"What?" She looked puzzled. "No. Mostly water aerobics."

"Lupe Sue is a big fan of the band," David said.

"I am!" She beamed at Hector and the others. "But only since David gave me your CD the other week. I'm listening to it every day." She was excited for us to shoot the music video in her restaurant. "Order whatever you want," she said. "It's on me. Everything's good here."

"This is true," said an older man at the next table who'd been listening to us. He sat across from who I guessed was his granddaughter. The little girl had her elbows on the table and was staring with dejection at the taco in front of her. "You can take *my* word." That was when he pointed at the little girl. "She's just grumpy because it's not a slice of pizza."

We talked about possible shooting dates. David had Lupe Sue sign a location release form. The waitress took our orders. I decided on the enchiladas de mole. For so long I'd been doing little film projects where, if I needed a location, I'd do it guerrilla style, and so I'd forgotten how nice it felt to be welcomed into a place where they want you to shoot. Often I'm shooting and directing my own personal projects, and I don't have the time or the resources to go out, hat in hand, asking if I can use someone's house, restaurant, shop, whatever. Also, I don't do well with rejection.

Now, here was sweet Lupe Sue, buying lunch for us as we brainstormed on how best to crawl and climb around her restaurant with cameras and actors. Yet we had nothing to offer her. Well, nothing tangible. Clearly, she was thrilled to be at the table while Hector explained his concept for the video.

"The song, well, it's a working-class story. Blue-collar guy, that'll be me. Waiting tables at the family restaurant. We'll fill the place with loads of extras when we shoot. There'll be scenes shot in the kitchen, behind the cash counter, all over the place. The rest of the band all have jobs here. In the kitchen. Bussing tables. Running the cash register. Things are crazy. People shouting for food. Chaos. But good chaos. Community. Family." The old guy at the table nearby was coughing. I glanced over, but he just smiled and put a finger to his lips. He was listening, and he winked in approval. "As I work," Hector continued, "I'm singing—well, lip syncing. And at some point, the action dissolves, or maybe it's a hard cut." Hector stopped and held up his hands. "Bam! We're in a dark and smoky club."

The coughing got louder.

"I'm up on a stage singing into a microphone. The audience—our extras—are the same as the people from the restaurant, but dressed up for a night out."

Chuco, the accordion player, was getting into it. "And I'll still be wearing my hairnet!"

The coughing had turned to choking. The old man had his hands at his throat. His granddaughter watched in distress. Hector looked over. He rose and stood behind the old man. He performed the Heimlich maneuver so naturally and so smoothly that I don't think many other people in the place even knew what happened. A small piece of brown meat came out of the old man's mouth. He sucked in his breath and muttered something in Spanish. Hector peered down at him. The man's eyes were big and his shoulders slumped, but he grinned and nodded. He was okay.

"Yeah, hairnet," Hector said, returning to his seat. "I like that. And we're in aprons. All that stuff. David, have you lined up the Melodeon as our nightclub?"

I turned toward Lupe Sue. She was staring at Hector with her hand over her mouth.

David grinned, shaking his head. "What the hell was that?"

"I think it was the carne guisada," I said. I pointed to the old man, who looked down at his plate sheepishly.

Chuco began laughing and said something too soft for me to hear.

"What?" I asked.

Hector shook his head. "Chuco has been threatening to quit the band for years and start his own death metal band called—" Hector looked around the table with his hands out.

All the band shouted in unison: "Carnage Guisada!"

Lupe Sue was still holding her hand to her mouth, staring at Hector.

Chuco shrugged. "It gets less funny each time we say it," he said.

ORION'S FEET ON THE WATER (SEPT. 25)

I'd gotten up before the sun to run for a few miles along the San Antonio River, just south of downtown. This was all part of the new regimen. No alcohol. Clean up the diet—no more eating crap. Run every day. My life was drifting dangerously off course. Off course from what, I wasn't so sure. But drifting, it was.

It had rained last night—a welcome relief after one of the hottest and driest seasons in decades—and I had to break my stride a couple of times to avoid squashing the little spade-foot toads that had hopped onto the paved path. A bike zoomed by, its blue-white LED headlight shuddering rhythmically each time it rolled over one of the seams in the pavement. I overtook two women jogging at a shuffle, shadowy forms no more substantial than cobwebs high in a corner. I caught a scrap of their conversation. Something about "Scott," who had "lost his appeal months ago." A cluster of egrets advanced from the opposite shore into the water. Their white bodies reflected off the surface, along with two stars I recognized as Orion's feet. Just before I went beneath the railroad bridge, I looked up as a low-flying helicopter made its way north toward downtown.

On my return trip, half an hour later, that helicopter was still up there, circling. Instead of turning off the trail onto my street, I crossed the pedestrian bridge and continued on, curious as to what was happening. The sky had warmed to a pastel pink hue, and as I rounded a bend in the path, I saw a dozen emergency vehicles. All the activity centered around Probandt Street near the railroad crossing. At first I thought a train had derailed. As I approached, a cop, stepping from his squad car, shot me a look, so I hung back. I noticed Beto, a photographer who ran an art gallery a few blocks away. He was riding his bike across Probandt toward me. He rolled up, telling me that the Nopalitos Bar and Grill had burned down. The fire trucks had just finished putting it out. He pulled his chunky DSLR from his messenger bag and showed me several dramatic shots of the blaze while it was in full swing. Before I could gather more information, Beto jumped back on his bike and hurried off. He shouted over his shoulder that he needed to post the pictures on his blog before the *San Antonio Express-News* scooped him.

I decided to head back home by crossing the river over near the Blue Bird Arts Complex. As I walked down the slope, I heard a quiet, raspy voice call my name. I spun around. I finally saw a face peering at me from the shadows of the cement tunnel which lets the run-off from the streets drain into the river.

It was Lawrence, the cook at the Nopalitos. I was surprised he remembered my name. I'd only spoken to him once. It was about six months ago when Pandora Salazar and I shot a music video at the bar for her band Chingolandia. I climbed up closer to Lawrence. He motioned me to sit down beside him at the opening to the tunnel. He wore a grimy t-shirt, cut-off shorts, and flip-flops. He was covered in soot and smelled awful.

"Jesus," he said, and then fell into a coughing fit. When he regained his breath, he told me he'd been woken by "a loud pop, like an explosion." I gathered he had a room in the back of the bar where the owner let him live. "Before I figured out what was happening, the whole place was going up."

"You need to go tell someone," I said as calmly as possible. I tried to make eye-contact, but he shook his head.

"Not going to happen."

"But they might think you didn't get out."

"They'll figure things out," he said. "Eventually."

I tried to get him to at least follow me home and take a shower. I offered him some clean clothes. But nothing was going to coax him from his hole alongside the river. "Look," I said, growing frustrated. "Be reasonable."

"Reasonable?" There was a frantic edge to his voice. "Reasonable? That would be nice. You ever heard of the Isabella Stewart Gardner Museum?"

"What?"

"In Boston. I worked there as a security guard. I was paying my way through the New England Conservatory, and—"

"Hey, yeah," I said. "That big art theft. They made off with a Vermeer, and, um—"

"A Rembrandt, and two by Degas."

"That was like ten years ago."

"Twenty."

"What? Are you saying that you…?"

"Fuck, no! It's when this all started. No one believed my story. About the guys breaking in. Tying me up in the basement. Like I'd tie myself up? I lost my place at school. The papers were after me all the time. Cops. FBI. Thinking I'd slip up or something? I took a job on a cruise ship in the Indian Ocean to escape from all the bullshit. Playing trombone in a goddamn light jazz band." He rambled on about years of bad luck. His band leader drowned snorkeling with him off Madagascar. Some sort of incident with a hot-air balloon in Albuquerque. Then it started fragmenting, each story crowding in before he'd finished the last.

I told him to sit tight. If he wanted to stay in his little hideout, fine, but I would get him something to eat. It only took me twenty minutes to run home, drive to Lila's Tacos To Go, and return to his tunnel. But he'd already left. So, I took a seat where he had been. I could still smell the rank odor of soot and sweat. I ate both of the bean and cheese tacos and drank one of the worst cups of coffee I'd ever had.

From the darkness behind me, I could make out the sound of people talking. I thought it was Lawrence for a moment, but then I realized I was hearing the firefighters. Their voices bounced through the storm drain from where they were packing up their truck on the other side of Probandt. The only words clear enough to understand were, "well, shit, that was a long and hot morning."

Of all the places in the neighborhood that could have burned down to the nub, why did it have to be the Nopalito Bar and Grill? But I guess neither fate nor arsonists take requests, and there are times when each of us has to take what is thrown our way and figure out how to proceed. Even if it meant dropping out of sight, once again, like Lawrence. Eventually popping up somewhere else, like those toads, and presenting himself to the world as a fresh new being. God, that sounded appealing.

GONE TO GROUND (OCT. 6)

"I need a man I can trust," Johnny told me.

It was nine-thirty on a Tuesday morning; my head pounded with a hangover. I was wearing boxer shorts and a long-sleeved t-shirt. It was the first week of October which, in south Texas, is usually just an extension of summer, but this morning the weather changed. I shivered with my front door open, though it wasn't much warmer inside. I tried to decide if I would invite Johnny in. I really didn't want to.

"Get dressed and meet me as soon as you can," he said, running both his hands through his hair.

"What? Meet you?" My tongue stuck to the roof of my mouth. "Meet you where?" He pulled the screen door open, grabbed my right hand. He began writing an address with a Sharpie on my palm. "Oh, please don't do that," was the best I could manage in defense of my person. But he didn't stop, and I hadn't the energy to yank my hand free.

"Hurry up, man. Hurry up. Great things are happening!" He turned and left. I leaned out. He wasn't in a car. He was walking away down the street. I stared at my hand. 246 Cedar Street. Why was that familiar to me? I shrugged—I'd figure out soon enough—and then I lugged my protesting carcass into the shower, doing my best not to wash off the address.

Last night was stupid. I had managed to live the virtuous life these last couple of weeks, running every morning, refraining from drinking. I wanted to blame it all on my neighbor, Allison, but that'd be wrong.

When I returned from a weekend camping trip yesterday, there was a bottle of tequila on my porch with a note from her. She had moved back to Texarkana to take care of her mother and didn't have a chance to say goodbye, so, well, here was a little gift. I should have stuck it away in a cabinet. Or poured it out. But I didn't. Everyone's leaving town, it seems. And me, too. Well, at least leaving the neighborhood. Where I'll go, I'm not sure yet. Back on Wednesday, my landlord told me he'd sold the property, and I needed to be out by the end of October.

Before I headed out to meet up with Johnny, I chugged down some ice water, hoping it'd help with the headache. 246 Cedar, I now remembered, was located above an underground spring. Or so Johnny was convinced from a footnote in an obscure edition of Cabeza de Vaca's journey. The book's passage hinted at a sacred cavern of treasures. I guess Johnny still believed that the two of us had discovered that long-lost natural water source.

I walked the five or so blocks to the address. The house was a two-story Victorian affair with massive white Corinthian columns. Like many of the grand old homes south of Alamo Street, it had fallen into a sad state of disrepair. I could see Johnny in the backyard talking on his cell phone. He stood beside a large yellow backhoe. As I walked down the side of the house, I glanced up to nod at the two guys sitting on the porch smoking cigarettes. The day was beginning to warm up, though they both wore sweaters, and one had on a knit cap. The man with the hat was Kelton Dermott, the executive director of the Prometheus Performance Company. I'd heard he lived in the neighborhood, I just had not known where. I felt weird walking into his yard, so I waved and said, "Hey, I'm with that guy over there." He responded with a tiny dip of his head. I assumed his frosty behavior was connected to my having resigned from his theater company, although he'd never showed much interest in me even when I was in his better graces. Whatever. I continued on toward Johnny.

"No, ma'am," Johnny said into his phone. "I'm not putting in an order. I'm just asking if I can have it on reserve?" He paused, listening. "Really? How interesting. I'll think about it." He hung up. "Good lord," he muttered, "you'd think it'd be easier to place a jackhammer on reserve. But they want a deposit and all kinds of stuff." He took a breath and held up one of the little notebooks I use. He grinned. "Look familiar?" It did. It was the notebook I'd had back in April when we'd been in the tunnel. The one directly below us. I'd used my GPS to plot out where the tunnel ran in relation to the streets above. And the inlet of the water coming from the supposed historical sacred spring was under our feet. Clearly Johnny planned to dig down to reach this spring and the cavern it was supposed to contain.

"Are you nuts?" Those were my first words. Johnny shrugged his shoulders. Before he could speak, I jumped back in. "To use equipment like this and to dig within the city limits, you need a permit. Do you have a permit?"

Johnny scratched his head. "Um, maybe if we built a fence so no one could see us."

"Yeah, fine, but again, you need a permit to build a fence. How did you even get this backhoe?"

"My cousin, Leon. Remember? Sarafina's husband. His father owns a cemetery over on Applewhite Road near the Donkey Lady Bridge."

"This is bad, man. You're gonna get busted. I mean, who'd you get to run this thing?"

"You know," Johnny said, his voice serious. He walked over to the backhoe and leaned against it. "You can be so negative." He took a breath. "Has it occurred to you that I know how to operate one of these? I learned a lot when I was in the Army. This baby," he said, patting the machine, "is a pussycat. I can make it dance the cha-cha-cha." Johnny moved away from the backhoe. He paced about, looking at the street. "It's a line-of-sight issue, yeah? All we need is to block the view of what we're doing." He clamped his hand over his mouth, taking a couple of deep breaths through his nose while looking at the ground. I was about to say something pithy about him digging his own grave. He dropped his hand and turned to me with a grand smile. "Problem raised. Problem considered. And now, my friend, problem solved." Johnny bent over his cell phone and punched in a number.

"Junie, it's me," he said. "What? No, me, Johnny. What were you thinking? Look, I've got a perfect place for you to park your camper. It's in King William. There's only one thing, the guy who owns this place, well, he's an eccentric. He wants you to get the Winnebago here before noon." He paused. "Are you still asleep? Yeah, that's noon *today*. Can you make it?" He paused again. "Perfect. It's 246 Cedar. We'll be looking for you."

"That's your plan?" I asked, trying to sound accusatory, but I couldn't keep from laughing.

"It's a beast. A giant beast of a moveable fence. Code compliance will have no clue what we're up to."

"What about, you know?" I had lowered my voice and pointed toward Kelton and his friend on the porch.

"That was the easy part. They think I'm with the city making a repair on a water main." He tossed the little notebook to me. I grabbed it midair. "Let's make sure we're digging in the right place," he said.

I had no intention of getting hauled off to jail with an empty stomach, so I stepped close to Johnny and tapped his sternum with my index finger. "Look, you dragged me out of bed before even my first cup of coffee."

Johnny's eyes widen. "Oh, man, sorry. I guess I wasn't thinking. But, no problem. I'll walk over to the Pik-Nik and get you a couple of barbacoa tacos and a Big Red. It'll fix you right up."

"Don't be imposing your culture on me, dammit! Two bean and cheese tacos with a cup of coffee. Cream and sugar."

"Fine. But while I'm gone, I want you to mark out—"

"Go! Tacos! Coffee!"

Johnny placed his hands on my shoulders. "I'm so glad you're helping me with this." I tensed, afraid he might kiss me. He squeezed my arms and walked away, out toward the street.

I studied my scribblings in the old notebook I had given to Johnny. Using the GPS on my cell phone, I realized that he'd placed his markers too far in. I plucked from the ground one of his little flags made from a coat hanger and a duct tape triangle painted fluorescent orange. I replanted it about twenty feet away, closer to the neighbor's freshly painted picket fence. After pacing off the diameter of the tunnel, I sunk another flag.

Within the hour, after coffee and tacos, Junie Lee Vargas showed up. He positioned his Winnebago precisely where Johnny had instructed. Junie stood beside me as Johnny turned a key and the backhoe roared into action.

"Where the fuck did he get that thing?" Junie shouted to me.

"Out by the Donkey Lady Bridge," I replied. Junie nodded. It made sense to him. "I guess the real question is," I said, "how many of us are going to be sitting in a jail cell before this day's over?"

I was impressed by the careful and smooth manner in which Johnny operated the backhoe. I'd cautioned him that the concrete tunnel was beneath four to six feet of dirt. And I could be off on the horizontal position, one direction or another, by as much as five feet.

"Johnny has permission to be doing this?" Junie asked.

"The owner's on the porch," I said. "Johnny said he talked with him."

"Kelton, the theater guy?" Junie asked.

"Yeah."

"That guy doesn't own shit." Junie shook his head with a smirk.

"Bet he just rents." He pulled out his cell phone and began pushing buttons. At first we had some neighbors checking us out, peeking over fences, staring out windows. But they soon lost interest. I assumed they thought we knew what we were doing. "According to the Bexar County tax records," Junie said, reading from his cell phone, "this property is owned by François Maillard." Junie sighed. "Maybe you know him as Frank Maillard?"

"Yeah," I said. "I know Frank Maillard." A hole began forming in my stomach. "And by that, I mean I know *of* him."

"Asshole is famous for having no sense of humor," Junie said. "And more lawyers than I have cousins."

We were interrupted by an unpleasant scraping sound.

"Thar she blows!" Johnny shouted over the thrum of the backhoe engine.

Junie and I watched as he repositioned the backhoe so that his trench shifted two feet to the south. He went down four feet and there was another scraping noise, this time in a higher pitch.

"We have arrived!" Johnny stood up, hands clasped above his head like a boxer posing beside his prone opponent.

Junie walked across the yard and climbed up beside Johnny atop the huge machine. He placed his mouth against Johnny's ear. Johnny listened. His eyes widened. At that moment, I heard honking out on the street. I moved back so I could see around the Winnebago. A polished black Cadillac Escalade with tinted windows was parked at the curb. The driver rolled down his window. I saw the beady eyes and receding hairline of François "Frank" Maillard, hated real estate mogul. He honked the horn again. I turned and noticed that Kelton and his friend were no longer on the porch. The rear door of the Escalade opened. Two burly men in the black tactical trousers and tunics favored by private security forces stepped out. They peered up and down the street, assessing the general situation, before walking past me and stopping to look up at Junie and Johnny.

Johnny stiffened, as if preparing himself to flee. But then he smiled and sat back in the seat. He said something to Junie that sounded like: "Save yourself!" As Junie jumped to the ground, Johnny pulled back a lever. The backhoe growled. The clawed bucket rose up high and dropped down into the hole, banging on the exposed cement surface of the tunnel.

"He's snapped," Junie hissed in my ear.

The men in black circled the backhoe, uncertain what to do. Frank Maillard walked past me and Junie. He stood looking more perplexed than angry as Johnny dropped that backhoe bucket again and again onto the top of the tunnel. Chunks of cement flew out of the trench.

Junie spun around to face the driveway. "The fucker blocked me in with his SUV," he said. Then he grinned at me. "Well, we'll see about that." Junie climbed into his Winnebago.

A horrible crash came from down in the trench. "Ah ha!" Johnny shouted. He stood and jumped into the hole. I ran up alongside the backhoe and peered down, standing there at the edge alongside Frank Maillard and his two goons. Johnny had managed to knock a hole through the huge underground pipe and was lowering himself through it and into the tunnel below. He stopped for a second, with just his head poking out. He looked me in the eyes. "You know where to find me. Don't forget the bolt cutters!" He slid into the darkness and was gone. The three men turned to me as if noticing me for the first time.

"Who the fuck are you?" Frank Maillard demanded. Before I had time to think of a plausible answer, the two security men shifted their attention to something going on behind me. It was Junie, putting his Winnebago into gear. I watched as he took off, slowly at first, across the lawn, the huge tires chewing up a cactus garden and flattening a couple of small dogwood trees. The RV bounced over the curb, missing the rear bumper of the Escalade by inches, and headed down Cedar Street.

Frank Maillard and his men rushed to their SUV and were soon in pursuit of Junie Lee Vargas.

I walked home, collected my bolt cutters. When I reached the entrance to the tunnel under that old cypress tree, there was no padlock. The gate to the tunnel stood wide open. Johnny was nowhere to be seen. I didn't stick around. I would check up on Johnny, but he'd changed his phone number. I decided to let it all work itself out and went home to crawl back into bed.

BEYOND THE BAMBOO (OCT. 15)

I'm the only person I know who dries his laundry on the clothesline. There's an electric dryer on the back porch beside the communal washing machine, but I never use it. I like how I can hang up my clothes and forget about them. Hours later, when I remember, there they are. Dry and ready. We have no alley on my street. The back fence which I share with the neighbor on the next street over is a simple wire hurricane fence, but in their yard is a dense stand of bamboo, so thick that I can't make out their house. All I know about them is their dog. Peachy. He's a spry but quiet little dachshund who always comes pushing through the bamboo to watch me string up my wet clothes. He sits there patiently, studiously. On those occasions when I hear a guy on the other side of the bamboo call Peachy by name, the little dog begins wagging his tail, and it is only with a forced deliberation that he manages to break away from the show (meaning me) and push his way back home, toward the voice.

Today, I was unpinning from the line a black dress shirt that I needed for tomorrow's gig, videotaping interviews of minor celebrities at a comic book convention. It was a windy autumn day, and when a strong gust rolled into my backyard, I found myself looking at Peachy to see if he might be entertained by the pecan and sycamore leaves I felt playing around my ankles. But, no, he kept his eyes fixed on me. Well, on my hands. And as I noticed his head shift, I also saw a black form fly past my ear. It was my shirt, billowing up into Peachy's bamboo. It cleared the fence and became tangled up there just long enough for Peachy to stare in amazement, jaws agape. I heard the shallow intake of breath.

Then the shirt fell down beside the dog. The silence was broken by the clatter of a pecan falling onto my tin roof. Peachy snapped up the shirt, and they were both gone.

Everything fell silent. Not even the leaves stirred. I called, softy. "Peachy! Here, boy!" Just the way his master called. I tried louder. And even louder. But nothing.

I was wearing shorts and slip-on Vans without socks. I got up on the fence, trying to keep my legs from the wire metal prongs on top. I made the mistake of reaching out to steady myself on a shaft of bamboo. I went down fast. But the ground on the other side of the fence was soft. I made sure no one had seen me, and I slowly pushed my way in through the bamboo. Coming into the open of my neighbor's yard was like in an H. Rider Haggard novel, when the hero pushes aside a palm frond to reveal the inexplicable Lost City of Whatever. I marveled at the beautiful, thick grass. A lush stand of ferns beneath the shade of a grapevine arbor. A line of manicured loquat trees. Most amazing of all, a swimming pool. I had no idea this Shangri-La was here. My backyard could boast nothing more than nettles, dandelions, and a rusted Weber grill.

I spied Peachy sitting on an Adirondack chair with a cushioned seat. He had my shirt up there with him, draped across his forepaws. I moved with caution, so as not to cause him to think it was a game. When only ten feet away, I experienced a trifecta of sensory input. They all happened pretty much at the same time. I smelled burning clove. I heard the reverb guitar from Donavan's "Hurdy Gurdy Man" buzzing from tiny speakers. I saw a slim young man, barefoot in jeans and a t-shirt, reclined in another Adirondack chair, wearing blue-tinted glasses, headphones, and smoking a black clove cigarette. He had his eyes closed, nodding his head to the music.

I realized I was on all fours on the grass, coaxing a dog with kissing noises, while in someone else's backyard. I stood up. The man in the blue glasses must have had his eyes open enough to see my movement. He slid off the headphones, pushed his glasses up on his head, and smiled at me.

"I'm so sorry. Didn't hear you come in."

"Um, well." I pointed back to the bamboo. "I came over the fence." He kept smiling. And he waited. "Your dog got my laundry. Well, a shirt of mine blew up in your bamboo…"

The man pivoted in his chair. He remained sitting, but placed his feet on the grass. He glanced at his dog. "Peachy!" he said. "Bring it here!" The dog leaped down, his tail thrumming. He carried the shirt to the man and laid it at his feet. "I'm so sorry about this. My name's Warren." I gave my name.

Peachy wandered over to the pool. I watched him pace along the edge near where an inflatable mattress floated. He studied the situation for no more than five seconds. With a determined little hop, he landed on the mattress. He shot a look of satisfaction toward us, then curled up and went to sleep.

"Is he safe on that thing?" I asked.

"What do you mean?" asked Warren.

"I mean, you know, if he falls off."

"Oh. Then he'll do the dog paddle." Warren examined my shirt. "I hate to break it to you, but it looks like my little sweetie has torn it."

"I'm sure I can fix it."

Warren waved me off. He stood and walked to his back door. "I'll get you fixed up in a jiffy. Come with me."

Inside the kitchen, Warren introduced me to Scott, a tall gawky man with shoulder-length blond hair pulled back behind his ears; and Babs, a puffy middle-aged woman wearing a chartreuse apron over a conservative pantsuit. Babs had a bouffant of airy lacquered apricot hair, and a pair of turquoise earrings large enough to be strapped around a championship wrestler's midsection. Warren amended my name by adding, "the charming man from beyond the bamboo." Scott and Babs were assembling a salad. As she cleaned mushrooms with a little brush, he sliced them with a chef's knife. It seemed they had been enjoying the cocktail hour, and both chattered at me, voices overlapping. I gathered that Warren and Scott lived together in the house, and Babs, Scott's mother, was in town for a visit.

I mumbled something along the lines of: "How nice."

"Mother's visiting from Maryland," Scott said while retrieving tomatoes from the refrigerator. "She's retired after a long and storied career as a political lobbyist. She's got the dirt on everyone. Everyone *important*, that is. And," he said, lowering his voice and turning to me, "I'll let you in on a secret—"

Babs cracked open a can of ginger ale under Scott's nose. He recoiled from the spume and sneezed.

"Hey, you don't even know what I was going to say," Scott said with a soft whine.

Babs laid a hand on my cheek, and as quick as it was there it was removed. "I have many secrets," she cooed. "And this one here knows that I treasure each one of them." She shot a nasty glance at her son that wasn't nasty at all. "Speaking a secret makes it something else. Something trivial. It gets turns into simple, tawdry gossip."

Warren left in search of his sewing kit. Babs steered me to a seat at the kitchen table. She put the can of soda in front of me. Scott placed a glass of ice and a bottle of bourbon beside my ginger ale. Scott and Babs continued with their salad preparations, entertaining me with stories, mostly those concerning what an "ineffectual mouse of a man" Scott's father was. Even though the two beverages, when mixed together, created one of my favorite cocktails, I ignored the bourbon, sipping the ginger ale from the can.

***

I remembered the first time I was introduced to bourbon and ginger ale. I was eighteen, living in Worcester, Massachusetts. I'd found an apartment in an old house that had been turned into an Orthodox Jewish temple. At that time, I only had the vaguest concept of the history of the Shabbat goy, but it hardly mattered. My little apartment in the back no longer had a job attached to it. The duties once carried out by the gentile tenant were now all automated, and thus I became simply the kid who rented the apartment. There was a patio on the side of the house with a hammock and several chairs. I used to sit there reading and writing. The man who lived next door was with the congregation. He was quite well off, and his house was massive. Everyone called him the Commodore. He'd been in the military, the navy, I assumed. Also, he had been mayor for a decade or so of one of the outlying towns. Now, he lived a comfortable retired life. Just him and his daughter.

The Commodore's daughter, Millie, never once spoke to me. I'd overheard someone from the neighborhood, a professor from over at the Polytechnic, refer to her as having something called Fragile X Syndrome, along with, as he put it, "profound complications." I took exception with the word "profound." I found it unnecessarily cruel. Millie lived in the coach-house behind the Commodore's home. She seemed able to take care of herself well enough. Millie was about thirty-five. She often came over to my patio while I read. Sometimes she sat in one of the chairs, stiff and staring into space. But, as often, she'd just be there, standing, pensive, as if waiting for something. She'd only look at me if I moved or said anything. When I spoke to her, she'd do nothing more than glance over, acknowledging that I spoke, and then her gaze would drift back off to an undefined spot.

The Commodore never came to collect his daughter. She never strayed beyond the property of her house or the temple. She had no interest in the busy street out front. She made me think of a tame deer, poised to flee, but no longer needing to. When I'd go inside, she never made any move to follow. She'd either wait outside or wander back home.

One day, the Commodore invited me over to his place for dinner. It was nothing special. Frozen pizza and a simple salad. We sat at the table in the Commodore's huge kitchen. He kept my glass filled with what he simply called a "highball." It was bourbon and ginger ale, mixed according to his measurements. He waited attentively for me to finish, so he could build me another one from the ground up. None of this idiocy of "let me freshen your drink." It was one part Old Crow whisky, three parts White Rock ginger ale. No substitutes. No deviations. And it was perfection. Like a tart and earthy cotton candy that eventually pulls you down into this cozy, fuzzy substrate.

His thick mustache belonged in another century. After every deep drink from his highball glass, he made a great presentation of wiping his upper lip with the back of his hand. The Commodore mostly ignored Millie, who, during my visits, was always in the doorway or seated at the kitchen table. Millie never looked at her father. That night when we were clinking glasses and sharing pizza, the Commodore lifted a finger (we were in the vicinity of drink number five) and drew my attention to Millie. She was standing in the doorway to the utility room, watching me.

"Millie is like a dog. Obedient, and asking so little." I wanted to tell him I thought Millie was more like a cautious deer, but I wasn't quick enough. "Ten years ago," he continued, "I had the foundation of the north wing jacked up to make it level again. The contractor stayed for the entire week in the coach house. Millie didn't live out there at the time. But I soon learned the two of them were…" He left the sentence unfinished.

Even though Millie was standing nearby, I didn't look at her. Or at the Commodore.

"I understand," I said.

"Do you?" the Commodore asked, using his fingernail to trace patterns on the condensation of his highball glass. "Do you understand? Fatherhood isn't like in the books or the movies."

I have a dim memory of my relief when the conversation shifted toward another, more mundane topic.

When the Commodore hung himself in his stairwell that winter, I found it odd that none of the obituaries mentioned the cause of death. Perhaps that wasn't so unusual with suicides. There was no mentioned of any surviving family members. Just the birth and death dates for himself and his late wife, followed by a lengthy list of his military and political achievements.

Millie, I learned later, went to live in a group home outside Rutland.

**

I drifted back to the present when I realized that Babs and Scott were asking my opinion of some reality television show I'd only vaguely heard about. "Is that the one where they all live in the same house?" I asked. Babs snorted at that. She shook her head to express a general sense of pity concerning my ignorance of such things.

Scott told me: "That defines so many of them. But, yes. Yes, they live together." He tapped the untouched bottle of bourbon beside me and lifted an eyebrow. I shook my head. He shrugged and continued. "Anyway, that's where this Ice Queen, Mona, comes in."

"What a USDA bitch," Babs said, hissing the final word through her teeth with terrible seriousness.

"And she's got this poor little nebbish guy—"

"He's a tap-dance instructor!" said Babs with sudden enthusiasm.

"She's got him wrapped around her pinky."

I noticed Warren enter the kitchen with my shirt. He tilted his head, and I followed him into the front of the house. Babs and Scott kept up their banter, apparently oblivious to my departure.

"They can be exhausting," Warren said as he peered down at the shirt in his hands. "But what can I say? I love them dearly." He rolled his eyes, but his smile conveyed enormous warmth. "Alright," he continued, turning the folded shirt so I could see it. "I've stitched it up nicely. Also, your collar button was about to fall off, so I sewed it tight."

"It looks great. Thank you! It's the only good shirt I have."

He turned to walk back to the kitchen and the door to the backyard. But I shook my head.

"I think I've done enough climbing over fences for today. I'll go around the block."

We walked out the front door, and I noticed that the fence surrounding the backyard came up to the side of the house. Peachy was staring at us from the other side, wagging his tail. He completely ignored a large chow with matted hair who sat in the front yard. I'd seen this quiet, slow-moving old dog wandering the neighborhood for at least two years.

"We call her Brownie," Warren said of the chow. "She's always escaping from the neighbor's yard. She adores Peachy, but he pretty much ignores her."

"Life showers us with surprises that aren't always kind," I said. Warren nodded in agreement at that. I waved to him and walked home.

LITTLE ALTARS (OCT. 23)

There's a lonely stretch of road on the southside of San Antonio between the old Spanish Missions of San Juan and Espada. It runs along for a mile parallel to the Southern Pacific Railroad tracks. Many people in town are familiar with this region, as the southern reach of the road makes an abrupt turn and crosses the notorious Ghost Tracks, a railroad crossing purportedly haunted by the children who died when their school bus was struck by a train. It's a good story, but the problem is no one can find any newspaper report covering the event. I ride this road at least three times a week on my bicycle, and from my experience, if ghosts haunt this area, they most likely would be from the carcasses of the family pets dumped out here. It's easier than digging a hole. Every few days, I encounter a new box or trash bag surrounded by a cloud of flies and stench. There are live pets abandoned here too—I see them eyeing me hopefully as they cringe at the fence-lines of the surrounding farms. There are also three roadside altars along the road, those sad markers where a drunken or dozing driver lost control of his car and perished unseen and alone.

I had wrangled a photography show at an Alamo Street gallery for Día de los Muertos, which was just a week away. My plan was to shoot a dozen of the more interesting local roadside altars, but I hadn't yet taken a single photo. However, I learned last night that the music video I made for the band Resistencia won first prize at the Seguin Film Festival, so I felt a warm sense of purpose and motivation. Time to get back to work!

I decided to begin with one of the altars about half a mile from the

Ghost Tracks, as it was the only one of the three that showed any signs of upkeep. It was early afternoon when I pulled off the road in my truck. There was a chill in the air and the trees clustered across the road from me were still shedding droplets from the heavy rains that morning. I grabbed my tripod and camera and walked up to the large live oak tree. Four tall votive candles stood at the base of the tree, each with about an inch of rainwater in the glass holders. Further up the trunk, a heavy iron grate that looked like it belonged to a barbecue grill had been nailed to the tree. Attached to the bars of the grill were all manner of sentimental objects: a weathered, sodden teddy bear, white silk flowers, plastic beaded necklaces, some cards with pictures of saints, a tiny gift-shop acoustic guitar, and a rosary with pink beads.

The clouds, which had been running low and fast on my drive out, were breaking up and the sun began throwing pleasing shadows. I set up the shot with the grill in the foreground—I was zoomed in as tight as my lens allowed, so that the train, when it finally made its appearance, would be massive and imposing in the background. A slow shutter would smear its motion like a river surging by. Now it was just a matter of waiting. I toyed with the idea of reframing the shot to include a crude carving in the trunk—*Yolanda 4 Ever*—but I wasn't sure if it was part of the altar. At the sound of a car approaching, I swung around. It was an old, metallic green El Camino. It slowed and rolled to a stop in the grass between me and my truck. Conjunto music with a heavy bass line and a strident accordion came from the open windows. A young woman sat in the driver's seat watching me from behind sunglasses. Beside her sat an old man in a baseball cap reading a newspaper. The twisted front bumper was held fast with baling wire.

The music stopped. The woman cut off the engine, which dieseled onerously with a low throaty cough before finally dying. That was when I heard the long, wavering train whistle. I glanced back toward the tree and the train track beyond. The train had just rounded the bend near the cemetery across from Mission San Juan. It was coming in fast, and

I tried to ignore the woman who climbed out of the car. She began walking my way. I needed to get this shot, because who knew when another train would come along? I saw, from my peripheral vision, that she had stopped about fifteen feet from me. She took off her glasses and crossed her arms.

When the train was about to enter the frame—the sound of steel wheels rumbling along iron rails with the whistle screaming crashed into me like a physical thing—I squeezed off a shot. I took another three exposures with different settings and placements. Then I put on the lens cap, like a diner, placing his napkin on the table to indicate he was done with his meal, and I turned to the woman with what I hoped was a pleasant, cordial smile.

We stood there, facing one another as the train lumbered by. She pointed with her folded sunglasses at the tree. "You're not messing with that, are you?" she shouted. I didn't make out the words at first over the noise.

"What? Oh, no. I'm just taking pictures." I said this all slowly and loudly. She furrowed her brows. At that point the final train car sped past, snatching with it the thunder and high-pitched metallic squealing, and dragged it all away. "It's for a photography show." I added: "At an art gallery."

"Oh," she said, with an understanding dip of her head, as if art explained everything. "It's just that if my mother saw anyone messing with this, she'd be sick. This is for my little sister, Yoli." She walked to the tree, fussing with the silk flowers, reshaping the wired fabric petals. "Come back with your camera next week. Me, my mother, and my nieces, we'll redo it. We freshen it up every few months." She wore an orange t-shirt, faded jeans, and flip-flop sandals. Her hair was pulled back into a high ponytail. She was about thirty.

"She was in a car accident?" I asked.

"What?" She stepped over for a closer look at my camera.

"Your sister."

"Oh." She slipped her sunglasses into the front pocket of her jeans. "It was up there," she said, pointing to the rise of the train tracks. "She was walking along the tracks with her boyfriend. They were drunk. Some guy said he saw them pushing each other as the train was coming up. Just pretending. Kids do stupid stuff. Sergio, her boyfriend…well his parents sent him to live with his grandparents in Laredo. It was an accident, everyone knows that. But, well, the kids at school and everything." She bent down to empty the water from the candle holders and stood up with a sigh. "Come on back next week. It'll be pretty." She smiled at me and walked back to her car.

"Hey," I said. "When did this happen?"

She turned. "On her birthday," she said. "On Yoli's birthday." And I watched her get in the truck with the old man and drive off.

GOVERNOR'S REPRIEVE (OCT. 31)

My finances aren't in the best shape. Here it is Halloween, and I can't even justify buying a couple of bags of candy. Well, the fact is, I have money socked away, but I need it for my move. My landlord gave me a three-day extension. However, as the end of the month is tonight, that means I need to vacate the place by Tuesday. I still don't know where I'm headed. A different city. Yes, I think I'd like that. And probably out of state. I'd forgotten how exhilarating it is to have a life-changing and irrevocable plan in place. One that is absolutely devoid of details. Barely a plan at all, I guess.

The sun was just going down over the top of the huge house across the street. When I moved into this neighborhood ten years ago, that house was a ramshackle affair, the quintessential old haunted house. But this is the King William historical district, and this street, like all the rest of this neighborhood, is feeling the lick of fresh paint and the thrum of contractors' diesel trucks as the gentrification process kicks into high gear. My humble duplex is the only rental property left on my block. And once my landlady gave the property over to her son, he was canny enough to make a few repairs and unload it. I have no idea what he sold the place for, but it will certainly continue a trend of increasing affluence in the neighborhood. This stage of the betterment of Southtown will have to happen without me.

This is the end of a decade of Halloweens on this street. For me, I mean. Also, it's the first year in a long time without Kat sharing the porch and passing out candy. She's back with her shiftless boyfriend.

They're living in Houston. If I can believe the gossip, they actually got married. So, this year I'm reverting back to the way things were before Kat. Retreat into the shadows to peer through the curtains at the crowds of children and their smiling, indulgent parents winding through the neighborhood. It's important to keep the lights out and stay as silent as possible. Don't attract the attention of the hoards of kids scouting for candy if you have nothing to offer them.

I was playing an early John Cale album at low volume. The shelf above the fireplace held a dozen flickering votive candles, and I sat on the floor taking inventory of my firearms. Well, my father's guns. But when he passed away twelve—or was it thirteen?—years ago, they all became mine. I've sold most over the years. He left behind quite a few. They were squirreled away all over the used bookstore he owned in Dallas. I remember him telling me once that he wished he could have a more diverse business. A combination book shop, gun store, and bar. All his three passions merged into one breathtaking emporium. I guess we don't share the same passions. Now I'm down to the final two. A rifle and a pistol. I know a guy who runs a lucrative tattoo shop over on South Zarzamora who would give me enough for the both of them so that I can make it a good bit further down the road toward the next chapter of my life. My mother would shake her head were she aware of my plans. She's an accountant, and I was planning to divest some assets. That's all I do. And this she knows. I found myself with an array of mediocre holdings a few years back. Rare books and guns. I've been turning gold, and a small amount at that, to shit ever since. The antithesis of alchemy.

It's not just about the money. It's also the winnowing down of possessions. I have been purging for the last few months. I am down to an inflatable mattress, a bicycle, a laptop, camera equipment, clothes, kitchen stuff, and the guitar I still haven't learned to play. Everything was ready to be boxed up and loaded into the bed of my truck.

I had made a call to the tattoo artist, Javier Ortega. It was his machine which answered. "Javi, it's me," I said. "Look, I have a couple of toys that go bang. I'm cash poor, so that puts me at your mercy. Give me a buzz." Leaving candles burning is something I don't usually do, but I was just heading across the street to my neighbors' place, and I didn't want to return to a dark house. I slid my cell phone into my pocket and headed out.

Trip and his wife Minnie live next door to the mansion across from me. They do it up every Halloween and, as their neighbor, I have a standing invitation to their seasonal parties. So I walked into the fray of Halloween, Southtown-style. Cars inched along the street, kids and their parents swarmed the sidewalks. People were all in costume. Everyone laughed and shouted. Trip and Minnie had covered their front lawn with a dozen painted styrofoam tombstones bearing the names of famous American gangsters and murderers—Al Capone, Ted Bundy, John Dillinger, Jeffrey Dahmer, and so on. I walked up the steps to their porch. There was momentary lull in the trick-or-treaters. Trip, wearing an orange prison jumpsuit, was strapped into an electric chair. He had a big bowl of candy in his lap. His wife stood beside him with a stern expression. She dressed as a prison guard and was slapping a billy club into her palm.

"So, what's it gonna be?" she asked of me. "You man enough to pull the switch on this flea-bitten reprobate?" When she pointed with the billy club, I turned and saw a huge old-style electrical knife switch attached to the porch pillar beside me.

"Aw, please, mister," Trip sniveled. "I'm sure the governor's gonna call any minute now. Just wait. Please! Please wait!"

I muttered about how it was, really, too great a temptation. I pulled the switch. The sparks impressed me. They flew from the metal band across Trip's forehead and the other bands holding down his wrists. But it was the sound effects that had me laughing. A high electric hum and loud sizzling. Trip thrashed about, whimpering, and then slumped still, his tongue lolling from his mouth. "Wow," I said. "And was that the sound of frying bacon?"

Trip opened one eye. "Good ear. We recorded it this morning. First time I've had bacon in years. Usually she makes something awful from soy."

Minnie poked him with her baton. "You be quiet, or I'll have this man pull that switch again."

"Glad you made it," Trip said, opening both eyes and sitting up. "Food and drink in the kitchen, as usual. And if you could move on. There's a line forming behind you." I looked around and saw a witch, a vampire, a pirate, and two toddlers dressed as candy corn. I nodded to a few of Trip and Minnie's friends and relatives seated on the porch drinking wine, and I headed on inside. In the living room a bunch of teenagers—nary a costume among them—were talking loud and laughing, ignoring the giant-screen TV on the wall playing the *Bride of Frankenstein* with the sound off.

In the kitchen, Trudy looked up from the guacamole dip. She smiled and greeted me. We were the only people in the room. I returned her smile and began to fill a bowl with some chili off the stove.

"Make sure to add Fritos and cheese," Trudy said, moving around the island counter to show me where they were.

"Of course," I said, following her advice.

"Just watching your back." She leaned a hip against the counter, crossed her arms, and stared straight at me. I met her gaze and held it while eating my chili. I liked Trudy, but she was always playing a role, and constantly trying to bring drama into her life. I first met her when I moved to town. We had both attended a city-sponsored economic empowerment workshop for artists. It hadn't helped me one bit, but Trudy seemed to be racking up shows, sales, and a good amount of media coverage. She's about fifty. She used to teach, but as I understand it, took early retirement. Her husband does something with acoustical engineering, which doesn't sound like it'd pay that well, but they're clearly not hurting. They own a huge house two streets over. Trudy's a printer, mainly using an old style lithography process. Skillful, detailed work of a sexual nature, which is strangely meager in eroticism. I once told her that I loved her work because it made me think of robots having sex. She stopped talking to me for two years. Now, we're back to being friends. At least, I think we are. "I always see you," she said, "you know, out at events."

"This is an event? I just crossed the street to snag some free food."

Trudy turned around, opened the refrigerator, and removed a bottle of Lone Star beer. She raised an eyebrow. I shook my head, pointing to a bottle of Mexican Coke. She switched the beer for the coke and placed the lip of the bottle cap on the edge of the butcher block island and brought down the palm of her hand, hard. The cap popped off. She handed the bottle to me. I had to move fast to suck up the rising foam. At that moment, Trudy's husband walked in.

"Hey, man!" he said to me with a broad grin. "How's it going?" He slapped me on the back. He's one of *those* guys. He pointed at my coke and looked at his wife. "Out of beer?" Trudy opened the fridge to fish out a beer. She handed it across the island counter to him. "Thanks. Um, where's the opener?" Trudy pointed to one on the counter by the seven-layer dip. "Great!" he said, cracking open his beer. "Guess what? Trip's going to let me get in the orange jumpsuit and take over for a while." He pushed his glasses back and adjusted his tie. "I've never been in an electric chair before!" He hurried off.

"You know," Trudy said as she picked up a corn chip and began making abstract designs in the guacamole, "you're always nattering on about your poverty, your difficulty paying the bills. How every penny you save goes straight into buying more camera equipment." She stared at me and ate a chip.

"Guess I lack ambition," I said. I took a long sip on my coke. "So, what are you getting at?"

"I've a proposition. One that might interest you." Trudy raised her eyebrows, apparently to encourage me.

I guess I had my phone on vibrate, because I felt it go off in my pocket. I held up my finger to Trudy and got it out. My caller ID showed it was Javier.

"Dude," I said into my phone. "You're so prompt with the callback."

"I love me my toys," he said. "What are we talking about?"

Trudy eyed me with curiosity and not a little irritation. I turned away and lowered my voice.

"That Webley you're always asking me about."

"Finally! The Navy issue, right?"

"Yeah. Gonna be hard to find .455 ammo, but that's not my problem."

"How much?" he asked.

"Not done yet. This is a package deal. I need the money. I'll thrown in an SKS, in a fiberglass composite stock, and a thousand rounds of Soviet era surplus ammo. I'm wanting twelve hundred for the lot."

"How could I say no? Let's make this deal happen!"

"Great! Look, I could head over to your place tomorrow and—"

"Dude, I'm parked in front of your house. What's with all this Halloween shit? It's nuts here. And why aren't your lights on? You at a party or something?"

"I'm at my neighbors' place. You see that big mansion across from you? I'm in the house on the left. Come meet me on the porch." I hung up.

"Doing a little business?" Trudy said quietly, cautiously.

"Trudy," I said, with a playful wink. "People make proposals to me all the time. Sometimes, I say yes." I put down my empty chili bowl and left the kitchen. I'd thought I'd made a cool, clean exit, but the woman followed me all the way to the porch.

Javier walked up the sidewalk. He's a striking man, tall, muscular, with a shaved head. Even on cool nights like tonight, he favors wearing short-sleeved shirts to better display his tattooed arms. He had monochromatic portraits of Karloff's Frankenstein's monster, Lon Chaney's Werewolf, Bela Lugosi's Dracula, and Karloff's Mummy on his forearms and biceps. When he got to the porch, he was grinning at me. Trip glanced up nervously. Javier's an intimidating man.

"Don't fret," I told Trip. "It's the governor. I'm thinking he's here to give you a pardon."

Trip exhaled and relaxed, realizing I knew this guy. Javier crossed to me and we exchanged a hand-clasp and an abrazo. I leaned in and quietly explained that "the goods are on the window seat when you walk in my door." I slipped my house key into his hand. Javier winked and nodded. He left the porch, walking back across the street.

Trudy's not very tall, and I felt her face press up against my arm as we watched Javier let himself into my house. "Don't you want to hear about my proposition?" she asked. I looked on as Trudy's husband suited up in the orange jumpsuit. He was grinning as he allowed himself to be fastened into the electric chair.

"Trudy, I don't know what I can offer you."

She put my hand in hers. Thought better of it, and released.

"You're good with video editing software, right?" she asked.

"Yes."

I realized she was gazing across the street as Javier carried a long object wrapped in a blanket from my house and into the trunk of his low-slung black Lexus.

"I want to animate my lithographs to make a short film," Trudy whispered, her head tilted closer to my ear.

Javier returned to my house. Then stepped out lugging a heavy box. A thousand rounds of steel case ammo can be a burden. He placed it in his trunk and then slammed it shut.

"You want me to make a film for you?" I asked.

"Not quite," Trudy said. We watched Javier return to my porch, lock my door, and began walking toward us. "I want to hire you as a tutor. I've spent a thousand bucks on the best video editing software money can buy, and it's kicking my ass."

Javier walked up onto the porch, ignored Trudy's husband sitting in the electric chair. He dipped his head at Trudy; she smiled up at him.

"We happy?" I asked.

"Happy? Best Halloween ever!" Javier lifted the edge of his guayabera, discreetly showing off the Webley tucked into his jeans. Trudy's eyes got big. The Webley Mark IV is an inelegant pistol. Brutish and ugly. Not the sort of thing one would expect from Victorian Britain. It looked like something built for one purpose. To seriously mess you up. Javier opened my jacket and put an envelope into the inside breast pocket. We repeated the abrazo-shake, and he was gone.

"Aren't you going to count it?" Trudy asked, both her hands clamped on my forearm.

"There's a gentleman's code involved," I said. If she could play a role (and I was not exactly sure what game she was playing), so could I. "Here," I said, giving her one of my old business cards—Labyrinth Productions. Before I walked off the porch and headed home, I told her to give me a call.

I wonder who has the phone number on that card these days? Maybe it's someone who can help her. But probably not.

THE HAND-FEEDING OF
OPOSSUMS (NOV. 2)

It was my last gig in town before I turned over the keys to my apartment and drove out toward the city limits and beyond. I had received a call from my friends over at Carnaval de San Quilmas, an arts nonprofit which teaches dance and drumming in a decidedly Brazilian manner. They have gained a good deal of recognition by being a staple of the grand parades during Fiesta. They wanted me to videotape their annual Día de los Muertos performance in Hemisfair Park. The parking was usually a pain downtown in the evenings, so I grabbed my camera and my monopod and walked. By the time I got there, the sun had just set. The drummers and dancers were in place, their ornate costumes flashed with battery-powered LED lights.

The performance began out in the Plaza de Mexico with drumming, slow and steady. Then the dancers in their white gauzy gowns emerged from the shadows over by the side of the UNAM building. The crowd in the plaza made way for the dancers, who began moving in a fluid, circular path. I had the camera running. I moved along with the dancers, matching their speed. The high limestone walls of the adjacent convention center were lit from below, and that reflected light was just enough for my camera. As the drummers increased the tempo, I found a place to settle for a few minutes, so as to shoot some stationary footage.

I saw Wesley Foster sitting perched on a low wall, watching the dancers. He was alone. I wondered where that new wife of his might be. I sat beside him, and, positioning the monopod just so, continued to shoot the performance. It soon became apparent Wesley was off his meds.

"It's the voodoo," he said. "What they're doing." He seemed only vaguely aware of me. I then realized I was still wearing the black mask with silver sequins that Darlene, one of the dancers, had given to me, mostly as a joke. All the drummers and dancers wore masks or face paint. "It's right out of Africa," Wesley continued. "This dancing. This drumming. The old religions don't belong here. We're new people in this country, right? The Orishas, or whatever dark spirits they're conjuring up, have no regard for the likes of me or you." He looked up at me. "Can you feel it? They're chipping away at the wall between this world and the other. When that wall cracks, well, it will not be good."

He turned back to watch. I was glad to be wearing a mask. Wesley was correct about the Afro-Caribbean elements. It's actually a stylized ritual, but as is often the case when what was once a solemn offering to the gods is allowed to be performed in public spaces, the sacred mixes with the profane, resulting in celebration as much as invocation. I like to think that's why the outlandish costumes of Carnival and the festively painted Catrina skull faces of Día de los Muertos evolved the way they have. It allows the more serious communicants, who are crying out to the old gods, to mix freely with the carefree secular celebrants. The music, the chaos, the swaying and spinning of bodies, are all things to all people. And here, behind a mask, you can hide your identity, agenda, allegiances.

And tonight, here we were—yes, with my mask I was one as well— all as anonymous as any of us could hope. I moved in closer, peering through the viewfinder of my camera as I weaved through the crowd of onlookers. The dancers created a circle in the plaza, with the drummers joining them, moving and banging faster, getting louder—really leaning into each beat. The dancers began pulling people into the center, dancing with them. Children and the elderly were chosen first, as they have fewer inhibitions. But, soon, everyone was churning in a rotating disk of humanity and swirling tulle. It was all flashing lights and hypnotic drumming, loud and urgent. You heard it in your chest, and your feet and fingertips answered back that primal call. Eventually, with a final, trembling and exhausting crescendo, it was over.

I noticed Wesley as he stood up from his seat on the low wall. He glanced around, uncertain. Then he wandered off.

My camera has two slots for media cards. I had set them to record simultaneously, so I could have a copy for my own archives. I walked over to Tomás, the music director for Carnaval de San Quilmas. He and his drummers were gathered together, packing up their instruments. I removed one of the SD cards from my camera and gave it to him. He thanked me and handed me an envelope of money.

"Drop by the studio when you're back in town," he said. I nodded. For some reason, I had not told Tomás I was moving away. What I had told him earlier in the week was that I was leaving town for a few days, so I would appreciate it if he could pay me the night of the gig.

As the crowd dispersed, I too slunk away. I walked across the plaza, taking the steps down into the Grotto. This is the terminus of a blind tributary of the famed San Antonio River Walk. The Grotto is under the convention center. No one was down there. I wandered past a series of artificial waterfalls. The water flowed through a couple of pools before emptying into the downtown segment of the river. I enjoyed listening to the echos made by the gurgling water. There was a low ceiling with recessed lighting. Steel rails kept you from falling into the shallow pools, which were lit from below. When I finally made my way to the far side, with the dark nighttime sky above me again, I was officially at the River Walk. High up on the wall of the convention center was the gigantic curved mosaic by Juan O'Gorman. As I stopped there to admire it, I realized I was standing beside one of those river taxis. They resemble the tourist barges, but are smaller and faster. You can rent them—in fact, like a taxi.

"Dude," the driver said to me. I had startled him. Maybe he'd been napping. "I hoped to pick up a few fares. There's an event happening up there, right?" He hooked his thumb the way I had come.

"Yeah. A big crowd. But no one's coming this way."

"No worries. So, where you headed?"

I was about to tell him I wasn't a tourist and just wanted to enjoy a good walk. But then I changed my mind.

"How much to take me to Main Plaza?"

"Five bucks," he said.

I handed him the money and, once I had climbed in, he started up the motor.

The River Walk is a series of pathways that snake through downtown below street-level, following the river. We were on a side channel which loops around the River Center Mall. As we puttered through the lagoon alongside the mall, I pulled my camera from my bag and took a few shots of reflection off the water. We passed under some foot bridges and moved into an area where large cypress trees are covered with white Christmas lights. Then we took a turn to the left.

"Hey," I said. "Isn't Main Plaza the other way?"

"Oh," my driver said. "You know your way around. You in a hurry?"

"No. Not at all. I was just afraid you heard me wrong."

We rounded a bend at the Arneson Theatre. This is an outdoor amphitheater, with the seats on one side of the water, and the stage on the other. The taxi came to a halt at the edge of the stage. I saw that a large opossum was hunkered down in the dead center of the performance space. Its fur shone blue from the halogen incidental lights shining from a nearby live oak. When the guy cut the engine on his boat, the opossum headed our way without caution or preamble.

"I call him Elvis. Of course, he could be a she. But then the name wouldn't work." I started running the camera as the critter approached.

I heard the tick-a-tack of those little claws on the raw and unvarnished wooden stage. The taxi driver held out a large bone-shaped dog treat. The opossum stopped, sat up on its haunches, and reached out to take the treat. It had a white face, large black eyes that were all pupil, and its long, opened snout filled with sharp teeth was somewhere between comical and terrifying. It sat there, not five feet from me, holding the treat in it claws. It munched away, unconcerned with our presence. "When I first began seeing Elvis on the stage," the guy said, "I knew I wanted to make friends. I looked up what do possums eat. I should have asked what *don't* they eat. Man, they're just like us. Meat, fruit, cereal. But also bugs and stuff." He started the engine back up, using a button near the throttle arm. Elvis glared at the driver with a baleful expression at such a breach of dining etiquette. But the animal kept eating. The driver placed two more Milk-Bones on the stage near the opossum and we were off again.

"I found Elvis liked dry dog food best. But those bigger tour boats spook him. And when he gets scared, he can't grab up a mound of dog food and run away. Give him these big Milk-Bones, and he's got something portable." As we glided along, I replayed the video clip of the opossum. And because the boat sat lower than the stage, it was a terrifying perspective from which to see that beast scurry straight toward the camera.

Later, as I walked up the steps from the river to Main Plaza, I heard the energetic music of Resistencia, that rock en español band with accordion. They were playing on a stage next to San Fernando Cathedral. The audience was modest at about fifty people. At a nearby table someone was handing out complimentary pan de muerto and styrofoam cups of steaming champurrado. I crossed over to a bench in a quiet corner of the plaza and sat down to review the video I shot of the dancers and drummers. I was so engrossed, I didn't hear the two guys approach. The first thing I noticed was the smell of marijuana. I looked up. They were watching my video. Two guys in their forties. One was scruffy—his blue jeans worn to a white mesh of fuzzy threads at the knees, and one of his boots was reinforced with duct tape. He had a beard, a knit cap, and a ripe smell. The other fellow was Renaldo Jiménez, a local artist who I had been introduced to on several occasions, yet who never seemed to remember me. They were drinking from 16-ounce cans of Lone Star beer wrapped in a brown paper bags.

Renaldo gave me a wink. He sipped his beer and wiped at his mustache with a sleeve. He turned to the other guy, speaking to him in rapid Spanish, gesturing to my camera. Then Renaldo asked me: "Was this over in Hemisfair?"

"Yeah, Renaldo. I just came from there."

At the mention of his name, Renaldo blinked. Then he moved in to look at me closer in the dim light reflected off the Cathedral. He still didn't recognize me. And it wasn't like I was still wearing the mask. Over the years I've resigned myself, I suppose, to not being remembered. I feel I must lack something (I don't know what) that so many others have that allow them to etch their, well, *essence* onto the minds of others.

I was wondering if I told him that just six months ago he had cajoled me into dancing with him on Johnny's balcony. Would he remember me then? But I kept silent. Renaldo only laughed, tilting his head back, assuming I knew him because of his local notoriety. He gave me an elaborate courtly bow. "A lover of the arts," he said.

He then fired up a joint and handed it to me. I took a deep drag and gave it back. He explained that his companion—who, as I had presumed, he had just met—had recently made his way from Mexico. "Doesn't speak more than seventeen words of English. And most of those are off a McDonald's menu. He's tried for years to get into this country. Four times he's been caught and tossed back. This is the furthest north he's ever made it."

I introduced myself to the man from Mexico, welcoming him to America as best as my poor Spanish allowed. When I said my name,

Renaldo squinted his eyes for a moment as if it sounded familiar. Then he shook his head. Nothing. He extended his hand, and I took a couple more hits off the joint. They made their goodbyes. I watched as they left, a cloud of smoke billowing around them.

I headed home along the River Walk until I came to the steps up to Cesar Chavez Boulevard. Back up on the street level, I made my way to South Alamo Street. I walked past the bars and restaurants, and the galleries and bed and breakfasts of Southtown. I only wish I could say that those tokes off of Renaldo's joint had an impact. Not so much. But a walk through my neighborhood at night is always pleasant and full of small surprises. Tonight it was the white fluffy face of a dog sticking its head through a cat flap of someone's front door. The dog could barley get its head through, so I knew it'd not be able to get out. It did not pay any attention to me. Rather, it focused its attention on a slender orange cat seated on the porch eyeing the dog with obvious displeasure. The cat got to its feet and swatted the dog on the nose, causing it to immediately retreat. The cat took its time, licking the paw that displaced the dog, and then it sauntered through the swinging plastic flap into what I assumed was its home.

My truck was parked in my driveway. I pulled back the tarp to look at the boxes and other items I had loaded into the bed. It was all unmolested. I stowed my camera equipment behind the passenger seat. Then I climbed the steps of my porch and let myself inside one last time to the duplex I had called home for so many years.

So, here I am right now. Sitting in the dark, perched on the window seat in an empty apartment. And when I finish typing out this last blog entry from San Antonio and upload it via the tethered hotspot from my cell phone, I'll power down my laptop and give a final inspection of this place to make sure I'm not leaving anything behind. Next, lock the door, drop the key into the mailbox, and get into my truck. Head out of town.

It might seen odd, beginning a major road trip at midnight. But I have to say, there's something exciting about having the sun come up, revealing a radically different environment. Also, I don't want to have to explain to my neighbors if they ask me why I'm leaving town with no warning. The fact is, I don't have an answer to that question.

My plan is to get onto Highway 90 and head west. Maybe stop at a gas station in Hondo, or a town further out to fill up the tank. And then? I don't know yet. Or *maybe*, instead, I should take the highway in the other direction. It has been engrained in my head for so long that the place to start over, to reinvent oneself, was somewhere to the west. What about, instead, driving all the way to New Orleans? See if Rachel is serious about her offer. Besides, there's this wonderful po' boy shop off Magazine Street she introduced me to, and I have been dreaming about it for months.

I'm conflicted. Shall I flip a coin?

* * *

ERIK BOSSE

After ending a career in the antiquarian book trade, Erik Bosse moved to San Antonio, Texas. For over a decade he honed his skills as a writer, filmmaker, and creative collaborator in that city. During those years he worked for several art and cultural nonprofit organizations When not busy as project manager, program documentarian, or marketing director, Erik kept busy with creative work. He directed several music videos, produced a couple of plays, and collaborated in a series of multimedia public art projects. He also wrote a series of short stories that were eventually woven into the novel, *Tales of Lost Southtown*.

Erik currently lives in New Orleans with his partner, Laurie Dietrich. He continues to write and do film work. He has been published in *Rum Punch Press*, *The Bitter Oleander*, *Maudlin House*, *Razor*, and *Unlikely Stories*. Much of his work can be found on his website: erikbosse.com

www.ingramcontent.com/pod-product-compliance
Lightning Source LLC
Chambersburg PA
CBHW070413310726
48977CB00003B/667